AT THE

END

BOOK ONE OF

THE ROAD TO EXTINCTION

JOHN HENNESSY

INNOVATION TODAY PUBLISHING
GO INDIE

An Innovation Today Book. Go Indie.

This is a work of fiction. Names, characters, places, and incidents either are the product of the author's imagination or used fictitiously, and any resemblance to actual persons, living or dead, business establishments, events, or locales is entirely coincidental.

Cover art by Brett Carlson
Edited by Brittany Yost

http://www.johnhennessy.net

ISBN-10: 1475171889
ISBN-13: 978-1475171884

By John Hennessy

Novels
THE ROAD TO EXTINCTION TRILOGY
Book One: *At the End*
Book Two: *Into Cinders* (Winter 2012/13)

THE CRY OF HAVOC SAGA
Book One: *Life Descending*
Book Two: *Darkness Devouring*

Praise for Life Descending
"As good as *Game of Thrones*."—Stella Blackmore,
Night Owl Reviews
"A masterpiece."—Reviewed by Rita V for *Readers Favorite*
"A riveting read."—*Midwest Book Review*
"Endlessly imaginative."—*Kirkus Reviews*
"Hard to quit reading."—Robert Medak, *Allbooks Review Int.*
Finalist in *ForeWord Magazine's* 2011 Book of the Year Awards
—fantasy genre

Short Stories
A Stalker's Game (free eBook)

To my Grandpa John
whose enthusiasm to read each
chapter the day it was finished
week by week
propelled the story onward.

1
They're All Gone
Darrel

They did it; they really did it.

The Catholics put an end to the birth control industry, eliminating contraceptives by over 97%, from what I understood. How? I should have paid more attention in school.

The room became darker the longer I stared at the ceiling. Everything was so still, so quiet. It was almost as if I lived on top of a mountain, a lone man, in a sanctuary of solitude. This was far from any sanctuary. The alarm clock on the nightstand pierced my ears as if it sought to kill me. I hated that sound, always had, and probably always would. Although, this would probably be the last time I listened to it. Would that be so bad?

I reached to my left to shut off the harsh noise. I moved as if a reptile waking up in the cold, blood running slower than slow. Numb to the world now, maybe, but I had never experienced this feeling before; I could have misinterpreted the emptiness. My finger must have made it to the correct button because the sound finally ceased.

The room glowed with electronics. I couldn't remember the last time I saw complete darkness. My computer: a tiny metal case smaller than a shoebox that perched on my desk, silent as it slept, lit most of the room. From what I was told, old computers always made humming noises, cooled by fans. I'm not sure what cooled that bugger, but I'd never heard a peep out of it. On the wall above my desk hung the Ultimate Resolution Display, a marvel of the twenties, I believe. Considered garbage in comparison to the shelved items on the current market, but it worked consistently. My eyes darted to the 3D contact lenses resting next to the silver metal clock. Quickly, I inserted them with painless ease. They didn't change my dark-blue eye color like some contacts did. I hated those kinds.

I plopped down into the roller chair, awakened the cursor, and ran a search for the world population. Still 38,638,347,313. No one would ever change it again, probably for the best.

I cleared my throat, always a bad habit of mine.

I drifted into the kitchen, possibly thirty minutes later, or maybe three; I didn't know where time went. But it passed almost at a creep that I'm certain of. Well, I'm not certain about anything anymore, but about as certain as I dared to be. The neo-plastic countertops were bare; they even sparkled in the rising sunlight that found entrance into the house through minor slits in the blinds. An empty fruit bowl sat near the raised edge of the counter, waiting to be filled again.

I cleared my throat. My eyes glazed over, the fruit bowl vanished, hidden in a mist that did not exist.

The world came back as a finger nudged a spoon that sat in wait for me on the counter. The countertops were designed to look like wood, a modern kitchen. I had wondered what modern kitchens looked like half a century ago, probably bleak stainless steel. I had seen part of one before, about five years ago, as it was updated to neo-plastic, a type of super plastic that I knew nothing about. Again, I should have paid more attention in school. Maybe.

I poured a bowl of cereal. Sugarcoated wheat flakes, I could have eaten them every day for the rest of my life, but I didn't think they would be around much longer, then again, I'm guessing neither would I. Time escaped me again, as by the time I made it to the couch, the flakes were soggy. Damn.

The couch was as comfortable as ever. Now this was a sanctuary, a haven, at least for the time being. "Uhrm. On," I said loud enough for the sensor to pick up my voice. The brand new screen lit up. Immediately, a news anchor—a pretty woman—dressed well in a tan suit, came on.

"Good morning and welcome back. The time is three minutes past the eight o'clock hour, Tuesday, the twenty-fourth of March, twenty forty-eight. Today, so far it is estimated that another two million people have gone missing in the Seattle metropolitan area . . ."

"Channel 227," I groaned. I couldn't listen to the news anymore. Cartoons on the other hand I could watch, they did not remind me of the disaster happening outside. A rat jumped out on the screen, almost real. A cat chased its tail, but the rat had better plans, ones involving dynamite. So unrealistic, only people killed things with explosives. I loved it.

All the blinds were drawn down, as I hoped to ignore the street, and the odd, high-pitched noises that periodically came from it. A while later, I thought a midmorning nap seemed appropriate, falling asleep to the boom of cartoon violence.

A creak from the front door stirred me. My chest tightened. The end at last, I hoped.

The creak grew louder, followed by silence.

Something bumped the piano in the room off from the foyer. A curse escaped, floated into the air, and was eventually picked up by my sub-average listening skills. I sat, encased in ice. I heard the blood in my ears. I thought maybe a heart attack would kill me first. My short brown hair bristled like a porcupine. I could feel my rosy-cheeked complexion paling.

Four limbs touched the ground like a cat, fairly soft, but I picked them up despite the voices coming from the TV. I concentrated so hard on the sound that it was all I could hear.

They drew closer, slow, as if they imitated a sloth. The last step I heard was at the end of the couch, just on the other side of its arm. My head was probably centimeters away. I don't think I breathed. My heart thudded against my ribs, as if it were going to split me in two. I waited.

An almond-shaped head popped out from behind the arm, two round, burnt eyes stared at me from behind nifty spectacles. "Darrel?" a voice said, but I was on my way out. Blackness surrounded me, engulfed me; it took care of me, like a warm electric blanket.

Water splashed my face. I guess that worked, because I woke up, wet and screaming. Curse after curse, all the ones I knew, I let them fly.

"Calm down, bromigo," a voice tried to soothe me. The almond head dropped into view in front of me. I erected myself with my back against the couch. I didn't trust what I saw.

"Félix?" I gasped. I coughed some, still short on breath. I cleared my throat. Shocked, I just gaped at him. I never thought I'd see his dark, pecan skin again.

His long face turned into a smile, presenting his luminous white teeth. "Yeah, it's me. You going to pass out on me again?" he asked, nervous. I saw his hands twitch, scared. He ran his shaky fingers through his short black hair.

"No. At least I don't think so. I could use some water though." A second later he was pouring me a glass. I never thought simple water could taste so damn good. "Thanks," I managed, setting the empty glass on a neo-plastic coaster. Mom hated watermarks.

"No prob," he said. He poured himself a glass, sat down in the chair next to the couch, and stared at the animated bullets coming right at us. "Can I ask you something?" He shifted in the velvety fabric, turning to see my expression.

My eyes were still a little unfocused, but my mind felt sharp, guessing as to what he was going to ask. "All right."

"Why are you watching cartoons?"

"You see the mark on the door?" I asked him. I heard the shakiness of my voice.

"Yeah, I did."

"That's why," I answered. I turned back to the showdown, two red-stashed cowboys settling a dispute with a duel.

"You should be watching the news, to understand what's going on," he remarked.

"Is that what you've been doing?"

He nodded.

"Do you know what's going on?"

He shook his head.

"Then I'm just going to watch cartoons, okay?"

"Well that's not logical, it just means no one knows yet," he said. He took another sip from his glass.

"Félix, why are you here? Better yet, how are you here? Yesterday the news said not to go outside, that it's unsafe; I haven't seen anyone on the streets for over a day."

Whatever I said struck a wounded chord in him. He buried his head in his lap, sobbing.

I heard a muffled, "They're gone."

Damn, so many.

"Mine too," I said. "Taken the first night, yours?"

"The second," he replied.

His words were stifled by a cough, but I understood. "So last night was your first night alone?" He raised his head and nodded, taking off his glasses to dry his cheeks. "Well don't worry, they'll be back." I didn't know what else to say, more than likely all my words would be lies. "You want to play Death Squad?"

"No," he said. I think that was the first time in two years that he didn't want to play. "I want to watch the news."

"Uhrm. There's no point. It's been the same news since yesterday morning," I told him.

He stood up, angered. "Billions of people are missing, your parents, my parents, don't you care?"

"Yeah, I care. But she's not saying anything new, none of them are. They don't know anything."

"But maybe they do now, when did you last check?" he asked, hope unconcealed in his words.

I scanned the clock on the TV. "Less than an hour ago."

He shook his head again, not listening.

"I'm telling you nothing has changed."

He ignored my words; he needed to hear good news. "Channel 0002," Félix yelled. The same news anchor appeared on screen, streaming the same broadcast she had been for the last several hours.

"Today's current estimate has peaked at 38 billion people missing, about 13 billion more globally than yesterday." She changed her tone; maybe something new was coming to break her from her repetitive blathering. "Surprisingly, the first two nights occurred without a trace of recovered video footage, but last night a French woman caught on camera quite a disturbing sight, using an antiquated 1998 camcorder. We have managed to interface the outdated technology." They rolled the footage: a mellow-toned French woman shot a distorted image of a nighttime street at least three stories below. A few city lights illuminated parts of the sidewalk, where large, fuzzy dots crossed under them in single file. The image went in and out, alternating between darkness and a strange static screen I had never seen before.

The camcorder played back a harsh noise drawing closer, high-pitched scratches that sounded as if claws dug into the building's side, climbing. As the sound grew louder, the camera began to shake more, as though an endless twitch struck its bearer. "Do you see anything?" a man's voice asked in French before the TV translated his words into English.

The camera withdrew from the window, still focused on its frame. "Spots," she replied. "Could be people down there." The sound advanced faster for a few seconds until it ceased altogether, stopping near the window.

"What is that noise?" the man asked with a tense voice.

"I don't know," she replied, less afraid than her male counterpart. She edged closer again. "Maybe a squirrel."

The silence coiled fear in me, ready to discharge, but my eyes remained glued to the display despite the anticipation of horror.

"Too big," the man responded. The camera crept to where the footage had started by the window, but before it reached its destination, a claw swiped it to the carpeted flooring. The lens recorded nothing but blackness after, yet an audible short scream burst forth.

"Estelle . . . Estelle?" the man whispered, almost choking in fear. A rush of footsteps ran at the camera, then carried the device off into more darkness.

The news anchor reappeared. "That's all the footage reveals, a giant claw, larger than a Tiger's. From this, we know whatever the creature is, it is capable of scaling vertical walls. The man escaped his apartment and found his way to a news station still in operation around seven this morning . . ."

I couldn't listen anymore. "Channel 227, priority one," I spoke clearly. The TV recognized the command and changed back to a cowboy riding away on a horse as the sun set.

"What are you doing?" Félix screamed at me. His eyes had been just as stationary as mine, fixed to the screen. "They have new information, change it back." My silence awakened a fury in him that I had never witnessed before. His skinny fingers curled into a fist with eyes targeting my face. "Channel 0002."

"Access denied, setting priority one in activation," the speakers communicated.

"My dad added the setting so that my little cousin would stop switching the stations," I said.

Félix stared at me, surprised. "Figures, you don't know anything about electronics." His arm trembled in agitation.

Would he really strike at me?

"All right, dude. Calm down." I put up my hands and swallowed. The dryness of my throat gave way to slight tears. "Channel 0002," I commanded. No use arguing when he felt passionately enough to make fists.

In size, I was much bigger than him, but I had little heart to fight in real life. I thought him the same, but it looked like my opinion turned out wrong. Clearing my throat, I seized my empty glass while he refocused his attention to the screen.

Words that overflowed with panic were blaring out of the speakers.

The rushed voice did not slow as the TV transitioned to a new image: the Space Needle climbed in the distance, failing to compete with a multitude of newer buildings that dwarfed the symbolic tower. The sound faltered, skipping over a few words. An instant later, it cut out altogether. The camera zoomed in, the screen blurred unable to draw the pixels fast enough. The screen adjusted to an image hovering above the city. The picture began to follow the sound in its collapse, flickering between static and skyline.

The image stabilized for a moment.

Félix gasped.

"No way," I muttered, staggered by the inconceivable spaceship that floated near the Space Needle, poised for possible destruction. "You believe it?" I asked.

He shook his head.

Of course he didn't. Despite the hundreds, maybe thousands of imaginary spaceships my eyes had encountered, nothing prepared me for what I saw. I had flown ships that looked and felt so real; I sometimes began to believe they were, but not anymore. Not anymore.

A news chopper flew towards the great machine: five black and red ovals, like a bee's abdomen the size of skyscrapers, trailed behind a slightly larger oval, connected by support beams that curved at peculiar angles, almost as if made for aesthetics instead of reinforcement purposes. A strange red light glowed at the butt end of the five, emitting trace amounts of a crimson gas that disappeared soon after it encountered the firmament.

The chopper drew closer, almost within a few body lengths to the front oval. The camera zoomed in again, concentrating on the one section, and as the pixels adjusted, dozens of curved poles that extended out from the nose of the body and attached to the rear, all came into sight.

The ship looked more complicated than the interior of the human body, including the brain. "I guess graphic designers got it all wrong," Félix said.

I nodded my concurrence.

"Invasion?" I asked, though I didn't know how I expected him to reply; it's not as if he would have known any more than I did.

The display cut out again. When it returned the chopper was descending beyond a rate that suggested control; it was crashing, heading for the waters of the Sound. The camera attempted to keep track of the chopper, but a second later the screen went haywire, producing only static.

I twisted to meet my friend's utterly stunned face. "Invasion," I repeated. Panic hit Félix, but I think it hit me harder. I ran, skidded, tumbled, and clambered to the front window. Curses were the only words that left our mouths, in an echo similar to a fading song chorus.

I brushed aside the curtains.

Normal. Everything still looked the same, except no busy cars to be heard. "Did you see anything on your way over?" I asked.

"Not a thing," Félix replied. "Maybe they are only in the bigger cities. Seattle is only an hour away by car."

"Then how come everyone is gone? No, I think they're here, somewhere . . ." My arm twitched, then my leg gave out, sending my face to the carpet.

"You okay?" he asked, twitching as well.

"No . . ." I said. It was the end, happening just like in Fury of War and Our Descent, the two games I played most before the release of Death Squad. It was now. "What do we do?" I lay there, motionless. I couldn't do this. I couldn't survive.

They would get me . . .

"Do you know anyone with a telescope? Maybe we can look for ourselves, to see what's out there."

"I remember Jacob Moletti had one," I replied.

"He goes to U-Dub, doesn't he?"

"Yeah, he does, and from what I understand it's changed him drastically. All he does is drink now." Or did. Probably taken now, and it's doubtful the aliens gave out free cocktails.

"Well, we should go take a look to see if it is still there."

"Do you really want to know?" I asked. I didn't. I'd seen too many bug-eyed aliens on screen, at least enough to discourage my curiosity to go and search for them.

He slumped down next to me, hands twitching as if attacked by an epileptic fit. Taciturnity became our mood. What was there left to say? Goodbye? The time had long passed for such sentiments, too many people taken unexpectedly.

Time betrayed me, for the next time my eyes crossed the kitchen clock, only twenty minutes had passed, but I swear the sun should have been settling down for bed. Félix laughed when he saw me staring at the clock, flustered.

"You know it's funny, all we've ever done is play video games, and now when it comes to it, all that training means nothing," he said, still laughing.

I turned to him. "Training?" I said. His meaning was lost upon me.

"Don't you think we've been trained for this? The military does the same thing for combat simulations," he said. His grin widened.

"Except they have people screaming at them, they have people instructing them, they have other tests besides combat games," I countered.

"True . . . but still . . ." He wanted to say something more, but stopped himself.

"You really think we should go to Jacob's?" I said, not entirely excited for his answer.

"His father works for NASA, doesn't he? That's why his parents split?"

"From what I understand, yeah. You think his father tells him secrets . . . stuff like the existence of aliens?"

Félix propped himself up using the window ledge. "All I know, bromigo, is that I can't watch cartoons waiting to die . . . waiting to be taken." He hastened to the kitchen, where he began to empty the knife block. He was always using the Spanglish word bromigo, something passed on by his cousins in San Diego. I had tried it out once, but it didn't roll off my tongue so well. I had always performed poorly in Spanish class.

"What are you doing?" I asked. Uncertain as to what he intended to do out there, on the streets that promised our demise.

"What's the first thing you learn before playing Our Descent online?" he asked, frantically scouring through drawers. He placed older knives next to his assembled weaponry.

The answer came easily, probably a saying I'd repeated a million times since I had heard it years ago. "The well armed take advantage, whether physical or intellectual, all are assets to the soldier," I said without fault. For some odd reason the saying sparked a feeling of courage in me. It ignited a strange passion that I'd never comprehended.

"Then let us be well armed," he said, raising his eyes from the collection of blades to meet mine, now ablaze with the will to fight. I placed the thought of surrender in the shadows of my mind.

I jumped to my feet, invigorated. "My dad's tools," I yelled. His eyes glinted at the idea. We raced to the garage, lined with woodworking implements. I clutched one of the several electric handsaws, charged by the sun. "The batteries should last years, unless the aliens block out the sky." All at once, the adrenaline ran dry, replaced once again by fear.

Years . . .

How long could we really survive? Video game campaigns ended when you shut off the application. A Nightmare was beginning to unfold in my mind.

A hand landed on my shoulder. I jerked. Félix smiled. "Let's just make it to Jacob's first." I'm pretty sure I nodded. His effort to comfort me freaked me out more.

I tried repeating the energizing motto, but its power lessened the more I recited it. Félix held up a hatchet, twirled it around. He eyed it for a long time, then asked, "Why does your dad have a hatchet when he has all of these saws?"

"Beats me, my father is a strange one, he probably used it to chop up wood just for fun." I searched around, nothing resembled any real weaponry, then I remembered my neighbor. "The Troll," I shouted unintentionally.

"What?"

"The Troll," I repeated. "He has all that hunting gear."

"I'm not going anywhere near that place. What's wrong with this stuff?"

"The range," I said. My fingers glided over the sharp teeth of a blade. "None of this stuff has any range; it's all last resort gear." He nodded, he hadn't thought of that either. "Best to fire from ten meters than to slice from one."

"All right, but if he's home, we're dead."

"Uhrm. We're dead if we don't go, too," I added. "Uhrm." The thought of leaving the house started to agitate me, my throat felt as if it would never be clear again. "Uhrm."

"You all right? You're clearing your throat more than normal," he observed.

"Guess it's not a normal day."

His lips moved to one side of his face in a half-grin. "Guess you're right about that. Let's put this stuff in a bag with some food and get going. Might take us a while to get to Jacob's and I don't want to be out in the dark."

We gathered the equipment, grabbing any spare blades and accessories. My dad's utility belts proved useful for stuffing knives into as well. In twenty minutes we transformed ourselves from scared-shitless teenagers into scared-shitless teenagers with garage weapons.

Ready for departure, I surveyed the street through the peephole. Nothing. I hadn't heard a dog bark for two days, and I hadn't heard a bird since yesterday, but then I wasn't listening for them either.

"Uhrm. Ready?" I rotated so that I could see Félix.

He carried a handsaw in his right and a hatchet in his left. "I wish I were."

I nodded and opened the door. Slow and with caution, at least I tried, but the damn thing sounded off like a siren, alarming anything within a thousand meter radius with its impairing creak. An exaggeration on my part, probably, time would tell shortly.

I lived at the end of Rhododendron Way, which hadn't change much in the last twenty years. In fact, Bellingham hadn't changed much. Still relatively small, fewer than 200,000, still considered progressive in its collective views, from what I understood anyway.

The Troll was different. I didn't know why he didn't live up north in Lynden, probably would've fared better there, but then again, I knew little about the man. Except that he favored hunting, boasting an arsenal fit to take down a small militia on his own. No one on the block had liked that.

The cul-de-sac presented us with more cars than the usual Tuesday afternoon. Extra vehicles dozed in driveways all down the street, probably never to be woken again. We slinked into the front yard, crouched behind some flowers I had never bothered to learn the names of, mostly because my mother rattled them off as if I already knew them. I examined the neighborhood.

Dead.

The same symbol marked all the doors that I could see: a slanted line with three lines pointing upward, like a tilted E, colored black and red. I turned back at the engraved marking on my door, my eyes flooded, no stopping the tears. I wanted to run back inside, sit back down on the comfy couch and watch cartoons, so that I could pretend that everything was fine. Not a chance. The TV had died like everything else around. Damn.

I glanced at Félix; his face was the same. We weren't soldiers . . .

I could not say for sure how long it took us, but we made it to the Troll's house, three houses up and across the street. "His house is marked," Félix noted in a tone full of apprehension.

"Yeah, but he could still be alive, after all, we are . . ." I said. We spun around to meet each other's stares. Neither of us had thought about that. Our houses were marked, yet we weren't taken.

"The foil?" we said in unison.

"But that was just for fun. It doesn't do anything," he said. Two years ago, we had put foil up above our beds, for protection from aliens, of course. It started as a joke at school, I scarcely remember why, and neither of us had bothered to take it down since.

"Maybe we should wrap ourselves in it," I suggested. "Just in case."

"Yeah, all right, I guess it couldn't hurt."

I nodded. My skin pimpled from a shiver, the silence of the street was starting to eat at my already fragile nerves. We confronted the mark on the door, then snuck inside, the Troll's properly lubed hinges produced no noise. In the kitchen, we stocked up on more cutlery, as his were top notch, sharpened to perfection. Conveniently, the Troll had three large boxes of foil that we used to blanket our bodies.

We crept down the stairs, but our furtive steps seemed pointless, nothing jumped out of the dark at us.

"Over here," I said, heading towards an old armoire covered by dust. The whole room matched, decaying and dusty. I opened both of the doors to the furniture, where several bows greeted me, including an ancient one without any technological enhancements. Hunting blades hung on the inside of the doors, a few of them the size of small swords.

"No guns," Félix observed.

"Guess not." I snatched one of the newer bows, and a pair of goggles fell to the floor, a small dust cloud puffed up upon the impact. I scooped up the pure black goggles that looked like ski goggles. After I extracted my 3D contacts, I put them over my eyes. I flipped the switch on the side and the room lit up in black and white. "Wow, I can see everything."

"Infrared. There are lights on the side of the goggles." Félix pointed to a light, then grabbed his own pair.

"Slick."

"Expensive."

"Yeah, I bet," I said, pulling back on the bowstring. "Except for that." I nodded at the ancient bow. "Don't know why he would keep that around."

"Probably worth a ton, bromigo. It looks like an artifact." He touched the heavy wood, careful not to knock it over. Eventually he selected one, stowed a bundle of arrows, along with half the hunting blades. The other half I took, placing the deadliest looking one in a soft sheath that I wrapped around my calf. The Troll had three quivers, one probably as old as the ancient bow, the other two maybe a few years past their prime, but they held together.

I scanned the room for anything else viable for combat, but came up empty. Pictures of the Troll and hunting companions hung on the wall, displaying their acquisitions. I'd never seen such a spitting image of the fantasy creature; the apt nickname described the man in full detail.

I turned back to Félix.

"Ready?" Félix's voice was as shaky as my sweaty hands. I hoped I would never have to fire the bow; I would never hit a target with such rebellious nerves. A sickness attacked my stomach, climbing up my throat. I saw the ceiling above before the goggles went flying from my head.

Félix sprinkled cold water on my face as I came to. "Hey," I said weakly. He handed me the bottle, but it was hard for me to pour. He guided the bottle for me, my hands still quivering. "Thanks."

He nodded. "Forget it."

"Time?" I asked.

He pressed a button on his wristwatch. It lit up for a second. "Three," he answered.

Good, it had only been ten minutes or so, not the end of the world. Not yet. He helped me to my feet. "Maggy," I mumbled.

"What was that?"

"Maggy, I forgot about Maggy," I said, searching the darkness for the goggles. I found them under an antique chair.

"You think she made it?" he asked.

"Uhrm. She was in on the joke, too. Remember?" I took a step and wobbled, almost collapsing again. He reached to support me. "I'm fine," I said, waving away his hands. "I'm fine. Let's go check out her house. We have time before it gets dark."

"Sure, sure." I was glad to hear his sympathy.

When I had first met Maggy a few years ago, before we became close friends, I had the biggest crush on her. Funny thing about that, it never actually went away. I think she had always known how I felt, girls always seemed to know, but they were excellent at concealing any awareness. That was probably to make it less awkward when their feelings didn't match.

We met daylight again in the Troll's backyard, which connected to the Railroad Trail that wound all around Bellingham. My foot sunk into the soft dirt, mushy from last night's rain. On the other side of the trail, a fence stopped us at somebody's backyard, too high for me to scale.

"There's a gate over there." Félix pointed to the next neighbor down. The latch was simple, a fence more to keep dogs in than people out. No dogs chased us as we crossed into the front yard to Lake Crest Drive. We crouch-walked along the sidewalk, passing a few houses until Crestline Drive. Her bright yellow home shined, as if it smiled in the overcast.

We stopped on the porch, whispering what to do if she wasn't there, or if it was a good idea at to know at all. The foreign symbol marked her door. I gripped the handle. "Okay," I sighed.

I twisted the knob.

A knife struck the molding. In a panic, I swiveled, pushing Félix off the porch as I jumped away. I heard a strange shrill scream. It was my own. My heart had pounded playing video games before, but nothing compared to this. And the heat. It was the worst hot flash, the temperature lingered only in the 40's, maybe low 50's outside, but my skin sweated as if it were in the high 90's. I gushed like a waterslide.

I spotted a few bushes and hid behind them, desperately trying to calm my breathing; it was as rapid as a fully automatic bursting 5000 rounds per minute. Félix joined me a second later. "You all right?" he asked. I nodded, drawing in a deep, deep breath.

I had dropped my bow, so I reached for the sword-like knife resting against my calf. The blade shook and shook. Damn my nerves. I looked over at Félix. He nodded as he drew the same conclusion I had come to: aliens.

I cleared my throat a hundred times, the vein in my neck bulged as if a thousand snakes shot through it in rapid succession.

We charged around the corner, yelling war cries. I threw the knife, but it more slipped from my hand than anything, rotating in the air like a saucer. Félix fired an arrow towards the door, but missed, only to hit the doorbell. My knife didn't make it that far, as it thudded into the stairs of the porch.

Maggy stood in the doorway, eyeing us with complete disbelief. "Jelly? Tortilla?" She was carrying two steak knives but dropped them once she saw us. "You morons . . . you're alive . . ."

At that moment, I hoped the wetness around my crotch was sweat. "IQ," I said. I ran up the steps, hugging her skinny body as tightly as I could muster, though my muscles trembled, aquiver with fear. I released my weak hold. "You tried to kill us."

"You tried to kill me."

"Even?"

"Even," she replied. "You guys made it, how?"

"Do you still have the foil hanging above your bed?" Félix asked.

She nodded, her long, sleek black hair swaying with the movement. "We think it has something to do with that."

She giggled. "Is that why you guys are as shiny as a new quarter?"

"You guessed it, bramiga," he answered. "You should wrap yourself as well, just in case it's true." She led us inside, where we sat on the couch while she neatly dressed herself in foil.

I stared at her beauty, probably a bad habit I should deter, but I didn't know how. She was short, thin, and an Asian-American that actually lived up to the old stereotype: she was a brainiac. Her yellow eyes stunned me for a few moments every time I looked into them. "When were your parents taken, IQ?" I asked.

"The first, yours?"

"Same," I replied.

"The second," Félix said, taking a sip from a water bottle. I had already engulfed half a container in the few minutes since we had sat. The icy liquid helped steady my out-of-control heartbeat.

"Sorry, Tortilla, must be a little harder." He didn't reply, just slowly drank his water. "Jelly, can you help me?" She struggled to wind the foil around her back.

"Yeah," I said. I didn't mind her nickname for me, even though it meant I was bigger, it also implied a sweetness, like Santa Claus and his bowl of a stomach. She gave it to me because the only thing I liked more than sugarcoated wheat flakes were jelly-filled donuts, raspberry or strawberry, it didn't matter. Félix never complained about his either—she called him tortilla because for an entire month last year he had eaten tacos at lunch with a specific kind of soft tortilla shell, and I guess the name sort of stuck after that. His mother never cared for it, that's certain, always making sure that Maggy understood that they weren't Mexican but Salvadoran. Why it mattered though, I never understood.

When she finished with the foil, she concealed it under thin clothes. "So I don't look like the dorks you two look like," she said. When she was done poking fun, we explained the plan, the journey to Moletii's house. "I'm in, bromigos." She was good enough at Spanish to pull off the word. I think Félix had always liked that.

"You'll need gear." Of course, she already knew that. She played just as many video games, and spent just as many hours taking down opponents as we did. Packed with kitchen utensils and a replica axe from *Lord of the Rings*, she added in a few more things that we had forgotten, chiefly, a change of clothes.

"Isn't the axe a little heavy," I said.

She laughed. "It's not the 20's." She tossed me the axe; it was as light as the hunting knife. "It's neo-plastic, probably stronger than that blade you have," she bragged.

With a smirk, I handed it back to her.

"You two ready?" Félix asked. "It's almost four."

"Ready," she said. I nodded. We went down the porch and looked both ways. "West Birch Street would be faster, we'll just have to cut through a few yards."

"Guess no one will mind," I said.

"Unless they are alive. Maybe we should look for survivors on the way," Félix spoke up, nocking an arrow back, primed for engagement. I copied him, though I doubted it would make a difference, the damn thing would fly ten meters from anything I aimed at.

"We have about three and a half hours of decent daylight, if we look too much, we won't make it there before twilight, and I don't have any nifty goggles," Maggy said. She started towards the cul-de-sac, axe raised, her eyes on duty, alert.

I followed close to her right, so Félix trailed to her left, putting her in the middle. She could probably take us both, but that didn't matter, something instinctual made us bookends. After two cluttered yards, we hit the pavement of West Birch, and the silence finally tore into me.

"Are the rounds of a dead end called a cove-va-sac or cul-de-sac?" I asked. I had loosened my hold on the bowstring, but the perfectly aligned arrow did not move regardless of the applied tension.

"I think it is cul-te-sac," Félix countered.

Maggy laughed. "No, it's definitely cul-de-sac."

"I think it is cove-va, myself," I said.

"Have your phone?" she asked. I shook my head. Félix dug around in his pockets but came up empty-handed from them all. I doubted any of us had gone somewhere without a phone since the third grade. Weird.

"Well, it shouldn't be hard to find one," Maggy said. The conversation numbed the high levels of apprehension, at least enough for us to breathe at a regular pace. "Let's try that house." She pointed up the road to a two-story baby blue home with yellow trim.

The front door was locked, so Maggy swung her axe at the crack where the door met the frame. The fake wood splintered after a few hard strokes, and with one hard kick, she threw it open. I stared at Félix. Neither of us knew she was so tough: built like a kitten, but as deadly as a cougar.

It looked like any other house I'd seen, moderately clean, some dirty dishes on the counter, a recycling pile too tall to ever be taken out in one trip, and in the living room a spotless jumbo TV bracketed to the wall in front of a couch.

"There's one." Maggy spotted a phone beside the toaster. She pressed a button then slid her nimble fingers across the screen to unlock it, finding the voice input button. "Define cul-de-sac," she said.

The phone searched for a few seconds before a woman replied, "A street, lane, or passage closed at one end, a blind alley."

"Yes! Ha!" She showed us the spelling.

"Lucky, that's all," I said, but there was no stopping her triumphant, smug grin.

"Shh," Félix uttered. "I think something else is in the house." I listened. Nothing. It was enough to creep all of us out, as I was the last to bolt over the threshold of the door. We let up on the gas when we rounded the corner where Birch forked off into east and west.

"Probably just our nerves," Maggy said when her lungs caught up. "Just nerves."

I cleared my throat a dozen or so times, downing water like a kitchen drain, but it didn't matter. Félix tossed me his inhaler after he finished spraying his throat. I shook it, counting to thirty. I shot the medicine into my mouth and held until a cough broke loose. Maggy took it next.

Asthma, I don't think I had known anyone who didn't have it. A plague of the twenty-first century, but medicine combatted it rigorously, making it little more than a nuisance.

"Ready?" Maggy asked. It didn't matter, though, whether or not we were, she took off towards Alabama Street. We were already over the hump of Alabama Hill, so at least we had that going for us, well, more for me. I was exhausted, yet the distance that I had covered was laughable at best.

I stopped when we started past the Lakeview Condos. "Spooky." The giant complex of expensive housing emanated a chill of death. All of the doors within the complex were marked just as all the neighborhood houses were. Félix tugged at my sleeve to press on.

Whatcom Lake came into view as we hit Electric Ave; the habitual

ripples of the water from boats and people were gone, the body of water lay motionless as any fluid ever could. The stoplight at the cross
street still functioned in its routine, signaling non-existent traffic. Still
no birds sang any jolly tunes, not even seagulls or crows flew in the sky.
It was barren, except for the heavy clouds.

We met North Shore Drive a block or so north, turning northeast
along the shore. We passed about four houses shielded by trees and
bushes, until an empty driveway gave way to a lone house. Maggy, observant as ever, regarded the mark on the door. "It's different."

We walked down into the drive. "What do you think that means?"
I asked. They both shook their heads. The symbol only had two lines
that pointed upward, colored solely black. Fearless, Maggy pushed the
door open so that we could peer inside. There was nothing dissimilar
from any of the other houses.

"Let's check it out," she urged.

Félix slipped in first, bow shaking but ready to launch. I refilled my
water after we concluded nothing stranger had happened compared to
any other home. The residents were missing, nothing unusual about
that.

Carelessly, we marched down the stairs to the daylight basement.

I heard a few crunches, as if bones were being crushed under extreme pressure. We rounded the corner. Indeed, that's what it was.

Horrorstruck, we all screamed. A short-haired beast that resembled
a lioness was hunched over a corpse, chewing down a slab of human
flesh. Surprised, it jumped up on all fours, standing two meters at its
shoulders. Two more arms sprang forward from its shoulders, jointed
in too many ways to count. At their ends rotated a hand with four humanlike fingers and two thumbs.

There was no time.

My arrow flew towards a bookshelf to the left of it; Félix's arrow
penetrated a tawny foreleg. A roar that sounded unlike a true lion, as
low and ominous as any video-game dragon, rattled our ribcages. I swallowed a hundred times; no more saliva existed to scream.

Maggy sprinted for the sliding glass door to our right, flipped up
the lever, and threw the door open. "Hurry!" she screamed.

Félix crossed the threshold last, stubbing a foot on the track; he
tumbled onto the wet lawn in a crash. A deadly paw stomped down on
his foot. He cried. We turned and saw the giant mouth, brimming with
scything teeth, about to crush his skull. Maggy pelted the alien with
steak knives. I launched the hunting blade sheathed around my calf.

Within moments, the creature was speckled with our weapons.

It roared again. My stomach quaked and gurgled. I nocked another dart and loosed it. It flew straight for its shoulder. As it hit, the alien twirled and stepped back. Félix crawled until he was able to stand. We darted for the lake.

A well-maintained motorboat, powered by the sun, was moored to a short dock, strangely idle in the creepy water. Maggy was the first to reach it. She jumped in. "No key," she yelled. I helped Félix settle down into a seat. The alien, now recovered from our startling attack, bolted down the slope of the lawn in an unimaginable burst of speed, twice as fast as any cheetah.

Maggy searched for a key. Félix handed me his hunting knife, and I slashed the cord, then pushed off from the dock. We slowly drifted away in the calmness of the lake.

Once the alien reached the shore, it stopped, stamped about for a second, then roared furiously.

"Maybe it's like that old, old movie, what's it called?" Félix said.

"*Signs*," Maggy replied.

"Yeah, maybe water will kill it."

As if it heard Félix's words, it defied his guess and rushed into the water, paddling hard after the boat.

"Find the key!" Maggy ordered. We scrambled in haste. Hidden or lost, it could not be found. As the creature swam, it used one of its humanlike hands to yank the arrow from its shoulder. Red blood, just like mine, escaped its body and dyed the water.

"Shoot it," Félix yelled at me.

But I couldn't. I was stiff. Dead. Already dead. Real fear doesn't exist in video games. I couldn't handle facing this opponent.

Félix looked up at me, his glasses still intact, then quickly snatched the bow and arrow, firing. It missed. He shot a second and a third, until at last it was upon the boat.

Maggy leapt forward with her neo-plastic axe and hacked off one of its human hands. She brought down a giant swing upon its head. The axe stuck, unable to be freed.

The alien cried as it sank. Bubbles surfaced: a reminder of its life now taken.

We sat in silence. "Alion," Maggy said after a while.

"What?" I asked.

"Alien plus lion, it's an alion," she laughed.

I thought about it for a second. "Nice, very nice."

Félix and I laughed, and she smiled. "Let's look again for the key," she said. She found a ring of keys in a dry box under the captain's chair. It was a good thing that Lake Dwellers were so trusting. If it were my boat, I would have kept the key in a safe, or at least someplace a little more hidden from thieving hands.

I checked over Félix's wound; it wasn't as bad as his cry had led us to believe.

We reached an expensive, neo-plastic dock on the northeast side of the lake. "It's only five thirty, so I think we're okay on time," Maggy said as she climbed out of the boat. "Moletti's house is on East North Street, and I think we're between Silver Beach and East Connecticut. You remember which house is his?"

Félix shook his head.

"I remember brick," I said.

"Brick is better than nothing." We nodded. The steps that led up the backyard slope wore me out, more than I thought a few lousy steps could. At the top, a high deck watched the sunset to the west, a great view on a clear day, but rainclouds were strolling south, always the backdrop of Bellingham.

We came again to North Shore Drive. "You know the area well," I said to Maggy. She smiled as we passed the East Connecticut sign. Finally, we stopped at the East North Street sign: it stood motionless, just like any other sign, but I had a horrible feeling that it would be the last street sign that I would ever set my eyes upon. Three houses up the road, we found an ugly gray house with brick siding climbing halfway up its walls.

The same symbol with two black lines marked the door. "I like that sign less than the one on our doors," I said. My heart was wild. I didn't want to go in.

Maggy gazed at us. "We have no other plan." She found two knives in her backpack: a butcher's and a chef's, each thick and sharp. I pulled out a handsaw. Félix gripped his last two hunting knives. Maggy rotated the knob.

A shadowy foyer greeted us, bleak and chilly. We crept in single file. My foot knocked over a glass bottle. We paused, silent and scared. The bottle rolled forever; I don't think it ever stopped. Maggy continued on. Straight ahead of the foyer connected a living room with a long curling couch that boasted seven cushions or more. In the corner of the room there was a TV fastened to the wall. It relayed nothing but static and emitted no sound. Bottles were scattered all across the carpet, coffee table, and the end tables. The house reeked of alcohol.

"Look!" Maggy cried. She ran to the couch where a sprawled body slept.

"It's Jacob," I said. "Is he alive?"

She put two fingers to his pale throat. "Yeah, just passed out, I guess."

"Look at this place," Félix gasped. He stared at me. "I've never seen so many bottles of alcohol, not even at your parents' New Year's parties."

"You think he'll get alcohol poisoning?" I asked, though I'm not sure why either of them would have known. They both shrugged. I walked into the kitchen with Félix not far behind. The counters were lined with unopened bottles. A dozen or more little green propane bottles glared at us from the floor.

"You think he wanted to blow himself up?" Félix's voice quivered.

"Don't know. IQ, come here." Maggy bounded up to us and gasped.

We all shuddered.

"Should we look for the telescope?" I asked. I didn't know what else to do.

"I guess so," Maggy answered. We searched the house for a while, until about six thirty; night crept upon us with about an hour before sunset.

We gathered by the couch. "Anything?" she asked.

"No telescope," Félix replied. "But I found an Apocalypse Room; it has a metal door, pretty thick too."

"That is good to know." She turned to me.

I shook my head.

"Well, I don't know what to do now; I guess we can look outside for it . . ."

"Uhrm. I'm not going out there now, no way. Uhrm. Forget it."

The backyard: a motion light turned on abruptly. We all hit the floor, crushing bottles and all. Curses, it was all curses after that. "They're here. They're here. What—what now," Félix stuttered, beyond panic.

"The propane," Maggy whispered.

"Huh?" he said.

"We blow the house with the propane while we hide in the Apocalypse Room; they're built to withstand bombs, so we'll be safe. You two line the house, and I'll put one in the oven." No one argued. She always had the plans, and we always listened.

A window broke somewhere in the house.

More curses sputtered forth.

Finished with the plan, we hastily lugged Jacob down to the metal room, and as we pulled on the door, a furry arm reached into the crack. Maggy picked up the handsaw.

The massive bone was as solid as neo-plastic, and it fought against the saw, but the alion finally withdrew its limb, cut halfway through. Blood splashed on the cold floor. When the door shut, no light illuminated the cramped space. Such complete darkness.

Claws, powered by tough, strong muscle, struck the door. No one screamed like on TV. I guess when fear is thick and real, they just didn't come out. My throat was so dry, so terribly dry.

"It will only take about a minute for the oven to get hot enough," Maggy said while stroke after stroke fell upon the door.

Silence overtook the room on our side of the door. My body quaked worse than a 9.0. I reached into my backpack and grabbed the goggles. I thought sight would calm me.

I looked upon a black and white world, with some gray, some cold gray. I saw Jacob's body in the back, still and lifeless. He had certainly had the right idea; there was no fear coursing through him now, no stomach pains, no nausea, nothing but blackness. I scanned the room until my eyes fell upon Félix and Maggy. They huddled together across from me, cozy and tender. I spotted their interlocked hands.

I had never felt so sick. So hot. So enraged. If ever an all time low existed, this was it. I cleared my throat over and over again.

The first tank exploded. The chain followed. I closed my eyes to peer at the darkness that blackened my thoughts. I waited, filled with hope that my tormented heart would cease, at the end now. At the end.

2
Empty Shelves
Maggy

Tortilla was holding me tight, his grip comforted and hurt at the same time. That's how hard he held me.

My head rested against his chest. For a while, I just listened to the *ba-bump-ba-bump* of his heart. This was my first time hearing it: it was the best sound in the world. It was so dark, and I was so relaxed, I wanted to fall asleep, but my mind jumped around as if I had had three cups of coffee.

I looked up at Tortilla. He was so peaceful, so incredibly peaceful. Well, I don't know if I saw him, or if I saw what I wanted to see. I couldn't see Jelly across from us. I was glad. I was glad he couldn't see us together. He would hate it.

I scanned towards the door: there was nothing but blackness. It held, solid. That's why they had named it the Apocalypse Room. I wondered if it did anyone else any good. The alions took people so fast, and who knew how they did it; I certainly didn't.

Finally, I let Tortilla's warmth overwhelm me. It soothed me into sleep, and there I stayed, probably for the rest of my life.

I rolled over, startled. I thought I had heard a roar. I thought I had heard that deep, monstrous roar. My leaden eyes stared at nothing, a void of black. Somehow, I had broken loose from Tortilla's clutch, so I labored to my feet, using the frozen wall as a prop.

The handle wouldn't budge, as if it were jammed. I tried over and over, useless. There were buttons on a keypad by the handle, so I fiddled with those, but they were useless, too. Until I hit a big one, like a space bar. All of a sudden, there was a computerized click. Pushing the door open, a sliver of light came in through the crack. It was devastating. I pulled back on the door again to reduce the harshness. After a minute or two, I kicked it open. It barely swung. A few of the hinges were bent, so I was happy that it moved at all. We could have been trapped in there, but maybe that would have been for the better.

I turned around and saw Jelly. He was staring at me, and the burnt room behind me. There were goggles on the floor next to his feet, and for a second I wondered if he had worn them while we were in the void. I hoped not. I really hoped not.

"We didn't die," he said, his voice sounded like gravel.

I smiled. "No, we did not. The sun is shining." I pointed up to the hole in the ceiling and the roof above it. The walls all around us were black.

"Yeah." He smiled. He looked relieved and burdened, burdened by something I knew he wasn't going to tell me about.

My stomach grumbled, using its weird digestive speech. "Did we eat yesterday?"

"I don't want to remember yesterday."

I nodded. That was fine, I guess. "Well, we need to eat today at least. Probably nothing left upstairs, but the neighbors might have something."

He turned around and grabbed a granola bar from a shelf. "And the Apocalypse Room. There's lots of food in here." He tossed me the bar.

I caught it, unwrapped it, and started munching away.

Jelly walked over to Tortilla, bent down, and shook his shoulder. "Hey, dude. Wake up."

"No thanks," Tortilla said, then rolled to his side, facing the wall.

"All right, suit yourself." Jelly attempted to wake Jacob, but he didn't stir. "He's still breathing."

I nodded. "Good. You want to look around?"

"I guess so, not really, though; I don't want to see what's out there." His eyes told me that he wanted to stay in the Apocalypse Room for the rest of his life, where it was safe. Safe. As safe as one could be in that cozy little box of a room.

"That's fine, I can go myself." The granola bar was in my belly now, so I grabbed two knives and headed to the adjoining room, a long hall that ended with stairs on one end and a sliding glass door at the other. The stairs were wrecked, impossible to climb up them, so I went and checked outside. Water pooled in the house, signaling that it had rained last night, which must have extinguished the fires from the propane tanks. Jelly was behind me, but it didn't seem like he was paying attention, almost as if he was dazed or something.

The air outside was cool. It felt nice on my lungs as they expanded. None of us had used the inhalers last night, and my chest had been tight, my throat had closed, for most of the time. Now I could breathe.

"Looks the same," Jelly said. He sat down in a black patio chair. The sun briefly smiled past the clouds then disappeared.

"Doesn't feel the same, though. Feels like it's dead out here." The air was calm, no animals . . . where had all the animals gone? I plopped down into a chair next to him. "What should we do next?"

He cleared his throat. "You're the idea maker. The planner. I've got nothing." He unscrewed a lid to one of his water bottles and took a huge gulp. He started to unwrap a granola bar when he twitched in his chair.

"You see something?"

He eyed me, disturbed. "I always see something these days. Whether or not they're there, now that's something I don't know."

I surveyed the area, but I didn't see anything, so I seated myself again and drank some water. "I guess we don't have to search for the stupid telescope anymore. I don't know why we did after we knew they were here." I heard a noise at the sliding glass door, and I whipped my head around and saw Tortilla bump into the frame. My blood instantly warmed at the sight of him.

"Hey," Tortilla said, his throat was dry and raspy. "Can I get some water?"

I offered him the bottle. He drank what was left of it in a hurry. "Good?"

"Real good," he replied. He dragged a third chair around to the door, so that he could view the backyard and beyond. I don't think anyone wanted to put their back to it, I sure didn't. "What are we going to do now?"

"Not sure . . . but we should probably wait for Jacob to wake up," I said. For some reason, all I wanted then was for Tortilla to hold me, to say that it was going to be all right. I needed that, but I knew he wouldn't do that in front of Jelly.

Tortilla glanced over at Jelly. "You okay, bromigo?"

I saw that Jelly's face was upset. He actually appeared to be angry, as if he were about to clench his fists. He didn't, though.

"Yeah, I'm fine. Just a lot to take in, you know."

"Yeah, I know," Tortilla said, smirking. "I think we should be dead, there were a lot of those propane tanks."

"But we're not," I reminded them. "We have to make a plan."

"Uhrm. You do that," Jelly replied in a heated tone. His face was changing to the color of chili peppers, red hot, maybe even hotter than that.

"You sure you're all right, you look like something is bothering you," Tortilla said.

"No, I'm not all right. Everyone is dead, and we're not. I thought I was going to die, but I didn't, now I have to live another day like a rabbit."

"You want to die?" I asked him.

"I can't do this. Can you do this? Fuck, I don't even know what we're doing!" he yelled, springing to his feet. "Uhrm. I . . . ." He was struggling to breathe. He gulped in air. "I—I don't want to live like a rabbit. Uhrm." He wobbled around on the grass.

I bolted to my feet. "Get an inhaler!" I screamed.

Tortilla sprinted down the hallway and came back with an inhaler, shaking it the entire way. He put it in Jelly's right hand.

Jelly pumped the inhaler once, sucking in the medicine in a deep inhale. He let it out and did it a second time. "I'm okay . . . I'm okay." He looked up at the sliding glass door, surprised.

I turned. "Jacob."

Jacob was staring at Jelly. "Darrel?" He staggered, wiping his nut-brown eyes. His longer brunette hair was as messy as the ruined house.

"Yeah, man. It's me. You look pretty bad."

"I bet. I feel pretty damn bad." Jacob examined us. "Félix?"

Tortilla nodded at him.

Jacob looked at me again. "I don't remember you, do I know you?"

"Not really. We went to Squalicum together, but that's it," I answered.

"That's Maggy Li," Tortilla introduced me.

He stumbled back, almost fell over, but Tortilla caught him and guided him to a chair.

"You need water badly, I'll grab you some," Tortilla said. He came back from the Apocalypse Room with a few bottles and a giant bag of turkey jerky.

"Thanks, I needed that," Jacob said after he drank his fill. "What the hell happened? How did you get here?"

"We walked here," Jelly told him. "Well, we also ran and boated across the lake."

"Didn't take a car?"

Jelly shook his head. "Didn't want to make any noise, draw any needless attention on to us. I don't know how to turn off those fake engine sounds the cars make."

"But you boated across the lake?"

"That was a last resort situation. We had no other choice. Aliens were gonna kill us," Jelly responded.

"Alions," I corrected.

"Right. Alions were gonna kill us," he said.

"What are you talking about?"

"They're here," Tortilla said. He sat down, and Jelly and I followed suit. "Aliens that look like lions, that's what's taken all the people. You haven't seen them? We thought that was why you drank yourself to death."

"I drank myself to death because there was no one else around. Everyone was gone, vanished, poof, you know. I drank because I didn't have a gun."

We all looked at him, his green face, bowls for eye sockets, stringy hair that looked as if it was falling out. He was in bad shape.

Silence overtook the patio.

"So what are you doing here?" Jacob asked after a while.

"We first saw the spaceships on TV," Tortilla said. "And we thought we would come here and use your telescope to see if it was true, you know, because your dad works for NASA and all."

"I have no idea what happened to my telescope, probably sold it in a yard sale."

"That's okay," I spoke up. "We know it's true now."

"So what are you going to do now?"

"Not *we*?" I asked. "You don't plan to stay with us?"

"Hell, I don't plan on living another day. I got a hundred bottles waiting for me upstairs. I thought I drank enough last night, but I'll be damned if I don't tonight."

"Actually, you don't," Jelly said.

"What do you mean, I don't."

"You don't have any more booze upstairs. Really, you don't even have an upstairs anymore."

Jacob ground his teeth. "What's that suppose to mean?"

We all glanced at each other, nervous. "They were breaking into the house—the alions—so we lined up those green propane tanks from the kitchen to the Apocalypse room, put one in the oven, and well, you don't have any more booze."

"Fuck! You blew up my booze!"

"And saved you," I added.

He looked at me as though he were thinking of strangling me. He jumped out of his chair and started pacing back and forth on the lawn, muttering curses. He really wanted to die, wanted to drink himself to death.

We left Jacob alone to calm down, outside on the grass. I gathered up our things in the Apocalypse Room, while Jelly and Tortilla looked at the food supplies on the shelves and hidden away in deep cupboards spaced along the back wall. "We should see where his dad is, maybe he could help us," I said, squatting next to our backpacks.

"I don't think he'll tell us, he's pretty lit." Jelly shuffled some canned goods around. "He doesn't want to help us."

"I never said I didn't want to help you." Jacob stood by the door, arms folded across his chest. "I just said I didn't want to be a part of your plans. My dad is in Pasadena, or at least he *was* in Pasadena. He was working at the Jet Propulsion Lab there, but I haven't talked to him in a few weeks."

We all turned to him. "You think he would help us?" I asked.

"Help you, how?"

"Help us get to somewhere safe. He might know somewhere we could go, to get away."

"I don't think there is anywhere to get away from these things. You've been outside, you traveled, have you seen anyone else?"

"We're alive, so others must be too. Why would the four of us be the only people who have not been taken?" I countered. "I don't know of anything else to do."

"We should go to a military base. That makes more sense. They are armed and trained," Jacob said.

"We?" Jelly said. "I thought you didn't want to be a part of our plan."

"I didn't, when I said that, but I thought I had a ton of fifths then. Now I don't," he growled. "Now I don't."

"Can't you get more?" Jelly asked.

Jacob laughed. "Are you serious? I was part of the raiding on the first day; the liquor from all the stores was cleaned out, the grocery stores and the electricity stations, all of them. I think a few others had the same idea. I went to seven stores to get what I had. That was on the first day . . ."

"So you're coming with us now?" Tortilla asked.

"Look, I can drink myself to death, but I can't shoot myself. I can't hang myself . . . I can't . . . so yeah, I'm coming with you. I don't want to wait around to die."

"Sounds good to me," I said. "But there is a flaw in your plan, the military bases will be primary targets, don't you think. Yeah they are trained, and yeah they are armed, so why wouldn't the alions hit them hardest?"

Jacob shook his head. "I didn't think of that. I suppose you're right. These things seem smart?"

"Smart and tough, incredibly tough." I snatched up the saw that I had used on the alion; it was slightly bent. "I tried to cut off one of its limbs last night, only made it halfway before it decided we weren't worth the trouble."

We all stared at the blade. None of us had any idea what had happened to the saw after the door closed, not in the pitch black.

"So what's *your* plan?" Jacob asked.

"We should go into the city to gather some weapons and other supplies, then start down I-5. It's a straight shot to LA, nice and simple, assuming no one else knows a safer or quicker route?" I received only silence. "You think your dad could help us?" I eyed Jacob, desperate for a reassuring yes. He gave it to me with a nod. "Head down I-5 until we get to Pasadena; it is near LA, right?"

"Yeah, it is. I'll also tell you that my dad was working on unmanned fighter spacecrafts for the IPDA, so he might know something about what's going on. That is if he is still alive." Jacob bent down and grabbed another bag of turkey jerky, opened it, and bit into a delicate piece.

I stood up, my brow scrunched.

"The International Planetary Defense Administration," he said when he saw my confusion.

"Oh, right." I sighed. I can't believe I had forgotten that . . . so many associations and administrations.

"So you want to go into town, eh?" Jelly spoke up. I could tell he didn't like that idea.

"It's not that far to walk," I said.

"I ain't walkin' that far," Jacob spat.

"How else are we going to get there, a car?"

"You're damn right a car." Jacob smiled as he fiddled with the door handle. "I know how to unwire the fake engine noise. We'll be as silent as a computer."

Jelly sighed in relief. "Sounds great to me, dude, show us the way." He grabbed his gear. We did the same.

Jacob spun around and headed outside. Jelly followed. Tortilla put a hand on my back as we left a few strides behind them. "It'll be okay, we'll be okay."

I turned back and stared at him. "I know." I felt a rush of comfort and warmth, and I stood on my tiptoes and kissed his cheek. He blushed. I turned around and fell in line.

When we came through the garage door, cinder and ash scattered as we tramped around. The two cars were melted, bent, and pliable. "Awesome. Just incredible," Jacob said. "You ruined my cars."

"And saved your life," I chimed in again.

"And melted my cars . . ."

"What about your neighbors?" Tortilla spoke up, running a hand over the softened neo-plastic that used to be a hood.

"Yeah, they didn't make it . . . they're gone."

We left the piles of goop and ash behind. We were all furtive except for Jacob. He didn't care anymore, if he ever did. He just strolled on over to his neighbors, as if he wanted to be captured, but I didn't think he did. He broke a window into the house with a rock, climbed in, then went around to unlock the door for us. In the garage, two neo-plastic Fiat Tracksters sat in idle disappointment. One of the coupes was fiery red and the other was aquamarine.

"Which one do we want?" Jacob asked.

"The red one," Jelly said. He ran to the door, opened it, plopped down in the seat, and started feeling the wheel like it was the only thing in the world that mattered. I think I saw him pet it for the briefest of moments.

"Yeah, sure. Whatever." Jacob went to the hood. "Pop it, bro." Jelly popped it, and Jacob started to tinker with the wires.

"This is so slick," Jelly said when we walked over. We piled our backpacks and the bows into the trunk. "This must be brand new, a few weeks old at most." It was good to see Jelly so ecstatic.

Jacob slammed the hood down. "Too bad you don't get to drive it." He disappeared inside the house and came back jangling a set of keys. "Haha, suckers!" He laughed in a squeal that hurt my ears.

"Where did you find those?" Jelly asked, excited, but saddened that he didn't find them first.

"They were hanging on some hooks in the kitchen. Now scoot over."

Jelly got out and went around to the passenger's side, flipped the car seat forward so that I could duck into the back, and eagerly jumped in after I was buckled. Tortilla got in on the driver's side.

"Are we ready to have some fun?" Jacob asked, also excited. He put the magnetic keypad in its holder on the dash and tapped the green ON switch. The car came alive with lights, silent, deadly to anyone listening to music, or looking the other way. That's why all electric cars had those fake engine noises. Jacob checked the car's vitals. "Full batteries, baby. We're ready to fly." He pressed the garage door opener. Soon we were looking at the bleak driveway.

"Don't kill us, please," I pleaded.

But it was too late; he had already pounded the GO pedal. We burst forth out of there like a fighter jet.

"I–I read an article on the Trackster. It can keep a speed of 300 kilometers per hour for over three hours. No other car in the world can do that," Jelly said. "Uhrm. It's one of the few cars that have a rectenna built right on top. This slick ride will go forever, as long as the bill is paid. The batteries will never deplete, though I suppose they could die."

"It gets it power directly from the electrical relay plants?" I asked. I had never heard of that before. Everything was on the grid. Six years ago, the twenty-year project to put solar panels in space was finally over, with the completion of the last Solar Station—one of five—that collected solar rays around the clock. They transmitted electricity as microwave energy, then converted the energy back into electricity at the electrical relay plants, where everything I knew about got its power. Cars were recharged at home, and at the electricity stations that replaced all of the old gas stations, not directly from the relay plants. "Incredible. So you never have to stop at an electricity station?"

"Never."

"Just incredible," I said. We could go all the way to California without stopping; I liked the sound of that. No, I loved the sound of that. I was enjoying the scenery when Tortilla tapped my shoulder.

"I don't believe it," Tortilla mumbled.

"What? What is it?" I asked. I scanned over his shoulder, out the window, but I couldn't see anything.

He jabbed his right index finger toward the lake, jamming it when he collided with the glass. A yelp escaped his mouth. "Crap that hurt!" He pointed with his left. "It's your axe. I see your axe."

"I see it too," Jelly said.

"You have an axe?" Jacob asked, incredulous. He zoomed along, turning with the winding road with precision.

"Pull over! Pull over!" I yelled. He pulled the car into a lakeside driveway. We scrambled out of the Trackster and broke for the shoreline. There it was, floating like the brilliant alion hacker that it became after it sunk to the depths of the lake. I picked it up and inspected it. "Yep, it's mine. See the initials on the haft." I showed them where I had engraved ML. I looked at Tortilla. "Good eye." I wanted to kiss him again, but I resisted the urge. I restrained myself, held it all back. I twirled the slippery weapon with both hands. "I'm back, baby."

"Were you ever gone?" Jelly asked me.

"My dwarven spirit was," I responded, putting my axe in the trunk.

We crammed into the car again, and off we went, zipping around North Shore Drive. Cars were scattered along the roadway. "People must have been taken while they were driving," Jelly gasped. "While they were driving . . ." He freaked all of us out when he said that, but no one spoke anything more about the possibility of abduction while driving.

North Shore was a narrow, two-lane road, and Jacob was driving faster than I was comfortable with, much faster. I glanced at the speedometer: 116 KPH.

"Can you slow down, bromigo?" I asked. We were all tense, I could tell.

"What for? I have it under control. You can't even tell that I'm going over 100."

I cracked my pinky fingers. "Because there are cars blocking the road. What if we come around a corner and there's a car that you can't maneuver past. You wanna kill us?"

Jelly started clearing his throat more. Too tense. The road was so curvy; it snaked like a river. We could hit a car at any moment.

I perched myself between the front seats, watching, waiting. As we came around a bend, I spotted the dead car, vacant of a driver.

Jacob dipped the wheel to his left, eyes on the car in our lane.

"Car! Car! Car!" I screamed. I had never screamed so fiercely before. I fell back into my seat, still buckled.

"What the hell!" Jacob shouted.

Another car drove right for us, barreling down the road as fast, if not faster than us. It honked its horn: BERN—BERN—BERN! We missed each other by a centimeter, I would guess. A mere centimeter. Jacob went straight into the ditch and out again, braking like a madman, not thinking but reacting. We halted in the middle of the road. My nose smashed the seat in front of me. Blood gushed for a second, then streamed down my lip.

There were a few groans as everyone settled; I don't know if they were mine. "Everyone all right?" I asked. My voice sounded broken to me. My head swam, and my blurry vision didn't seem to want to go back to normal. My nose ceased bleeding, though, so that was a positive.

"Yeah," Tortilla uttered to no one in particular.

"Yeah, I am too," Jelly replied. He groaned. It was him who was doing all the groaning, I noticed.

I unbuckled to examine Jacob. He was out, fainted. "He doesn't look good. Why did we let him drive, he wasn't even functioning properly."

"He took the key," Tortilla said. "I don't know . . ."

Jelly got out, letting me out after him. We inspected the Trackster. "What a shame," Jelly commented. "It was brand new, and bam, a scratch." The neo-plastic body was light but incredibly durable, and even at the scary speeds we were going, the front bumper was barely even scratched. Neo-plastic, a life-saving material no one should have ever had to live without; it probably prevented a million deaths a day. "What a damn shame." He shook his head, but it hurt and some more groans followed. He eyed Jacob. "He's melted, completely insane."

"That's certain," I said. "Probably enough to be in an institution."

Jelly laughed. "What do we do?"

Suddenly, a roar flew by us, so deep and threatening; it promised vengeance. It came from the east, in the direction of Jacob's house.

"Oh, no. No—no—no—no—no! What do we do?" Jelly flew up his arms, clearing his throat over and over. His panicky movements disoriented me for a second.

"Stop it, Jelly!" I yelled. "Stop it. Panicking won't help, so stop. Help me move Jacob to the back." Together we lifted Jacob and plodded around the car, every labored step ached, but we got him into the backseat. "I'll drive."

Jelly's eyes pleaded with me to let him drive, but he said, "Sure, yeah, all right. You're the better driver." He hopped into the passenger's front.

I got behind the wheel. I didn't ask if they were ready, I clicked the four-wheel-drive button, locked it into drive, and looked out on the road ahead. I heard another roar and zoomed away, west, toward Bellingham. The Trackster was smooth. I had never driven a car like it. Especially since Jacob disabled the fake engine noise. It was so quiet as I hit 80 KPH. I had heard a gasoline engine a few years ago, and I don't know how anyone could stand such a noise-polluting machine; it was detrimental to my ears.

Most of the city's expansion ran North and South, leaving the lake rather undeveloped, which was nice. I liked living so close to it. It was so much quieter there. The parks, the people, for the most part, were all muted in comparison. Quarter-way up Alabama Hill, the tops of the skyscrapers emerged, long, bright towers covered in green solar panels. The organic compounds of the solar cells worked exactly like trees, but twenty times more efficient, or something like that. They also didn't expel oxygen, not yet anyway. They probably never would.

"Jacob is coming to," Tortilla informed us.

Jacob grumbled about his head for a bit. "I screwed up. I screwed up bad."

Tortilla smirked. "We're alive. You didn't kill us, not yet anyway."

"How are you feeling?" I asked.

"Like I'm going to puke my goddamn brains out," he answered. He loosened the strap across his stomach and chest.

"I bet," Jelly said.

"No, I mean it. Pull over." But there wasn't time. He retched a pool of death by his feet.

"Why? Oh, why!" Jelly shouted. We rolled down the windows and opened the sunroof. All useless, in the end, it was so bad; I almost added the granola bar I had eaten to the putrid smell.

"I'll just go to the bus station, and we can figure out something from there." No one argued. They rarely did. "There were people in that car."

"What?" Tortilla said, adjusting his glasses.

"In the car that drove us off the road, there were people in it. We're not the only ones left."

"I didn't even think about that," Jelly reflected. "It's so normal for people to drive cars . . . I didn't even think about that."

The conversation ended as we all contemplated on the fact that other people did survive.

It became harder to maneuver in the city, much harder. Cars jammed streets everywhere. It was silent, immobile chaos. The smell was getting to me, dizzying my head. I pulled into a Little Old Food Mart parking lot a few blocks away from the bus station. "We can walk the rest. I can't be in this car anymore."

Not a word from them, not one.

"You think we should check the grocery?" Jelly asked.

I nodded. "Yeah, stock up. They might have duffel bags that we can use." The slider doors of the grocery store opened as usual, a computerized bell rang when they did. We stood there, gawking.

"It's empty. All the shelves, empty. How is this possible?" Tortilla said. His words only earned shrugs. We went down the aisles: the canned goods, the cereals, the produce, meats, bakery, all of it was gone. All the consumables. The cooking utensils, neo-plastic water bottles, aluminum foil—that stuff was all left alone, barely touched.

"It's impossible. With all the people missing the first day, the people left couldn't have taken it all."

Then it dawned on us: people didn't take all the food, not all of it.

"So you think?" Jelly said.

"Yep," I responded. "I can't think of a better explanation, can you?" Of course he couldn't, and if he did, he didn't say it. "Let's get all the aluminum foil, fill some more water bottles, some medications. You know, stuff we can use."

"Aluminum foil?" Jacob asked with a furrowed brow. "Why do we need aluminum foil?" Then I think for the first time he saw that Jelly and Tortilla were covered in it.

"You just noticed that we're wearing it?" Jelly said. "Man, you must be melted. We've had it on this whole time."

"I think I am melted. I can't see straight, I can't think straight. Yeah, I think I am going crazy, or have gone." Jacob sat down on the tiled floor and drank some water. "It's certain, isn't it? I'm gone."

"If you think you're gone, then you're probably not all gone," I said. "Probably."

He smiled. "Thanks."

While Jacob rested, the three of us split up and searched the store, throwing valuables into duffel bags that we had found at the front of the store. The bags had the Little Old Food Mart logo on the sides, with the slogan: "Buy local, buy local, buy local!" They really pushed buying local, but then almost everyone did in Bellingham.

When we finished, we met up at the storefront. "What kind of medicines did you find?" I asked Jelly.

"Uhrm. Pain relievers, adhesive bandages, topical healing creams, hydrogen peroxide, a bunch of inhalers. I think stuff we'll need."

"Sounds great," I said. "All the maps have been taken, so it looks like I-5 is our only option, unless we want to get lost." They all nodded in silence. We exchanged what we had collected, to make sure nothing was forgotten, as best we could anyway. "Before we go, I have to pee."

"All right, we'll go across the street to the sporting goods store, see if any guns are left. Maybe some camping stoves." We had gathered up a lot of the cookware, but had nothing to use them with.

"Don't leave me alone, that's stupid. I'll only be a couple of seconds."

"I'll stay," Tortilla offered.

My heart leapt, some alone time at last. Even if it only lasted a minute or two, it would be nice.

"Yeah, okay. We'll be right across the street," Jelly said. They left and took a few of the duffels to put next to the Trackster.

"I'll be quick," I told Tortilla. "So we can talk about . . . you know, what to do and all."

He held a cleaver in his hand. "I'll be right outside."

The bathroom was cleaner than I thought it would be, which was nice, a real bonus for the day. I laughed when I noticed that the toilet paper was out. The place had only electric dryers, too. Luckily, I had some face tissue in my pockets. I hated blowing my nose in anything else. When I came out, I didn't see Tortilla.

"Tortilla?" I said loudly.

The bathroom was in the back, down a hall. When I made it to where the hall joined the main store, I saw a sliver of Tortilla, across the walkway, one aisle back from the aisle in front of the hallway. He slowly crept to the edge of the shelves, and put his index up to his mouth as we made eye contact. He pointed to my right, and I spied an alion crouched low, sniffing at two of the leftover duffels, filled with cookware.

Its powerful nose detected us. It knew we were there. After a few more sniffs, the alion jerked its large head our way, sighting us instantly.

"Run!" I screamed, terrified. But Tortilla was horror-struck, petrified . . . immobile. I sprinted right at him, grabbed his hand and yanked. I yanked so hard he nearly fell over. The alion knocked over a shelf, starting a chain reaction, like dominos all lined up, tumbling over. I could hear them: CLUNG–CLUNG–CLUNG. How many were there between us, I didn't know, but we didn't stop. We passed the end of the aisle; I felt the air pushed toward me as the shelf toppled over behind us. We still didn't stop.

The alion roared, throwing laundry detergent jugs off its body, toward us. They smacked the floor a meter away. I didn't take a moment to turn back to see if it pursued us. We cleared the sliding doors and bolted under the overcast sky, heading for the sporting goods store.

"Darrel! Jacob!" Tortilla bellowed.

"Back here," Jelly replied. "By the guns." A sign in the back hanging from two chains pointed us in the right direction. When we found them, Jacob was loading an old handgun. Jelly held a shotgun. "I forgot this is a used sports store. Most of this stuff is from the last century."

"Alions!" I stammered. "In the grocery–chasing–escaped . . ."

"What?" Jacob said, straightening up. "You saw aliens?"

"Yeah, *alions*."

"Don't worry, I'll shoot it," Jacob reassured us. "Grab a gun, figure it out. We have nine of them, and enough ammo to last a while." I picked up a pistol. "Nice choice, a Heckler and Koch USP. Should be easy enough for you."

Tortilla picked up a pistol too, but different than mine. Glass broke at the storefront. "We gotta move!" Tortilla said. "Head on, or out the back?"

"Are you crazy? Out the back," Jelly answered. "I'm not going head-to-head with those monsters if I don't have to."

"Let's go," I whispered, heading for the backroom. An exit sign hung above a door to the right, so we took it. We filed into a cramped and smelly alley. "We'll circle around." I led the way and stopped where the alley dumped into the street. "I don't see anything."

"Then go already." Jacob pushed Jelly, who fell into Tortilla, who collided with me. I hopped forward, catching my balance. I rushed for the car. The hatchback was unlocked, so I hit the latch button underneath an overhang. SPEESHH–it shot up. We gathered our gear, bulky and burdensome bags. I slung my axe over my back from a cord that I had fastened to it. Tortilla and Jelly grabbed the two bows and quivers, even though we had the guns. I didn't ask why.

Something moved in the corner of my eye. I spun to my right. The alion galloped down an aisle, coming our way; in seconds, it hurtled over the window frame, out into the street.

All I heard was the gun blast.

The alion crashed into Jacob, claws out. But a bullet went right through its eye socket. It rolled away from Jacob and caught its feet, stabilized. With blood oozing out the hole in its face, it charged for a second run.

I heard another gun blast.

A second bullet struck it, through its throat. It fell over, coughing, struggling to breathe. It was horrible to listen to as it sucked in and blew out: KLEHH–AH–KLEHH–AH. Then it started to gurgle before it died, blood shooting out its neck.

Jacob stood up, staring.

Tortilla had his arm extended, shaking as he held the gun. We all looked at him.

"You saved me . . ." Jacob said, his voice cracking. "I almost got you killed . . . and you saved me."

"Well, hopefully you'll do the same for us when the time comes," Tortilla said.

Jacob nodded. "You saved my melted brain." He didn't say anything more, no thank you, no yeah, I'll be there to watch your back, nothing but: you saved me.

I gazed at Tortilla. I wanted to kiss him again, but the time wasn't right. All I said was, "You did good."

"Yeah he did!" Jelly exclaimed. "The well armed take advantage and you took advantage!" Before any more congratulations could be given, another roar echoed in the city.

"The buses, they're big enough to push cars out of the way, let's take one of them," I suggested.

"Good idea." Tortilla started eastward for East Champion Street. "Hurry." We ran off, right behind his steps, except for Jacob, who lingered at the carcass of the alion.

I turned around and saw him staring at the dead beast. "Come on, dummy!"

He raised his eyes to me. A shadow covered his face, dark and foreboding. He didn't reply but started off after us.

The road turned south and the bus station was right around the corner. Cars were everywhere, parked at the meters, and dead in the street, blocking it. A few buses looked as if they had been pulling out when the people aboard had been taken. I heard screeches down at the cross street, glanced over and saw three alions charging.

"They're coming! Get inside, get inside!" I shouted.

Tortilla pushed in the doors of the closest bus. We scrambled up the steps, and Jacob vaulted into the driver's seat. "No way, bromigo," I laughed. "Get out." I threw my hand back behind my head. "Get out now."

"All right, all right." He scurried off to the back.

Luckily, the key was still locked in the ignition pad. I pressed the big green ON button. It fired up. Tortilla had shut the doors, and now they locked as the bus came to life. I stomped down on the GO pedal, and the tires squealed, then with a jolt they shot forth. I twirled the wheel to the right and headed up East Champion, a one-way going the opposite direction, but I figured no one would mind.

By then, they were upon us. They were smart, too. They went right for the tires. I watched as they slashed the two outside back tires. Fortunately for us, the buses had three tires in a row, just in case something happened to one, the other two, or even one, would support the bus for a decent enough distance. The alions failed at slicing the inner tires.

So they gave up. Instead, they changed their tactics, running alongside the bus. I swerved, trying to squash their guts, but they were nimble, far too nimble. I took a right on Ellis: it was nice not having to stop for traffic. I lost track of two of them as I studied one in my left mirror, gaining distance, almost to the front tires.

I swerved again.

On agile paws, it leapt away.

Tortilla was also observing the alion. "I think I can shoot it." He closed one eye and aimed.

"Open the window," I shouted back to him. "Glass could go in your eye."

He slid the window to the side and locked it in place. "Hold the bus steady."

"I can't." I took a left up Lakeway. The alion faded back for a second, hopped over a glossy silver coupe, dodged another, and sprinted up to where it had been before, near the front tire.

"Shoot it! Shoot it!" I heard myself scream. It echoed down the bus. It sounded as if it existed only in my head though.

I glanced at the mirror and saw the longest, deadliest claw lacerate the outer tire. I skidded right as Tortilla fired. It missed. I steadied the bus out. He fired a second shot. I spotted blood around its shoulder.

"Again!" I cried.

PAP—PAP. I glimpsed the alion going headlong into a tree on the median. I turned right, up the on-ramp to the fourth and highest layer of I-5. I had hated the interstate before, always so crowded. But now all the cars were stopped, easier to pass, skipping from lane to lane, maneuvering around them as if I were in a high-speed chase. I guess in some way I was.

My attention had been focused on Tortilla and the left, but now Jelly's high-pitched screaming became clear: "We're dead, we're dead, we're dead!" He repeated it over again. "One of them is skipping on the hoods of the cars."

Then all of a sudden I heard THUNK on top of the bus.

Jelly—in complete hysteria—pointed his shotgun at the roof. He discharged the cartridge. Another THUNK. Debris fell from the roof. "I think I got it."

We waited. I checked all my mirrors, but I didn't find anything, not even the third one. Then I heard scraping, as if nails were digging into metal, on the roof. A paw busted through a window near Tortilla, reaching, striving to slice one of us to pieces.

In a panic, Jelly launched a round. A roar followed as the paw exploded. He aimed up again, to where he thought the beast was perched, then pulled the trigger. The spray of shots hit fur, flesh, and bone. Blood trickled down the holes like disgusting red rain. The body rolled off the roof going BUMP—BUMP—BUMP the entire way.

I heard a cry of glee come from all three. I checked the mirrors again, but I still didn't detect the third one. But then something caught my eye at the door; the alion was galloping alongside us, trying to pry the doors open with its two humanlike hands that jutted from the tops of its shoulders.

I sped up. Cars were everywhere. It became difficult to dodge them. Then all five lanes were blocked. I had to smash through them or fly off the side through the guardrail.

Jelly leaned over the driver's chair. "Go up the middle," he advised. "Right up the middle."

I nodded.

The bus plowed into two bumpers, crushing them in an instant. We came out all right, still intact. I peeked at the door: the alion barreled along with us, keeping pace. My mouth gaped. I thought it was impossible, but there it was, alive.

"Shoot it." I nodded toward the door.

Jelly sighted the alion and flinched back.

When I looked back at the road, two cars blocked my path. Filled with terror, I slammed on the brakes and slid to the right, smacking the alion. I lost control, and the tires decided to rebel, keeping course for the meter-high steel barrier. I tried to steer away.

We bulldozed right through the guardrail and plunged over the side of I-5, four levels up.

I stared through the giant glass windows, looking down at the earth, a big patch of wet soil beneath us. The bus rolled in the air so that the right side would collide first. Jelly, Tortilla, and Jacob held on to the overhead rails, screaming. I gripped the steering wheel, every muscle locked up. I didn't want to die. I wanted to kiss Tortilla one more time.

I closed my eyes and waited for my world to end.

3
The Lonely Road South
Darrel

BOOOOM.

The crash was so loud. I held on to the overhead rail that spanned the distance of the bus. My body jerked in the impact. My neck whipped back then forward. It felt like it snapped. I released my grip and fell to the broken glass, landing on the crumpled frame. I just lay there, unable to breathe. I wanted to inhale but couldn't, not even a short breath. I tried to gulp in the air, but I felt like a fish out of water. Everything was warm around me. My head swirled. It was nice. Then I saw black.

I came to as Félix poured water on me. It was three times now that he had done that, three times in two days. I choked in air, coughing and coughing. He handed me an inhaler. "I shook it already."

I put it to my lips. The mist flew down my throat and expanded my lungs as I held for thirty seconds. I clicked down the silver tube again. The life-saving spray shot down in sweet relief. "Thanks," I managed.

He nodded, wiping his spectacles. "Yeah, bromigo. I'm going to check on Maggy."

"Uhrm. Yeah, okay."

He replaced his glasses and climbed over the bus seats to the front

where Maggy was strapped into the driver's seat. She looked unconscious. I could barely make out the chair in front of me, everything was
blurry, unfocused. I was so dizzy. So damn dizzy. I put my hand to the
floor and slid over some glass that slit the outside of my palm. "AHH!"

"You all right?" Félix asked, looking at me as he crouched next to
Maggy.

"Cut my hand on some glass."

"Sorry." His gentle voice was full of sympathy.

"How's Maggy," I asked. I pulled myself up using the edge of the
tilted seats.

"I'm okay, Jelly. Everything is just spinning, that's all," Maggy said,
her voice high and grating. Félix gave her some water, then an inhaler.

"Yeah, same for me," I said, rubbing my eyes as I stood upright. My
feet were planted where the window used to be. I turned and searched
for Jacob. He had been holding on to the bar a few rows behind me,
and I found him sprawled out on his back, unmoving. He had dozens
of scrapes, some bruises too. "Jacob is in bad shape." I reached down
and checked his neck for a pulse. His blood was still pumping. "He's
alive, though."

Félix walked over to me, hunched over. "If he makes it I think I'll
try to make him a medal for being so resilient."

I laughed. "I bet he makes it. I mean, he's trying to kill himself, but
I'll still bet that he survives longer than all of us."

Félix smiled. "Yeah." He turned and unlocked one of the ceiling
hatches, kicked it out after a few hits, and crawled through. "Come
on."

Maggy slowly made her way over and crawled out. I followed after.
We examined the wreckage. The bus had crashed into softer soil, but it
was bent and crumpled, really scrunched together.

"How did we survive?" Maggy spoke softly. "How?" She looked over
at Félix.

He shrugged. "The wonders of neo-plastic. People have survived
way worse."

"Have they? With I-5 a level above the ground, we fell five levels."
She paused calculating. "That's over 20 meters."

It was hard to digest. I inspected the bus, walking all the way
around it. I shifted to peer up at the fourth level of I-5. "I think we
should be dead, too. It just looks impossible."

"Don't you remember that plane crash a few years ago? All twenty-
odd people survived because of neo-plastic's resilience and the way it

compresses. No one was even critically injured. It's the stuff of miracles . . ." Félix backed up from the bus a couple of steps. "Where is the alion?"

"Huh?" Maggy asked.

"There was an alion running alongside us, remember."

We all backed up, slinked around to the other side, and paused. "You see what I see?" I asked.

"Yep, bromigo." Maggy crept closer to the back wheel well. Two tawny paws stuck out, crippled, visibly shattered. "The rest of the body must be under the bus."

I edged up next to her. "How did I miss it? I walked all the way around." I was stunned, but relieved. No more hunters, no more alions to worry about, or at least, one less. I could barely take it. "I'm going to go check on Jacob."

Félix nodded. "Good idea."

I crawled through the hatch and checked Jacob's vitals again. I tossed some water on him, since it had worked so well on me. It worked on him too, kind of; he was already waking when the water hit his face.

"What's going on?" Jacob squinted at me with cloudy eyes.

"You'll be all right. Just take it easy."

"Do you have any gin?"

I laughed. "No, dude. I don't have any gin. Do you want some water?"

"What's water ever done for me? Do you have any vodka?"

I shuffled through a bag that had spare water bottles. "Yeah, I do." I offered him the water.

He snatched it up and drank it. "Damn that's good . . . that's good. Never had vodka taste so clean, so smooth."

"Well, make it last," I told him. "Here take this." I handed him an inhaler. He took it. "I'll be right back. Just relax. I'll be right back." I straightened up as much as I could, found the hatch, and crawled out. As cozy as it was in the bus, it was nice to be out in the open, breathing the untainted air. When I walked around the bus, I came upon something I didn't want to see, ever. Maggy had her arms around Félix, staring at him: my best friend. She rose up on her toes and kissed him. I twirled around as fast as my feet could handle and strode away.

"They were just friends yesterday . . . what is this? They were just friends . . ." I stomped around in the dirt. I had never really drank before, but I could go for some of Jacob's magical vodka, the real stuff.

My world was spinning, around and around. I puked my heart out a few meters from the bus.

Félix and Maggy came running up. "You all right?" Maggy asked.

"Oh, yeah, fine. I'm fine. Just a sour stomach or something, probably just needs to come out."

Félix grabbed a towel out of the bus and handed it to me. "Thanks," I said. He nodded. I found a water bottle and sat down, slouched against the bus. "What a nightmare."

"A little worse than a nightmare, that's certain," Félix said, his voice shaking. "We have some guns, some food, some water . . . but how far can we make it? It's a long road south."

I sucked down the water. "And we don't know anything about conservation. Every time I put a bottle to my lips, I drink half the container."

He smirked. "Yeah, me too, bromigo. Me too."

"But we have to try," Maggy said, her tone full of hope. "We all know it. Even that melted drunk knows that. We're stronger than you guys think. We'll persevere. That's what it's about, isn't it? The perseverance of the human race, that's our quality. It will be the alions downfall."

"We don't know anything about the alions," I countered. "Except that they have spaceships, they've taken about 99% of the population, they're smart, they're fast, and they look like lionesses. That's all we know."

Her eyes narrowed. "We know they bleed just like us, red blood and all; we know they can die."

"I–"

"No, we're going south. Together. That melted head, too. He'll make it."

I looked up at her. "He's already awake. He's fine, or should be fine. He thinks his water is vodka."

They both laughed.

"I bet he does," she said, chortling. She kneeled down beside me.

I eyed her. "You've got a plan."

"I've got a plan," she said. "Don't worry; I'll get us to Pasadena. All of us."

"I wish I had a head like you," I confessed.

She blushed. "The plan is to find the nearest on-ramp, find an SUV on the second tier, and take that all the way, under cover. The second level has always been the least driven, so we won't have to worry about so much traffic to bump out of our way. We'll be in Pasadena in a day or two if we drive without stopping."

I nodded. "Sounds like a plan, IQ."

"Tortilla and I will gather everything up, you rest there."

"Nah, I'm all right." I clambered to my feet with the aid of the bus. I was still holding the towel with puke chunks, so I tossed it towards the front of the bus, and we crawled through the hatch in single file.

Félix helped Jacob up and out the bus. We removed everything that was still intact and started to consolidate our inventory. I looked over our supplies. "So we have water bottles; some food; cooking equipment and utensils, including a stove we found at the sporting goods store; medicines; a whole backpack filled with aluminum foil; some towels, blankets, and toilet paper; and a whole duffel with knives, guns, ammo, arrows, and saws."

Maggy leaned against the haft of her axe, the head resting in the soil. "Too bad we left the other duffels; we might need more pots than this."

"If we do, we'll find some more along the way," Félix said. "We'll find what we need." He took an ammo box that read 9MM PARA-BELLUM on the lid and started to reload his gun the way Jacob had showed him a few minutes before.

"And make sure the damn safety is on," Jacob told Félix. "You don't want to shoot one of us. That goes for all of you." He shifted his narrow gaze on to us.

"So how is everyone feeling?" Maggy asked, changing the subject. "I have some big ugly bruises on my waist, shoulders, well everywhere."

"The cut on my hand is all right since I put bandages on it. Other than that, I have a few pretty bad bruises on my shoulders, arms, back, butt, and legs, but I'll survive," I reported.

"Pretty much the same for me," Félix said.

Jacob looked the worst out of the four of us. He was completely scraped up, bandages all over him, thanks to Maggy. "I'm not sure I can walk." Jacob was sitting against the bus and tried standing to his feet.

"If you can't, we'll support you," Félix told him.

"What about the weight from all the bags? We can't support him and carry all this stuff," I said. "I'm not that strong, and I'll get too tired long before we find an on-ramp."

Jacob took a step and collapsed. "Yeah, we need a new plan."

"Tortilla and I can go find a ride and drive back here," Maggy said. "Jelly, stay here and keep him safe." She pointed at Jacob.

I nodded. "That's not safe or smart, but neither is leaving this stuff behind."

They left, taking only three guns and the replica axe.

Jacob sat back down, bent over as he ate some jerky. "Why do you let her call you that?"

"Call me what?"

"Jelly. Why do you let her call you Jelly?"

I stared at him, my mind blank. "Don't know . . . it's endearing."

He laughed. "No, it's not. She's calling you fat, bro. She's not calling you the love of her life."

"What do you know? It's endearing, just leave it at that."

He didn't say another word on the subject. "You want me to show you how to load the shotgun?"

I was holding the weapon with both hands, across my stomach. "Yeah, unless you want the gun."

"No, I found these in the store." From a bag next to him, his own bag, he grabbed a pair of submachine guns. "I found these OMP2s while you were getting the stove. Probably just a couple of years old."

My mouth gaped. "That's the gun from Death Squad." I had never seen one in real life.

"The Optimum Machine Pistol model 2. These will rip those aliens to shreds. They fire at 2700 rounds per minute. Neo-plastic, you gotta love it."

"Why did you hide them?"

"Not sure, wasn't thinking all too straight. You know, melted brain and all." He smiled.

I smiled and handed him the shotgun. He let me hold the OMP2. It was so light; it probably weighed as much as one of my shoes. "Wow . . ." I whispered.

"Looks like you've used three of the twelve cartridges. See the loading port?" He pointed to the bottom of the gun in front of the trigger. "You press this button." He pressed a button on the right side of the loading port and a magazine detached. "And you get your magazine. It's an easy single column, so just pop them in here, and pop the magazine back into the gun and it will lock automatically. You can adjust the firing rate with this knob." He pointed to the left side of the loading port. "You can switch between automatic loading and pump-action by pressing this switch." He flipped a switch near the foregrip. "Either one is good, you might waste more cartridges with it on automatic, but it's nice not having to worry about loading when you're scared shitless, so it's your choice."

"I think I'll leave it on automatic." I accepted the shotgun when he offered it back to me. "How do you know so much about guns?"

"My mother was a cop in Seattle for a long time, and then in Bellingham. As I grew older, she decided to teach me, it was fun for her. She really liked taking me to the range." He stopped when he began to really reflect on his mother.

"Sorry," I said. I didn't know what to say to him, I didn't really know him at all.

"We've all lost, nothing to be sorry about. Nothing you could do, right? Unless you brought them here, unless you ordered them to take all those people and leave a handful . . . unless that was you, I wouldn't be sorry."

I was going to reply, but then I saw a police SUV speeding along the road about twenty meters to the west of us, the road that led to the freeway. "Look!" I flung out my hand and pointed.

"Other survivors?" Jacob asked.

It didn't take long for the answer to his question. Maggy skidded to a stop next to us with the window down, smiling. "You bums need a lift?"

"Yeah, and a drink," Jacob said.

"A lift is all I've got. Take it or leave it."

"I suppose I'll take it."

They jumped out and loaded up the car. I helped Jacob to the opened hood where he disabled the fake engine noise, then into the backseat on the passenger's side. After he was settled, I went around to the other side. "Nice ride."

"Figured it would be best to bump cars out of the way, you know, able to withstand it a few dozen times." Maggy pressed the GO pedal and we were off. "The batteries are at 72%, so we have a ways before we have to recharge, or find another cruiser. I wish we had that rectenna on this bad boy."

"Yeah, or some solar panels," I said.

Félix hadn't said much, and I didn't think he was going to; he looked pretty uncomfortable. I think he knew that I had seen them, or at least had some idea what was going on between him and the girl I had talked non-stop about for the last few years. It was hard to sit there, quiet. But I didn't know what to say to him either. Maggy on the other hand was great at pretending everything was cool, she always had been.

We rode along for a long while, nothing but quiet. The freeway wasn't far away. We were still in Bellingham. There were three more on-ramps before the gaps between them started to widen. The second level of I-5 was deserted compared to the fourth. It still made for awkward driving.

I got sick of the silence. "Do you think we'll see other people?"

"What?" Maggy asked. She was focused on the road.

"Along the road, do you think we'll come across others?" I placed the shotgun between my legs, the barrel sticking out of the lowered window.

"We saw people in Bellingham, I bet we'll see people on I-5. I just hope they're not crazy," Maggy replied. She slowed and nudged a '42 Sun Charger out of the way. It was a slick ride, but impractical. It would be useless on these dead, overcrowded roads. She accelerated when we passed.

"What's the time?" Jacob asked. He had been staring out the window with tired eyes. He needed some rest, that's certain.

"2:30," Maggy responded. "It's going to be slow going, that's certain. Hopefully we can get to Seattle before sunset. There might be a lot more people there since it's so much larger."

He didn't say anything more to her, and she didn't press him.

I looked over at him. "Why did you want to know the time?"

He shifted in his seat, sighing in pain. "I didn't, really, just a habit I guess." He returned his gaze to the landscape outside.

I guess habits wouldn't die that easily. I had a habit of eating, and I was hungry. I put the urge down.

Time crept by. Maggy pushed hundreds of cars out of the way. At least it seemed like hundreds. After every twenty minutes, I glanced at the clock on the console. It was torture, absolute torture.

The Seattle skyline came into view around 5:30, and by 6:30 we had a great panorama of the city. Under the setting sun, the orange sky was fading into a soft red glow. The buildings shined with lights, lit up as if a normal Wednesday night. A normal night with a spaceship looming above the skyscrapers, repositioned since Félix and I saw it on the news.

"I can't believe it's real," Jacob commented. "It's really there."

I squinted at the monstrous craft. "I had forgotten about it. I don't think anyone can believe it's real." I saw the crimson gas jet out the butt of one of the six sections. It was spooky to view.

"Why are the lights still on?" Maggy asked. She peeked out the window at the Space Needle and all of the skyscrapers that towered high above it.

"Did you turn the lights off in your house?" I observed the beautiful horizon and the enormous buildings.

"You got me there, bromigo." She understood. "Everyone was taken so fast . . ." She pulled over to the shoulder, so that we could study the spaceship better, and eat our delicious jerky and granola bars.

It was too hard to make out anything significant on the ship from our position on I-5. Still, we sat in silence and gazed at it as it hovered, suspended in the skyline like a mountain, dark and ominous, waiting to erupt its destruction on the land.

"What do you think they are doing up there?" Maggy asked.

"I don't want to think about it," Félix replied. "It can't be anything good."

"I wish we would nuke them already," Jacob remarked. "Blow them up out of the sky."

"Nukes . . ." Maggy whispered. "Have you guys thought about what happened to the Planetary Defense?"

"That it didn't work?" Félix shifted his eyes towards her.

"That we had no warning . . . that we didn't fire a single thing at them . . . almost like we let them in . . ."

I shuddered. "Let them in, are you crazy? Why would the governments let them come kill us?"

"I didn't say they did, I just said it was pretty easy for them to disable our defenses. They passed all of those missile and laser satellites, the launch bays on Earth, the long-range scouting ships and relay stations. I mean, it was like: POOF—here we are, we instantly shut down all of your weaponry, nice try, suckers!"

"It does seem that way. Maybe we did try to attack. Maybe the satellites did fire on them, and they were just too many, or too powerful for our stuff to matter," Félix said.

Maggy eyed him. "If we did attack, why would the news not report it, something so global . . . so threatening."

Félix frowned. "I don't have an answer to that." His voice was full of gloom.

"Hey, you guys see that? By the ship." Jacob pointed to a dot moving across the darkening sky.

"It's moving fast. Too fast to be a bird," Maggy noted.

"It could be a fighter jet, here to blow that big bastard up," Jacob said, hopeful.

The dot grew into a triangular shape, crimson gas spitting out its backside. It flew low, closing in on us, deadly quiet.

"Oh, god. Oh, god—you think they spotted us?" I said.

"Duck!" Félix yelled.

We all kissed the floor. A minute or two went by, nothing. Félix investigated the scene. "It's still out there, but now it's circling the city." We resumed our perches, watching as the smaller ship orbited the skyscrapers. Then I saw two rectangular objects launch from the alion craft. They rocketed right for the Space Needle. Each exploded where the beams converged to form V-shapes. The iconic flying saucer descended to the city streets below. Upon impact, it burst apart, as small infernos flew up like fireworks, and a thunderous echo ran through the city.

I sat there, stunned beyond dismay. Debris soared higher as the ship continued to circle the city. The bag of inhalers rested between Jacob and I, so I seized one and started shaking it. I shook and shook and shook. Then I pumped it into my mouth. I pumped a second. And a third. And a fourth.

"Jelly, stop," Maggy yelled when she saw me.

And a fifth.

"Grab the inhaler!"

Jacob reached for it, but his body was slow and damaged. Félix was much quicker. He snatched the inhaler from my clutch.

I let out a breath, woozy. "We're not going to make it . . ." I said.

Félix and Maggy turned their attention to some movement out the back window. I rotated around and spied people. People were fleeing, running down I-5, trying to escape the madness that had become the world. They ran right by our car. Another group of four, they sprinted right past our windows.

Maggy sprang out the door. "Wait!" she cried. "Wait!"

They all turned, shocked to hear human voices. They were clad in warm clothes and burdened with bags. Two looked about the same age as us, and the other two were young, probably not even in their teens.

The oldest looking of them, a man of late teens, maybe early twenties, stepped towards us, squinting. "Are you real?" he asked.

"Real, and well armed," Maggy replied. Her words were a test, to see if he played Our Descent.

"Assets of a soldier," the older girl spoke up.

The girl passed. Maggy laughed. "That's certain. Is the company of eight better than four?"

They looked at us, wary. "It could be, but people aren't the same, some are melted, some are wicked, out for their own survival, or their last pleasure before their death. You touch my sisters and I'll shoot you where you stand."

Maggy eyed her, amazed. "There is no threat from us, I assure you. We're going south to Pasadena, to see if we can find answers and safety down there."

The girl smiled, her thick luscious lips stupefying my brain. "I'm Penelope." She was a bit taller than Maggy, maybe by five centimeters or so.

Félix and I got out of the car. I stared at Penelope, and her beauty melted my body . . . brain, stomach, and heart . . . all of it. Copperish hair that verged on rufous flowed mid-back, thick and layered, but greasy from sweat mixed with product, combined with no shower. Her face drooped with exhaustion, her body looked to be on the edge of total collapse. Her deep brown eyes possessed an endurance that a rare few could claim.

"I'm Maggy." Maggy shook Penelope's hand. "This is Félix, Darrel, and the one still in the car is Jacob; he's pretty banged up." She didn't use our nicknames.

"This is my cousin, Mike, and these two little ones are my sisters, Jane and Amanda."

"Little ones, I'm not little. I'm a centimeter taller than her," one of the girls exclaimed, pointing at the sister of equal age. They were black-haired twins with blue eyes.

"Still shorter than me, which makes you little," Penelope said.

"Why do you think Pasadena is safe?" Mike asked, abrupt. He was tall and fit, with dirty blond hair. His green eyes burned holes through us.

"Jacob's father works down there at the Jet Propulsion Lab, we didn't know what else to do or where else to go, so we just figured we should start there." Maggy hoisted her axe onto her shoulder. "Where are you going?"

"South, out of Seattle. That's as far as we got in our planning. We just gotta get out of here," Mike answered.

"Well, you're welcome to come with us," I spoke up, looking at Penelope.

"We'll be fine on our own," Mike declared. "Just fine on our own."

"Mike, what are you talking about? It's been horrible on our own. We'd love to join you. We don't have a plan, and it sounds like you do. Something we could use."

"No," Mike objected, openly distrustful of us. "It's safer with just the four of us. We don't know them."

"Are you killers?" Penelope asked, directing her attention on to me.

"Just of alions," I replied, not thinking that they wouldn't have a clue what I meant.

"Alions?" Her voice inflected to a curious high.

Maggy smiled at her. "Well, if you've seen them, they look like lionesses. So I called them alions instead of aliens."

"We have seen enough of them to make your stomach rebel, that's certain," Penelope said. "Alions is pretty clever. I never thought about labeling them anything but monsters."

"We're not killers," Félix spoke up. "That's all we can say for you to trust us."

"Which is good enough a reason not to," Mike said. "Come on, Penny, let's get out of here." He motioned with his thumb southward.

I heard tapping on a window in the car, turned, and saw Jacob poking the glass. "Guys! Guys! The craft is coming this way!"

I darted my eyes to the city. The aircraft flew right for us.

"Get the guns," Maggy ordered.

I had left the shotgun resting on the seat cushion. Scooping it up, I ran to the other side of the car, in front of Jacob. Maggy and Félix lined up beside me, as if to protect the SUV. I was swallowing, all dry, painful swallows.

Just as the aircraft was about to fly over I-5, the bottom unlatched and dropped down like a mouth opening for a bite. Sliding, the alion shot through the air, descending like a cannonball, with a trajectory aimed at our level. By the time it reached the height of the fourth level, it uncurled. Immediately its four paws lit up with tiny bursts of white flames. Within a short, stifled breath it landed on a car, skidding across its roof.

I stared at the alion, rigid. A strange silver metal covered its paws like gloves. Through slits in the metal, five claws sunk into the neoplastic of the car, a death grip by any standard. I had watched a nature show on lions a few years before, and I remembered that the forepaw of a lion was strong enough to break a zebra's back in one swipe. I didn't want to think about what this beast was capable of. Probably strong enough to break an elephant's back.

It pounced onto a car two lanes over from ours, quick as a lizard's tongue catching a fly. The shotgun rattled in my grip. I couldn't steady it to save my life . . . and I needed to.

The alion was beyond intelligent. The four newcomers appeared to be unarmed compared to us, and it knew it; it knew we had projectiles, coming straight for us first.

Félix fired off a round and missed. The alion dashed out of the way, as if sensing the bullet coming. Maggy aimed and pulled the trigger, much to the same effect. I couldn't do it. My finger hesitated on the trigger . . .

It sprung from the car to the one behind ours. I stepped back, terrified. No air was going down my throat, and my lungs were starving as I wheezed. Suddenly it leapt at me.

Just then, Jacob exploded out of the car, knocking me back with the car door. With the two OMP2s clenched between his fingers, he shot off four rounds in burst fire, centered on the alion's large, muscular chest. It sounded like a tongue rolling: RRRR, but mechanical, precise, and lethal. The bullets and the alion greeted each other in a mortal embrace, the bullets passing through the beast without care of their quick meeting. In complete indifference, they continued on, out the sturdy back of the monstrous cat. Jacob spun out of the way. Maggy yanked me back, to the front of the SUV's hood. It struck the open door, breaking it from the hinges, landing on the shoulder of the freeway. Blood pooled like a puddle forming in a rainstorm.

"Let's go," Jacob said. He walked up next to the alion and smirked. "Gotcha."

Without warning, the alion swung a paw up at his legs, but missed, tapping the bottom of the SUV. Its last attempt to kill one of us drained it of what remaining energy it possessed. The alion's aircraft had flown on by, and now it circled around, heading for the main ship that clouded the city.

Maggy ran around to the driver's seat. "You coming?" She eyed the four newcomers.

Penelope looked at Mike, then turned back. "Yeah, we're coming."

Mike grumbled about it, but after the attack he seemed too scared to make any decisions and complied with a nod.

I helped Jacob into the front passenger's seat, as he could barely move, expending all his strength on the wild, life-saving maneuver. "You did it . . . you saved my life. Thanks, dude."

He nodded. "Just trying to help."

Félix and I crawled over the backseat, moving the bags aside. Mike climbed in after us. It was a tight squeeze. Penelope and her sisters sat comfortably in the three backseats.

Maggy started up the engines and began bumping cars out of the way. The brightness of the low beams worried us that we would be spotted, but it was difficult to see a thing with them off. She did her best to navigate the road for as long as possible without light, but eventually she had to turn them on.

Mike stared at us for a while, disgruntled. He looked as if there was something he wanted to say, but he never said a word, just narrowed his irritated eyes at us.

Penelope calmed her sisters, who had been screaming and crying since the alion landed on the car, even more so once it was dead. Now they just sobbed, clinging to their older sister, one to each side of Penelope, crying into her jacket.

Maggy pulled off I-5 when she saw the sign for Sea-Tac Airport. She parked in a driveway to a single-story duplex, shut off the engine, and sighed heavily. "We shouldn't go too far in the dark, it's too easy for them too see the lights. We can try to sleep here."

"You want to sleep here?" Mike asked sharply.

"That's what I said." She hopped out, grabbing her axe. She split the door by the handle, shoving the door backward, motioning everyone through. I couldn't believe how tough and resilient she was.

When I passed, I noticed the marking with three lines, which none of us had yet to figure out. The living room was spacious, with a long, three-cushion sofa, a love seat, and an inviting recliner. Maggy and Félix inspected the house for people and alions.

"Nothing here," Maggy reported, taking a seat on the loveseat next to Félix.

I wanted to plant myself in the recliner but gave it up to Jacob, who sorely needed it. Instead, I found a rocking game chair, pulling it up to join the circle. I stared at Maggy and Félix, not openly cuddling, but pretty damn close, their shoulders grazing. I switched my vision to Penelope, who was probably even more out of my league than Maggy. "So what happened to you guys? How did you manage not to get taken?"

The four newcomers sat together on the long sofa, Mike on one end and Penelope on the other, with the twins in the middle. Penelope looked at me with hard, tired eyes and swallowed. "Have you seen the symbols with two lines on the doors?"

"Yeah, we have. Why?" I think I was ogling by that time. I could tell that Mike hated it; I tried to stop, but it was a problem I had, a big one, eyes that lingered.

"You haven't figured out what they mean?" Her puzzled face

drooped.

"No, have you?" Maggy said.

"I have a pretty good guess," Penelope replied. "We were the only house on our block that had one, everyone else had three lines, and they were all taken the first night. All of my family was in the house; we all survived. But the second night . . ." she stammered. She broke into a sob.

"The second night was bad," Mike said. "I had been staying there for the week, looking for an apartment, luckily, I guess." He paused and swallowed a long, sour gulp of bile. "The second night, they came for us . . . to hunt us."

Félix choked on some water. "They came to hunt you?" He coughed in a fit, clearing his throat.

Mike glared at Félix, his jaw tight. "They leave the people with the two lines alone, so that they can come back and hunt. They're smart . . . and they like to play with us like a game. They're pack hunters, just like the lionesses in Africa."

"How do you know that's what the two lines mean?" Maggy asked.

"We met a couple who had the two-lines symbol on their door. They managed to kill three of them, and they fled down to the minimart we were staying in. This was last night. They didn't make it today. Anyway, they told us the same story . . . the same hell we went through on the second night, so it fits, I mean, I could be wrong, but I don't think I am."

"My house had two lines on the door, they didn't hunt me down," Jacob said.

"Yes they did, last night," Maggy blurted. "They weren't at your house for us, bromigo, they were there for you."

Jacob reflected on that; it was hard for him to think it through, since he had been passed out. He shrugged.

"So they are leaving some of us behind . . . to hunt us," Maggy said *sotto voce*.

"How did you survive the attack, did you kill them?" Félix shifted on the cushions, making them roll in a wave.

"Yeah, my uncle did. He had a classic revolver from World War I, a family heirloom. I don't know anything about guns, but I know it was a Smith and Wesson M1917. They displayed it in a glass case above their mantle . . . and he . . . well he had to use it. It only had six rounds, you know, only six. He used two on each one. After that, we had nothing but kitchen utensils. About two klicks from us was a pawnshop, so all six of us broke for it together on the second morning. There were no guns there, all taken, I guess. We went to a grocery store, but all the food was taken, but with nowhere else to go, we decided that the fire station a block away would be safer. That was on the third night, and they came for us again, as if they knew we had gone there. My uncle fended them off with one of those giant axes, while we escaped out the . . ." Tears were starting to slide down his cheeks. "By the morning, it was just the four of us."

All four of the newcomers were crying; it was hard for them, a lot harder since they had watched their loved ones murdered. It was slightly easier to cope, for me, as I didn't know what had actually happened to my parents. I assumed the worst. But maybe it wasn't the worst . . .

"I'm sorry," I said. "That's terrible." I was looking at the floor, shaking my head in disbelief and empathy.

We all started eating portable food, bars, fruit snacks . . . things like that. After a while, Penelope studied us a little closer, then realized something. "Why are you two covered in aluminum foil?"

"I'm covered, too, I just wrapped it underneath my clothes." Maggy lifted up a shirtsleeve and revealed my handiwork. Félix's aluminum foil, and my own, was starting to fall apart, with holes, minor rips, and big tears. It was time for a second application.

"But why?" Amanda asked, one of the twins. Both of the little girls had bright, wide eyes.

"You said you had the mark with two lines." Penelope nodded at Jacob. "But you three didn't. How did you survive?"

"All three of us had aluminum foil above our beds, so we figured that's why we survived, and well, that led to us dressing ourselves in it," I explained. "We have enough for you too."

Jacob laughed. "Aluminum foil isn't going to save us." He slid out of the recliner and dragged a bag to the center of the circle. "These are going to save us." He unzipped the weapon bag. Six handguns, two quivers of arrows, boxes of bullets, and knives galore stared back at us, disapproving of our ineptness, our inexperience, our complete lack of control to handle such deadly devices. Or maybe that was just what I saw.

Jacob turned his attention to the newcomers. "If you want to join us and survive, you'll need these, but if you plan on leaving . . . well, we need these."

"We all need each other," Penelope spoke up.

"Sounds about right," Maggy said.

Jacob snatched up a handgun. "Then take this." He offered Penelope the gun.

She debated with herself whether or not to accept the weapon, and by her slow reaching hand, it looked as if her desperate, scared side was winning. "All right." She finally gave in and took the pistol.

"It's loaded with nineteen rounds, so don't waste them. I'll show you how to load it, and how to put the safety on and all of that." Jacob went through the steps with her, then again with Mike when he chose a gun.

I went into the kitchen to see if the prior occupants had left any bread. I found a loaf in the fridge. When I closed it, there was Penelope just standing there; she startled me, and I dropped the loaf.

She bent down and scooped it up. "Sorry. I thought you heard me come in, it's a creaky place." She set the bread on the counter.

"It's all right. I'm okay. It's just, well you know. Don't think my nerves will ever calm down," I said, my voice faintly cracking.

"Mine either." She looked at me as if to find solace, or maybe just a regular conversation.

"So, you played Our Descent. Did you play online?" I asked.

"I was a two-star General, until the release of Death Squad."

I smiled at her. "You're kidding, a two-star, wow. I only made it to Colonel. You play Death Squad, too? That's awesome. IQ—I mean Maggy." I wasn't comfortable saying her nickname anymore. "Is the only girl I've met who plays on a regular basis."

She laughed. "Now you've met two. It's hard to pry me away. I'm in the Tough as Hell faction. What about you, are you in any well-known faction?"

I was still smiling. "No. We just made up our own, the three of us and a couple others from school." I started to open the bread bag. "You want a sandwich, there's peanut butter and jelly."

"No thanks."

Maggy walked to the edge of the kitchen. "Jelly, can I talk to you for a moment."

"Sure," I said. "I'll be right back. I want to know your rank on Death Squad." She smiled as I walked away.

"Let's go outside," Maggy said, so we did.

The air was fresh and cool. "You need something?" I asked.

"Yeah, I have to tell you something, something important that's kind of hard to say."

Oh man, I knew what was coming and I didn't want to hear it. I really didn't. I pulled a chocolate bar out of my pocket and began unwrapping it.

She saw that I wasn't going to say anything as I bit off a chunk of the chocolate. "Something happened in the Apocalypse Room, something that was a long time coming, though . . ." She sighed. "Though, I don't think you've noticed."

"You and Félix, yeah, I've noticed. Hard not to, you're my two best friends." I paced towards the car. "It's pretty weird. I mean—" I stopped myself. I couldn't tell her. I held it in, pushed it down my throat alongside the chocolate.

"I'm sorry," she said. "I didn't mean for it to happen, it just did. It won't break our friendship will it?"

I wanted to tell her to shove it, but I couldn't go sulk in my room; it was a different situation than normal, different than any situation I had ever been in. "I . . ." My sweating fingers let slip the chocolate bar. As it fell, I tried to grab it, and my foot swung forward, kicking the bar under the SUV.

"I'll turn on the lights." Maggy opened the driver's door and pressed the button for the vehicle's underside lights. Four small white lights illuminated the underside of the SUV.

I crouched by the back tire, but didn't see it, so I lay flat on my stomach and spotted it near the wheel on the other side. I jumped up and ran around, lying flat again, sliding under the car. As I crawled backwards, chocolate bar in hand, I noticed something weird-looking, as if it weren't a part of the car and wasn't supposed to be there. I grabbed at it, tore it loose, and brought it up with me.

"What's that?" Maggy asked.

I fingered the sleek black object: it was small, about the length of my pinky, and slightly thinner. "I don't know, it was attached to the car, but it doesn't look like a car part. I'm no mechanic or anything, but doesn't it look strange?"

"Yeah, it does."

I met her eyes. "We should bring it in, maybe Jacob knows what it is, or maybe that new guy knows something about cars."

"Good idea," she said. I started for the duplex's door. "Jelly, wait. Are we okay? I mean, you didn't say anything, and you haven't been acting like yourself at all today."

"It's just weird, that's all. I'll get used to it, I suppose. Don't worry about me." I walked off, into the duplex. Maggy entered soon after I did. "What do you think it is?" I asked Jacob.

Jacob inspected the tube, trying to pry the ends open. "It's not a car part, I can tell you that much. It's just a round cylinder of nothing, could even be hollow and empty."

Suddenly, one end flashed blue. "What was that?" one of the twins asked, curious.

Jacob scrutinized the end that had blinked. "Don't know."

"I can guess what it is, it's a locator beacon," Mike said, nervous and twitchy.

"Uhrm. What?" I said.

"They're tracking us, I'll bet." Mike snatched the object away from Jacob and waved it around. "Those monsters are tracking us!" His mood shifted drastically, now frantic.

"When would they have put it on the car?" Maggy asked. "We've only come across the one, and we killed it. You saw it all happen."

Jacob gasped, open-mouthed. "Yeah, we did kill it, but after I shot it, and it was lying there dying, it took one last swipe at my legs. It was a horrible shot, even bad for a dying beast, but now that I think about it, it clinked its claws against the bottom of the car."

"You think it stuck it to the car then?" Félix asked.

"Who's to say, bro? It's not a car part, and Mike, is it?" Mike nodded at Jacob. "Mike might be on to something. We should ditch it."

Mike was pacing back and forth. "Ditch it," he shouted. "We should just get the hell out of here and leave it behind."

"Nah, it's too dark, the lights are too bright. They have aircrafts that can spot us from the sky," Jacob stated.

"We've got to do something with it," Penelope said. "We can't keep it with us."

"What was that?" I said, breathing heavily.

The house went dead. Ears grew sharp.

"Are we going to die?" Jane asked, nestled against her older sister.

Penelope stroked her sister's back. "No, we're not going to die. We're going to find help; it'll be all right . . . it'll be all right."

"Let's calm down, we're all just a little spooked," Maggy said.

"We have to leave, we have to leave now," Mike argued.

"We just have to get rid of that thing, we don't need to leave," Félix replied.

Mike went over to the back window. The blinds were drawn down and closed. He still held the cylinder in his hand. He rested the gun on the windowsill and peeked outside.

I glanced over at him and the cylinder as it flashed blue again.

Without warning, two giant paws broke through the glass, digging into Mike's skull. The paws wrenched his body out the window, into the quiet night.

The twins were screaming, and Penelope looked utterly paralyzed.

My throat closed as my head swam with black-red streaks before my eyes.

"Get away from the windows! Get away!" Maggy screamed. She bent down and grabbed a second pistol. Félix did the same.

I put the shotgun to my shoulder, since it had bruised my gut earlier. Jacob had never mentioned how to properly fire it. I should have known from all the video games, but I just didn't think of it when the alions were around. I didn't really think at all, almost as if my brain just shut down, running away, leaving me only with nerves that hated the thought of real confrontation.

I yanked Penelope away from the window. "What are you doing, get away from there!"

Her eyes were glazed over, too foggy to see me right in front of her. Her sisters needed her comfort, her strength, but she was gone.

I knelt down by the sofa. "It's okay. It will be okay. I'll protect you. Don't worry, I'll protect you." Some instinct inside took over when I saw how fragile they were, how much they needed a soft voice to care for them. "Get down on the floor behind me." They slid off the cushions in a hurry, huddling.

My throat battled with me, not wanting to let any oxygen in, but I popped an inhaler in my mouth and sprayed. I narrowed my eyes on the broken window, with a sour feeling crawling up from my stomach, a feeling of imminent attack.

I bolted upright and fired.

The alion pounced silently through the large window, forepaws outstretched, gliding through the air like a dart. The spatter of shots blew the alion's face right off. The body thudded against the back of the sofa, throwing my legs out from under me. I smacked my head against its top. Despite the pillowy nature of the sofa, it scrunched up my nose. I flopped over onto my side, holding my face.

Félix crept near the arm of the sofa and peeked over. "It's just a pile of blood."

I got up and checked. All that remained of the alion was its huge body without a head. Blood was gushing out of its thick neck. "We gotta leave," I said, holding back the urge to puke.

"I'm with ya, bromigo." Félix nodded. He gathered up the duffels we had brought into the duplex.

Maggy went to the front door, key in one hand, pistol in the other, and her axe tied across her back. She threw open the door, scanned. "Nothing. Let's go," she whispered.

Félix hustled Penelope over the threshold and into the car. Jacob followed next, while I came up the rear with the twins.

Jacob opened the driver's backdoor, and as I lifted one of the twins into the car, out of the shadows an alion lunged at the second twin. I whipped around, grabbing the shotgun as it rested against the car body. I knew the recoil was going to hurt, but I didn't have time to bring it up to my shoulder, and I pulled the trigger with the butt stuck in my stomach. Another bruise was coming, that was certain. I groaned as the gun dug into me; it felt like the gun was going to come out the other side.

Jacob had jerked Amanda out of the way. At least I thought it was Amanda, but I had never been very good with remembering names. The shotgun spray blasted through the alion's chest and legs. It fell in a mangled mess of blood, fur, bone, and organs.

Jacob passed me Amanda, and I set her down next to her sister. Penelope scrambled over the compartment between the two front seats. She climbed into the back with her sisters, ducking low, squeezed together. They were bawling and with good reason. If I hadn't pissed my pants when Maggy had thrown the steak knives at us two days before, I certainly did then.

Félix hopped into the passenger's seat. I helped Jacob into the back and he scooted over so that I could get in faster. As I slammed the door shut, I yelled: "Go! Go! Go!"

Maggy had the car fired up, and she slid it into reverse, peeling out of the driveway. The police engine accelerated on par with the Trackster, and she wheeled us down a wide neighborhood street.

"Everyone all right?" Maggy asked. She didn't get much in the way of answers, mostly groans, and some nods out of her sight range.

I cleared my throat. "What the—"

BAM.

An alion smashed into my door. It was trying to run us off the road like in a high-speed chase in the movies. After its impact, it maintained a gallop alongside us, by my window.

"Faster!" I cried.

It bumped us again. The car wobbled.

The well armed take advantage, I repeated in my head.

Jacob tapped me on the shoulder. "Here." He handed me an OMP2. "Better than the shotgun."

I rolled down the window and just held down on the trigger. The recoil went into my wrist, less than the bite of hammering a nail into a wall, impossibly smooth. I didn't know how many bullets filled that beast, but it didn't last long.

Maggy drove on.

I hit the button that rolled up the window, exhaling the biggest, longest breath I ever had in my life.

We drove for hours without saying a word to each other. The only noise came from the newcomers in the back: they wept until the sun rose. In the morning sunlight, we zoomed along a lifeless road that connected to Tacoma.

Maggy drove so fast that she didn't notice the road spikes across the lanes until it was too late. She slammed on the brakes. POP—the front tires. POP—the back tires. Air rushed out, but they were cop tires, extra resistant. Maggy turned the wheel left, then right, then back again, out of control.

Even with my blood pumping wildly, I still heard her yell: "Hold on! We're gonna crash!"

I braced myself for the end.

4
What's Out There?
Maggy

I lost control of the SUV and we rammed right into the tail of a pickup truck. The airbags deployed, smashing my face.

I didn't know how long we sat there, but we just sat there, in the silence of the world. I pushed my face away from the soft pillow. It was so hot. I thought I was on vacation near the equator. Once my eyes focused on the steering column, I realized the truth, the situation of my environment. It wasn't a vacation.

I turned my neck toward Tortilla, and it popped several times, each one a moment of relief, followed by a dull pain. Luckily, Tortilla had braced his body well enough, using the door handle and the armrest. He had still hit the airbag.

He looked over at me, his face red and pulsing, and his glasses slightly bent. "Are you okay?"

I nodded. I stared at him, blinked, then opened my mouth to talk, but it was too dry as my words scraped against my throat. I found the water bottle that had rested in the cup holder, now by my feet. I took a drink. My eyes shifted between fuzzy and focused. "I'm having a hard time seeing."

He blinked. "Yeah, me too."

I peered out the windshield: three men stood, statues in the shadow of the street. "Hell."

Tortilla looked forward. "You thinking bad news?"

"I sure am." The pistol was still in the compartment under the main console. I snatched it up.

The three men walked out of the shadow, into clear view, boasting assault rifles over their shoulders.

"Bad, bad news," I said. They looked dirty, sweat-stained, and full of malevolence. In other words: dangerous. I turned the key. Nothing happened, not even a sweet sound that a possibility existed for the engine to fire up.

"Get out, princess. You too, spic," the middle one said. His lanky body looked strung out and aged, his back slightly humped. A huge, bushy beard hung under his chin, down to his chest; it was a frizzy clump of grayness.

"What do we do?" Tortilla asked. He grabbed his two guns, held them below the airbags, so that they couldn't see them from the outside.

"Don't know. I think they flattened our tires."

"Why would they—"

"Didn't you hear what they called you? We gotta get out of here," I said, trembling.

The others were starting to groan as they came to, disoriented. The crash wasn't that bad. The front looked as if it might be crumpled, but it could have been a lot worse if we had been going faster.

They lowered their rifles, aimed at the car. "Get out now!" the middle one shouted.

The one to the left of the middle one was tall, round, and empty-eyed, as if his mind was melted. He opened Tortilla's door, pointing the rifle in his face. "He said get out. So come on already, get out."

Tortilla was shaking wildly. The guns slipped from his grip. The guy yanked Tortilla out by his shirt collar and threw him to the ground. "What do you want? What do you want?" Tortilla screamed, his voice a few octaves higher than usual.

"The girl," the middle one said.

"What do you mean, the girl?"

"He's not very bright, chief. Freddy can have him," the big one said.

"Like a spic is something I want," Freddy said, the short, bald man to the left of the middle one. "Chief, I don't want no spic, you hear?"

"I never said you had to have him," the middle one said. "Get the other two out of the back."

Freddy took point in front of Tortilla, aiming at him with steady hands. The big one went to the doorless backseat and pulled out Jacob, who had passed out.

"What are you doing?" Jelly said groggily, gazing at the big man who held Jacob over his shoulder. He laid Jacob next to Tortilla. He went around the car and wrenched Jelly out of his seat, gripping his shirt by his chest. "Stop. What are you doing? Stop it. Put me down." The man dropped Jelly next to Jacob, smiling down at them.

"Come on, princess. I ain't gonna wait all day for you," the middle one said—the one they called "chief."

I stared at them, terrified. My heart was near the point of exploding. I couldn't move.

"None of them seem all too bright, chief," the big one commented.

"Looks to be that way, go grab her," Chief said.

The big one walked around the smashed truck.

I still held the gun, unbeknownst to them. I steadied my nerves to pull the trigger when the door opened. I waited as he paced around the truck, and with every step closer, my finger twinged, like sharp needles poking and poking relentlessly. I aimed right for where his gut would be when he was close enough.

"What are you eyeing?" the big one barked as he neared.

At the sound of his voice, the gun slipped out of my hand as I jolted. I needed the gun; it was my lifeline, my only hope. I reached to get it, but he knew I had something, and he rushed to open the door.

"What do ya got there?" He clutched my arm and squeezed with his massive hand.

I wiggled, trying to get free. No use. "Stop! You're hurting me."

"I can't hurt a cute little princess like you." He squeezed even harder. "Oh, we're going to have fun with you, little princess."

Out of the corner of my eye, I saw a shape pop up from behind the backseat. The gun blast rang in my ear. I stared at the man, gulping in air. Blood poured out of his throat. He staggered back and keeled over onto the sidewalk. The other two ducked in reaction. They couldn't see Penelope behind the tinted police windows. She shot through the crack in the open passenger's front door. The bullet blew through a window across the street.

The two men whirled around, crouching. "Where's it coming from?" Chief yelled. Another window broke up the street.

I unbuckled my seatbelt, found the gun under the GO pedal, and slid out of the SUV. I gingerly stepped over the big one, then wheeled around the front of the car and fired. Blood splattered around Freddy's left kneecap.

A shout burst forth as the man flew face first to the road.

Penelope shot off a few more rounds.

Chief twisted around and sighted me. I ducked behind the car. I ran around the backend, when I came around the corner, I saw Chief peering down at Jelly.

"Mr. Hammolin?" Jelly said, surprised. He coughed twice.

Chief yanked Freddy out of the road and into the building across the street. I fired at their boots, but every bullet missed its mark. "Get up, get up," I yelled. "We have to move."

Penelope threw open the hatchback, setting her sisters onto the concrete. "Through the store." She pointed to a jewelry shop to the left of the SUV.

Jelly and Tortilla lifted Jacob off the pavement. A spray of gunfire hit the SUV as they crossed over the threshold of the jewelry shop. I stooped down below the main window of the store. Bullets pierced the car and carried on to the storefront and its windows. The glass shattered.

"Out the back," I yelled. They nodded.

"The bags," Tortilla said. "What about the bags?"

"Penelope has the guns."

"We need the food and water. Your axe is in there, too," he reminded me.

"Give me some cover fire," I said. He nodded. We bolted out the door, crouched. I grabbed the bag of inhalers out of the backseat, while Tortilla shot off a few rounds, arms unfolded across the wrinkled hood. I tossed the bag to Jelly, who hunkered down by the doorframe. I crept over across the backseat, my heart racing. The assault rifle rounds made easy work of the car, but I was already in the rear, dashing out the hatchback with all the bags I could carry. "I'm good."

Jelly smiled at me when I reached him. "Almost as if we really were trained."

"Yeah, almost. We should keep going. Where are Jacob and the sisters?"

"Uhrm. Jacob woke up and took them out the back," Jelly replied.

Tortilla was running so fast, he almost toppled over us as he stopped in front at my feet. "Go." He grabbed a few bags and headed for the back. Jelly and I followed, loaded with our own duffels and backpacks. I had strapped my axe across my back, but it hurt with the weight of the pack compressing the haft into my spine.

Jelly whirled. "The bows."

"Leave them," Tortilla said. "We don't have time, they have assault rifles, bromigo. The bows don't matter."

Convinced, Jelly whipped back toward us and hustled out the backdoor of the shop. We emerged into a deserted alley, devoid of even recycling dumpsters. "Where do we go?" Jelly asked.

I inhaled a deep breath. "South. We keep going south."

Jelly squatted next to the twins. "We're okay. It's okay. We won't let them hurt you."

They stared at him, horrified, yet calm.

"Let's go," I said, pointing southwards.

"I don't think I can walk very far," Jacob said. "It hurts everywhere."

"You won't have to, just far enough until we can find our next ride," I told him. My lungs were expanding too fast, sucking in hot air, choking on white mucus. "You can make it."

"I could use a drink. Where is that vodka?"

The three of us laughed.

"Dude, you drank all that vodka," Jelly said. "It's gone. I told you to make it last."

"I don't remember drinking any more of it. Damn."

We began walking south, down the wide alley. Jacob had his arm wrapped around Tortilla for support.

"Uhrm. That was some nice shooting," I overheard Jelly say to Penelope.

"No, it was some nice luck," she replied. "Thanks for being so sweet to my sisters. They really need it."

"Glad to assist," he said, clearing his throat. I couldn't see his face, but I knew he was blushing. "I think they are the calmest out of all of us, but also the most scared. They're holding it together way better than I would if I were their age. How old are they?"

"Eleven."

"Yeah, I wouldn't have made it so far at eleven."

We came to the end of the alley, to a once busy street, seven lanes across. "Search the SUVs for keys. They'll be best," I said. I climbed into the driver's seat of some Lincoln. "No key."

"No key in the Honda," Tortilla reported.

"Yeah, no key in the Ford," Jelly said.

"Here! Found a key in the Nissan," Penelope shouted. She started it up. "We're good to go." She slid out of the seat. "You can drive. It's Maggy, right?"

"Yeah, Maggy. Long days take their toll."

"Yeah, I remember you told me yesterday, I just . . ."

"No problem." I didn't have any words of comfort, so I untied the axe and threw it in the trunk, then jumped into the rig, ready to peel away. Once the car was loaded, I did just that, turning back onto the main street, heading south. I didn't see the two men behind us anywhere, but that didn't mean they were gone.

"I knew one of them," Jelly said so quietly I almost didn't pick up his words.

He was sitting behind me, and I looked at him in the rearview mirror. "You knew one of them?"

"Yeah. You remember me always telling you about my crazy neighbor, the Troll. Well, the one they called chief, that was the Troll."

I scrunched up my face in disgust. "You sure, bromigo?"

"Uhrm. I swear." Jelly fiddled with an inhaler, tempted to use it. "He has a face you don't forget. I know he's a registered sex offender. He would have done . . ." He trailed off, not wanting to finish.

"You never told us that before," Tortilla said.

"Yes I did. You just weren't listening. It was a few years ago, on the day Battle We Cry came out."

He laughed. "Yeah, I probably wasn't listening."

Jelly continued to play with the inhaler, nervous. "Well, anyway, now you know." He began popping off its cover and replacing it.

The twins were asleep when I pulled into a driveway of a two-story home a few streets west of the main road we had been traveling on all day. We had made it to Tacoma, full of great towers, but we stayed outside the city, in the suburbs. Tortilla and I had inspected the entire SUV, finding no trace of a locator beacon. Hopefully the alions didn't have more than one design.

The house was stocked with cans of food, mostly soup, and we boiled three cans of chunky tomato and four cans of vegetables with beef. It was nice to have something hot in the stomach. So many lights were still on in the neighborhood that we didn't bother trying to hide in one room with one soft light for all of us. We did stay away from the windows. That memory was too fresh and real, too sickening to even consider looking outside. Once we were in, we were in.

We walked on our knees, out of sight from anything searching the interior from the outside, though our shadows were a problem, and everyone tried to stay still after we ate. Jelly, Tortilla, and I had taken off our aluminum foil garb. It was so noisy and crumpled up, none of us bothered to don new sheets.

Jelly and Penelope talked in a corner. It sounded like they were discussing video games, but I wasn't sure. The twins were asleep on a nice leather couch a few meters away from their big sister. Penelope giggled quite a bit; it was slightly irritating.

"You all right?" Tortilla asked as he caught me staring at Jelly.

"I've been better, that's certain, bromigo."

"You should be happy that she is here and talking to Darrel," Tortilla said. He scooted up on a nice dining chair with a tall back.

"She's just new, that's all. I don't know her. I think that's why I'm a little uncomfortable."

He leaned forward, gazing at me. "Well, she sounds pretty cool. She plays all the games we do. I think it will be good for him; it will help us, you know . . . he won't feel like the third wheel." He rubbed my leg, gentle and with care.

I smiled at him. "Yeah. I'll just have to get to know her." I drank some water, dehydrated.

He nodded. "Looks like we'll have some time for that. I'm going to go lie down, I don't know how any of us are still awake."

I yawned. "Good idea. We shouldn't turn off the lights, I think that would be a bad idea, maybe dim some of them."

"Yeah, I don't want the lights off either." He walked over to Jelly and Penelope. "We're going to sleep, mind if I dim the lights?"

"Go ahead, man," Jelly said. "Sleep sounds like the right idea." His eyes watered after he yawned. It went around the room, the contagious yawn. Jacob slept in a recliner, out minutes after we had eaten.

"I'll take watch," Penelope said. No one argued.

I lay out on the floor, in front of the couch that the twins were resting on. Everyone said their goodnights until at last sleep overtook the room.

I stirred awake when I felt something knock my arm. I opened my eyes and saw a thick black boot. It was nestled against my sprawled out forearm. I looked up and saw a shadow bent over me, and in an instant, the shadow retreated with one of the twins. My eyes popped. The boot sneaked back a few steps, silent. Then the light destroyed the shadow that hid the figure.

A wiry man held Jane tightly across her stomach, with a bright silver pistol digging into her temple.

I sprang to my feet. "What are you doing?"

"Shhh. I'm taking this one. I'm going to have myself some fun. You killed my partners, now I'm taking one of yours."

"We only killed one."

"Freddy was as good as dead when you wounded him. I couldn't let him suffer, oh no. But this one . . ." He squeezed Jane and she cried out. "This one is all mine."

Everyone else stirred awake when they heard Jane. "Penny! Penny!"

The Troll shoved the pistol harder into her skull. "Shhh, little princess. None of that now." He took a step back.

Penelope, who had fallen asleep slumped against the couch, now aimed a gun at the Troll. "Release her!"

"Oh no, this little princess is mine." He jerked Jane up so that her head blocked his throat. He walked backwards until he stood at the open front door. "You took mine." He laughed, a strange, treacherous laugh. He was completely melted. But he was spry, with agile feet, and quickly disappeared out the door.

"What do we do?" I asked.

"Is that even a question?" Jelly said, annoyed and frightened.

The hunt began.

We gathered everything up and crept out into the rising sunlight. "Look." Penelope pointed to an aluminum can in the driveway. She picked it up and inspected it. "There's a note inside."

"What does it say," Jelly asked. He stood in front of her, with his arms around Amanda, who kept asking if Jane was going to die. We had to ignore her after the tenth time.

"I want to play, oh, I want to play. Follow the trail. Follow the trail. At nightfall I'll have my fun, oh, I'll have my fun. Tomorrow I'll take the other one," Penelope read.

"What trail?" Jacob asked.

Tortilla ran out into the street and bent low to scoop up another can. "I think he is dropping cans for us to follow."

"Is this real? Is this really happening?" Penelope said. "Some melted bastard has abducted my sister . . . Aliens have abducted the rest of the world, this is all real?" She hung her head, tears overflowing. "All I did was fall asleep . . ."

Jelly wrapped his arms around her. "We'll get her back, don't worry."

"How do you know?"

"Because we have to. He wants us to find him, so we will," Jelly assured her.

"Let's get to it then," I said. I started up the SUV. The rest climbed in. Penelope and Amanda sat together in the back next to Jelly. Jacob sat in the front, and Tortilla scouted out the rear in the trunk space.

The driving was slow. Olympia shot up into view in the afternoon. "How many cans do we have?" I asked.

"Thirty-two," Tortilla replied. He kept our collection in the trunk with him. Why did we keep them, I didn't know, probably should have dumped them, but we didn't.

"Thirty-two," I whispered. The Troll had been leaving them in plain sight for us to find; he really wanted us to follow him . . . that was certain. I pressed down on the GO pedal after we collected thirty-three. He had led us to a fancy neighborhood, where the houses were mansions, with massive yards, pools, tennis courts, full-sized basketball courts, the works.

"There's one in the driveway to the left!" Penelope shouted.

I pulled in, and everyone hopped out, except for Jacob, who was sleeping off his aches.

Penelope snatched up the can. "There's another note inside. It says: Good, good, you found me. I'm inside where the lions await, guarding his prey . . . The sick bastard, I'll kill him, I will." She started for the door. Jelly followed.

"Wait," I spoke up. "I don't think he's in there." I surveyed the neighborhood. "I think he is in that one." I pointed to an even larger house, two houses down, across the street.

"What makes you say that?" Penelope asked.

"Look at the huge brick columns. There is a lion's head mounted to each one."

"Always so observant," Jelly commented. We all walked over to the mouth of the long driveway. The black metal gate rocked in the breeze. "So what's the plan?"

"Two of us go behind the house, two of us through the front," Tortilla said.

"We're not trained for that," I argued. "We might accidently shoot each other."

"Maggy is right," Penelope agreed. "We all have pretty shaky nerves right now." She bent down to her sister. "Sorry kid, you have to go keep Jacob company. We can't leave him out here alone."

"He's not nice," Amanda blurted. "I don't want to be alone with him. I'm going with you."

"You can't. I'll get Jane back, I promise. But you have to promise me that you won't go in there. A not-so-nice guy is much better than that monster in there. You understand?"

"We'll get Jane back," Jelly added.

Amanda nodded and walked off to the SUV.

I had two handguns. Tortilla had two handguns. Jelly carried Jacob's OMP2s, and Penelope loaded Jelly's shotgun.

She smiled at us. "I know how to use it. I've hunted pheasants before with my grandfather. Granted, this shotgun is older than mine, but I'll be fine."

Jelly nodded at her. "So through the front, or through the back?"

"The front," I said. I didn't have a reason to start there, but we were already there. I tried the doorknob; it was unlocked. "Ready?"

The all nodded, scared.

The foyer was barren, clean, and well lit in the daylight. The door swung open, and calmed as it hit the doorstopper. We scurried in, Tortilla and I went right, while Jelly and Penelope darted left. We crouch-walked to find cover.

Suddenly a resounding PANG pierced the heavy wooden door. An arrow stuck in the wood, just above the peephole. A piece of paper was rolled up around the shaft, by the feathers, taped. A carpeted staircase lay in front of us, but when I shifted my eyes there, no one stood where the shooter should have been. "He's fast," I said. I reached up and plucked the arrow from the door, unbinding the paper. "It says: I'm here, in this castle, but there are so many rooms. Pick the wrong one, and . . ." I spoke, trailing off as the note did. "That's all it says."

"Where should we start looking?" Tortilla asked

"We should sweep from the left to the right, to make sure we don't miss a room," I said. "Or right to left, it doesn't matter."

"Left to right sounds fine. Let's go." Penelope crouch-ran forward, into a living room. "It's empty." She pointed to a hall when we pulled up behind her. The hall connected to a den, a library, and a master bedroom, all of which were empty as well. We swept through the kitchen, dining room, a giant pantry the size of my bedroom, a family room, and two more bedrooms, but nothing was abnormal about them.

Tortilla positioned himself at the staircase at the right end of the house: it was the third one we had come across. He aimed up to the second and third floors, scanning. I edged up the stairs, trying to maintain complete silence; it was harder to do than in the movies. I was making too much noise, so I crawled back down and took off my shoes.

Everyone nodded at me, as they slipped off their own shoes.

I crawled up the steps again, this time without the squeak of my deteriorating soles. Penelope and Jelly followed, taking to the wings at the top of the stairs as I went to the corner of a hallway. I peeped around the side. Nothing. There was a closed door ahead of us. Jelly nodded towards it.

He knelt by the doorknob and twisted it slowly. The stale air in the room choked us. Jelly coughed and cleared his throat a few times.

Penelope ran to the bed and picked up something lying in its center. "It's a picture of my sister." She showed us the picture inside the frame. "Looks like she's in a smaller room, tied to a chair."

"He works fast, must have printed out that picture from his phone," Jelly said.

"Maybe. Let's keep moving," I said. I walked to the door attached to the room; it was a shared bathroom. "Guys." The urgency in my voice forced them into a run.

"What is it?" Tortilla asked.

I showed them another picture; it was gruesome. "I think he's a serial killer or something." A person's remains lay chopped up into pieces on a big slab of a countertop.

Jelly instantly turned away. "Why did you show me that?" He leaned against a high desk, clearing his throat, holding back his stomach.

Another open family room lay across the hall from the two bedrooms, and resting on the couch was another horrible picture. "You think he did this to these people?" Jelly asked. "I mean I knew he was melted, being a sex offender, but this . . ."

"Yeah, bromigo, I think he did it," I said. "We gotta find Jane."

After we searched two more bedrooms on the floor, finding two more pictures of mutilation, we sneaked up to the third floor. My stomach rebelled from the repulsive scenes framed ever so nicely for us. It was difficult to hold the acids in.

"That one," Jelly whispered, pointing a gun towards a shut door to the right of the stairs. He turned the knob, and I twirled around the frame, guns up. The darker room was full of shadows, and a silhouette of a man stared back at me. My slippery fingers clamped down on the triggers. The bullets whizzed past the figure. I fired again, this time the bullets pierced their target, carrying on through and into the wall. The shape remained still.

Tortilla ran over the threshold, stopping next to me. He flipped a light switch on.

I laughed, shaking. "A coatrack."

"So they can be confused for real people," he said, laughing.

I sat down on the bed, trembling out of control.

"So much for a surprise, our stealthy steps won't matter anymore," Penelope said. "Let's go."

"Wait, look at her, she needs a second," Tortilla whispered, rubbing my back.

"I don't have a second to spare," Penelope said. "You do what you gotta do." She bolted out of the room. Jelly followed her.

I sucked in a huge breath. "I'm okay," I said as I blew out the air. "Let's catch up."

Penelope was rushing into room after room, shotgun raised and prepared to launch a decimating spray of shots. I could see the anger and fear in her sunken, exhausted eyes. We stopped looking at the pictures left for us, no use doing what the Troll desired us to do: lose all of our senses and nerves.

Jelly opened the second-to-last door, and Penelope dashed in. We all followed in a hurry. We halted, staring at the Troll with the assault rifle at the back of Jane's head.

Penelope dropped the shotgun and whipped out a pistol from a holster wrapped around her ribs, hiding underneath her jacket. Her movements were as quick as a cat's, and fired straight for the Troll's head.

The bullet flew. Suddenly, glass shattered, and a hole emerged from where the bullet had struck the mirror wall.

"Move, and little princess here dies right now," the Troll ordered, his gravelly voice hurt my ears. "Drop your guns."

Jelly put his down first, then Tortilla, then I decided I would be too slow to get the best of him. Penelope kept her pistol raised, resolute and defiant.

"Come on, princess. You know you can't shoot me before I shoot her. Put it down. NOW!"

Penelope flinched at his shout. She released the gun, tears streaming in a torrent.

"Now here's how it's gonna go: I'm gonna have my fun with each of you, one by one. I have plenty of frames, nice frames that will do you justice, don't you worry."

"Why?" I stammered. "Why are you going to kill us?"

He laughed a sadistic, rough laugh, consistent with his harsh voice.

"Little princess, what else would I do with this house? Gotta make my parents proud, show them that I did something with it after they died . . . NOW ON YOUR KNEES!"

Jelly knelt first, then Tortilla, then Penelope and I both, our hands behind our heads, like on cop shows. It was instinct to place them like that, too much TV.

"It's okay, Jane. It'll be all right," Penelope comforted her little sister.

"Why would you lie to her like that, princess?" the Troll asked. "Didn't you see my last guests? How much fun I had with them? I have some great ideas for you, too." He cleared his throat. "What was that?"

"I'm going to kill you," Penelope repeated.

"Oh, sweet, sweet princess. You're on your knees, and I have a rifle."

"Mr. Hammolin, why are you doing this?" Jelly asked. "I know who you are . . . we're neighbors—"

"We *were* neighbors. But I noticed things are a little different now, haven't you? I also noticed that you took my bows . . . having fun with them?" The Troll laughed. "You take my knives too? I bet you did, maybe that's how I'll do you, neighbor. I'll use my precious knives, would you like that?"

I could still see the Troll, smiling in the fragmented mirror. "Why are you killing us instead of the alions?" I asked.

"Alions, what the hell are alions?"

"The aliens," Tortilla clarified abruptly.

"Don't remember asking you, spic. Keep your mouth shut."

Preoccupied with us, the Troll didn't notice Penelope rocking back on her knees, building momentum. She spun in the air, kicking. Her foot connected with only air, still a meter away. The mirror deceived my eyes, as the Troll stood much farther from us than what I had thought, and apparently, it got the better of Penelope, too.

"Oh, you poor, dumb princess. You didn't want to do that." The Troll moved forward and stomped down on her legs. Penelope cried out. He kicked her in the stomach, then her head. "Why would you be so stupid?" He unsheathed a knife at his belt with his left, then crouched beside her. He lifted the knife high, his eyes crazed, his brain melted; he gripped the weapon, preparing to strike.

PAHWKkk.

I turned and spotted Amanda, holding up two shaking arms, gripping a pistol. The Troll fell to the carpet, a hole through his brain.

"Amanda!" Jane cried.

I got up and went to the Troll, stealing his rifle and knife from his limp grip. "Check Penelope."

Jelly rushed to her side, feeling her neck for a pulse. "She's unconscious," he reported. "Is he?"

"I don't want to touch him," I said.

"If we leave him and he survives, he'll hunt us," Jelly remarked.

"Tortilla, take the twins. Jelly, carry Penelope, get them out."

Jelly shook his head, obstinate. "No, you get out."

Tortilla untied Jane, who was bawling her eyes out, then gathered up Amanda and rushed them out of the room. I went to the door and watched as Jelly picked up his OMP2s, aiming his right pistol at the Troll's unmoving body. He fired. The bullets penetrated his head, almost in a single hole. He lifted Penelope off the ground, and I went in to collect our weapons and the Troll's assault rifle. Boxes full of ammunition lay stacked in the corner.

We ran out of the house as fast as we could, gathering our shoes, all of us with full arms, except for the twins and Penelope.

Jacob slept inside of the car, unknowing of Amanda's absence. When Tortilla opened the driver's backdoor, Jacob jumped awake. "What's going on?" He peered at Jelly with Penelope in his arms. "Did he kill her?"

The twins climbed into the backseat with Tortilla. Jane was still crying, comforted by Amanda.

I opened the hatchback, loaded up the gear, clearing out some room.

"No, she's alive," Jelly said, laying Penelope in the flat trunk space. "I'll stay back here with her. Just get us out of here."

I nodded and closed the hatch. In reverse, I tore out of the driveway, heading for the main road we had come off, to the east. Up above the dash hung a GPS display, but it didn't work anymore, and I sorely needed it. I had never been down in Olympia; I didn't know any of the streets, except for I-5, as it ran through it.

I drove for a few hours, until the sun decided it was time for bed. I saw a sign that gave directions to a mall and followed it. We all needed fresh clothes. My spares were soiled, beyond stinky.

The mall parking lot was stuffed full of vehicles, and instead of navigating through the mess, I pulled up on the empty walkway, stopping at the front doors of the north entrance. "If there's a Luxury Mattress Town inside, we can sleep there," I said, hopeful. We all needed a decent night's sleep.

Penelope was coming round as we unloaded the SUV. "What's going on? Where are we?"

"At a mall, south of Olympia somewhere," Jelly informed her.

"Where is Jane?"

"Here," Jane said, walking up to the trunk, hands interlocked with her twin. "Amanda saved us!"

"What?"

"He was going to kill you, and Amanda saved us," Jane shouted happily.

Penelope looked at Jelly. He nodded that her sister was telling the truth. "Amanda did what no little girl should ever have to do, but she did it. She saved us."

Jelly explained everything as we made our way inside, and to our jubilation and relief, the mall had a Luxury Mattress Town.

Tortilla came up to me as I prepared my bed. He had found an eyeglass shop and fixed his spectacles with rubber-tipped pliers. "Crazy day, bramiga."

I smiled. "And I thought yesterday was crazy."

He smiled back at me. "You want me to . . . you know . . . sleep with you?"

My heartbeat skyrocketed, happy and confused. "Well, it's just . . ." I peeped over at Jelly and Penelope, who were making their beds next to each other. Jelly stopped Penelope and hugged her tightly. "Yeah . . . okay."

"We don't have to if you don't want—"

"I want to, Tortilla. I want to."

Jelly took first watch. I told him I would relieve him soon, but I'm not sure he heard me. We went to sleep with the main lights off and just the perimeter lights on. They hung around the edge of the store, glowing softly, a reassurance that if the boogeyman jumped out at us, we would see him coming.

5

Taken

Darrel

I awoke when I saw glass shatter, as two giant paws plucked Mike from the floor and out the window.

I sat up in the bed, sweating. It was cold and nasty, my hairs clinging to my legs. In the dim lighting, I could make out Maggy cuddling under heavy blankets with Félix. An unwanted sigh broke out. I turned my vision to Penelope and her sisters all bundled up together, tightly wrapped, and breathing softly. Beds of luxury: it was great to finally find some peace.

I didn't know who was supposed to be on watch, but whoever it was fell asleep on the job.

I grabbed a water bottle and walked into the silent mall. Minor humming came periodically from the food court area, probably the refrigerators. I passed a clothing store for young kids, then a sporting goods store, then finally I came to a store where I could pick out a few new articles. The racks were still full for the most part, not quite as devastated as the grocery stores.

After shuffling through the racks and finding two pairs of jeans that might fit, I seized a pack of boxers, in desperate need of a swap. I had soiled mine two mornings before, but I think everybody else had too, so no one bothered me about it. I strolled into the backrooms, searching for a shower. I found a single for men off to the side of the manager's office. The hot water felt like it was washing the last four days away. I had never taken a shower like it, and I didn't think I ever would again.

The new shirt fit nicely, but the jeans didn't fit, so I went and found a few more pairs, smaller sizes, since I guess I had lost some circumference. A plus, maybe, who could say. The dressing rooms were dirty, but the last one only had gum wrappers scattered on the floor, no big deal. I tried on the next size down, it didn't fit so well, a little loose, so I grabbed the next one, two sizes down. It fit well enough.

I was checking out the waistline when I heard a low rumble, like something caught in a throat, harsh and gravelly. I had brought one of the OMP2s with me. I had made enough noise that whatever it was knew where I stood. My feet halted. My breaths started coming rapidly. I tried to calm my lungs, but they wouldn't slow. I bent low to examine the room outside. When my eyes were level with the quarter-meter gap between the door and the floor, the door busted inward, smashing against me. I fell back.

The burst fire of the OMP2 rang in my ear. My eyes were closed and I shot around wildly, not caring where the bullets went. After a few moments, I noticed that nothing was attacking me anymore. I sat, slumped against the floor and the back wall of the changing room. The broken door was heavy on me. I pushed. Nothing. I couldn't get it off me. I crawled to the side, out from under it, and the door banged against the cheap, thin carpet.

Lying on top of the door, an alion gurgled blood, twitching. I jumped back against the sidewall, hitting my head against it. I aimed and pulled the trigger. Bolting to Luxury Mattress Town, my feet stumbled into each other with each stride, a tangled mess of effort. "We have to go! We have to go! Wake up." I shook the beds.

Jacob stirred first. "What is it?"

"Alions . . . they're here . . . I just killed one," I stuttered, out of breath and terrified.

Jacob cursed, threw off his sheets, and switched into a shirt he found the night before. "Where's my other OMP2?"

"I have it, here." I offered him the machine pistol.

He accepted it. "Thanks, thought I lost it there for a second."

I nodded. Shaking the others awake, I hurried them along, watching the entrance, and glancing all around the store in trepidation. "To the car," I whispered.

Penelope checked on the shotgun.

"Jelly, take the assault rifle," Maggy suggested emphatically.

"I don't think I can handle it."

Jacob smiled. "Bro, it's made so practically a baby can handle it. Trust me, it will be easier on you than the shotgun."

"Then I should take the shotgun." I looked at Penelope. "Don't you think?"

"No offense, Darrel, but I know how to use it," Penelope said. "You keep putting it in your gut."

She was right. The bruises on my stomach ached worse than any from the car crash and the bus crash. "All right, fine." I picked up the assault rifle, and it was peculiarly lighter than the shotgun. "Let's get going, before . . ."

Two alions stared us down from atop a pair of beds.

"Run to the back!" Maggy ordered.

Jacob, more recovered now, ran ahead. Penelope pushed her sisters towards the back. She whipped around and fired a booming shot.

The cats dodged the spray. Félix, bags across his shoulders, turned behind the twins and followed. Maggy fired her pistols, leading the guns ahead of the alion to our right. She twirled, falling in line behind Félix.

Penelope and I backed away slowly, each of us eyeing only one of the beasts. I kept sight of the left one, and she tracked the movements of the one to our right. "Go," I yelled.

"They're mine to obliterate," she said, overjoyed by the confrontation. "I'll kill 'em all!" It sounded as if the weight of death and responsibility had melted her brain.

I fired the rifle. Jacob had switched it into burst fire mode. The rounds exploded out of the barrel in smooth grace, each slug flying perfectly for its target. The bullets ripped the alion apart. Blood splattered in all directions. Fur misted the air. Its humanlike limbs fell to the floor, blown right off. After I saw the destruction the rifle inflicted, I turned tail and sprinted for the door leading to the backroom. I stopped at the doorframe and scanned for Penelope.

She fired blast after blast, hitting only air and bedding, screaming curses at the alion the entire time. Finally, the beast maneuvered around her, running directly at me. Its right humanlike arms pulled out something strapped around its right foreleg.

I fell back with a shock to my left leg. A bizarre tingle crawled up my shin to my spine, then to my brain; it was cold and nauseating.

The alion spun 180 degrees and shot the same thing at Penelope, who was chasing it down, shotgun raised. She fired as the object struck her.

The scattered shots pierced the alion all over, blowing off its right shoulder. It collapsed, twitching and gasping.

"Are you all right, Darrel?" Penelope called to me.

"Yeah, I'm okay. How about you?"

"I feel cold. I was hit by something."

"Me too. I feel dizzy and sick, but I'm not bleeding or anything," I told her. I reached for my leg where the iciness emanated. "There's a silver device in my leg." I tried removing it, pinching into my skin. "I can't get it out."

"Neither can I."

Then, all of a sudden, I saw a blue flash.

Then darkness.

I awoke to a thrumming, low and soothing. It filled me with tranquility and terror: tranquility because it sounded so peaceful, and terror because I couldn't stop it. I opened my eyes, and across from me in a black shiny pod with a transparent white door, lay Penelope, suspended. I tried to move my arms, but they didn't respond. Nothing responded, except for my thoughts that continued to spring out of nothingness. The thrumming relaxed me as I attempted to fight against it. But the harder I fought, the more relaxed I became, as if drugged into submission. I felt absolutely nothing.

I scrutinized Penelope's pod in semi-awareness: the black material reminded me of obsidian, polished and without rough edges, ground faultlessly. Three lights lit up her cage, two at her temples, and one above her head. Her eyes shifted around, as if examining my pod.

Without warning, a sound, harsh and deep, boomed into my ears: RAWRK . . . RAWRK . . . RAWRK. The lights inside Penelope's pod started flashing, as if malfunctioning. Then the door unlatched with a pressurized sound. A blue fog drifted out of her pod and into the room. She fell forward and landed on the black grating between the pods. She lay there for a while, though I didn't have a sense of time, so it could have been only a couple of seconds.

She clambered to her feet, using my pod as a prop. Pounding against the door, she yelled: "Can you hear me?"

I blinked twice.

"Good. I'll get you out of there." She fiddled with something off to the side of the pod, out of my sight range. She darted her head to her right, and her eyes popped in horror. "No!" She backed up a step, spun around, then sprinted away.

A moment later, a big blurry patch of fur ran by, heading for Penelope. I heard a clang. Silence overtook the curious room.

She staggered back into my view, gasping out of control, no inhaler in sight. Wobbling, she planted herself on the grating, her back resting against the pod she had emerged from. Closing her eyes, she calmed her breaths. Collecting herself, she stood, staring at me. "I'm okay . . . I'm okay," she panted. "There are some buttons over here that I think open these, so hold on, I'll be right back."

I blinked placidly.

She headed off to her right.

I heard a pressurized noise as the door abruptly unlatched. The same blue cloud engulfed the area as it floated out of the pod. Penelope stood in front of me, lugging me over her shoulders, then she gently planted my butt on the grating.

"How do you feel?" she asked.

I smiled. "Groggy."

"That's certain." She shut both of the pod doors and ran over to a station with blinking lights. She pressed buttons at random.

"You know what you're doing?" I asked, my voice grinding.

"Course not." The doors resealed, pressurizing. "I just hit the same button that I did to open it. I thought mine might be the button next to yours and it was." She smiled.

"Why didn't the other doors open?"

"Don't know, dude. They seem to be locked. None of the others will unlatch." She walked back over to me and helped me stand.

"How did you open your door?" I asked.

"I didn't. I guess it was an error. I don't think they intended it, especially that alien I killed."

"Alion," I corrected.

"Right, alion, whatever. It seemed pretty surprised that I was out and about."

I eyed her, exhausted. "How did you kill it?"

She opened her jacket and revealed a well-hidden knife. "I took it from your stockpile. I hope you don't mind."

I smiled. "I surely don't." I cleared my throat. "What about these?" I pointed to the object stuck in my leg. "I can't get it out."

"I think we have to dig it out," she said.

"What? Are you melted? I can't take a knife to my own leg."

"We'll have to do each other's," she said, serious. She slid out the knife from the sheath secured to her ribs.

"Uhrm. No way. Won't do it."

"You have a better idea?" Her face looked as bad as I felt, tired beyond recuperation.

I hung my head. "I don't think I can do it, Penelope."

"You have to. We don't know what these things do, but we both know it's nothing good. I'll take yours out first, okay?"

I nodded. We sat down on the grating.

"You have to lie still, though. Don't shake on me, I don't want to cut more than I have to." She rested the blade's tip to the side of the object. "Ready?" Before I could react, she dug the knife into my leg, underneath the object, and flipped it out, blood flying with it.

I screamed a terrible scream that would make a four-year-old proud. I started to wheeze uncontrollably. "You—didn't—wait—for—me."

"And you can't wait for me."

"I—can't—do—it." I was breathing far too fast. Red spots started appearing in my eyes, then large black gaps, then I was out.

I came to as Penelope belted out a cry of her own.

"You're much braver than I am," I told her. The hole in my leg was barely even a wound, oozing a tiny amount of blood.

She shook her head. "You're braver than you give yourself credit. You saved my sisters, on more than one occasion. You stared out that broken window, knowing that a beast was going to pounce right through it . . . you stood your ground." Her voice was warm and consoling. She smiled sweetly. "We should get going."

"And go where?"

"Do you want to stay here?"

I shook my head. "No."

"I don't know where to go, but I think we should look for a hangar bay, you know, for smaller ships."

I squinted at her, dizzy. "You want to fly off of here?"

"Yeah, dude. We're probably on the ship above Seattle, so if we find one of those smaller crafts, we can land it in the Sound. I have to get back to my sisters, they need me."

I nodded in understanding. "Why in the water?"

"Do you know how to land an alien craft?"

"Good point." I saw that it would probably be easier to crash in water than on land. "What if we don't make it that far?"

"I'd rather crash and burn than die aboard here," she said. "Wouldn't you?"

I nodded. "I suppose so. Which way do you want to go?" I looked around for the first time. Two columns of pods lined the room, opposite from each other. The long room went on and ended at a blue door. The end of the room opened up to another walkway.

"That door looks sealed, so let's go this way." She pointed to the walkway.

Standing to our feet, I noticed the hole in her leg, it was even smaller than mine. We emerged into a larger room that our room seemed to be a small section of, built in layers. I leaned against a railing, scanning down. Rows upon rows of pods layered the room. I looked up and it was the same. Across from us, hundreds, possibly thousands of pods lined the wall in tiers, facing outward, toward us, with a single walkway on each level. The pods were everywhere, and resting within each pod was a human: men, women, teenagers, little boys and little girls.

"I don't see any infants," Penelope observed.

"I hope we don't."

"I hope we don't see a lot of things I think we might see up here." Penelope surveyed up and down. "But I don't have any good feelings crawling up my spine."

"Uhrm. You think my parents are up here?"

"If they are, it would be impossible to find them," she answered.

I didn't like that. I squirmed against the rail. "Don't you think we should try?"

"If I knew where to start looking, I would say let's give it a go, but look at all of those people. It would probably take weeks to inspect every one."

"Then we have to figure out a way to release them all," I said. I inspected the walkway across from our level.

An alion spotted us, patrolling the walk. A deep roar echoed in the massive room.

"Run!" Penelope shouted. She headed in the opposite direction we had come. We stopped at the sealed door. "Do you see anything that looks like it opens it?"

Up and down the wall to the side of the door, colored buttons buzzed, waiting to be pressed. "Green means open, right?" I smacked the green one. A beep signaled our incorrect answer.

"It's probably a combination," she said.

I cleared my throat. "That could take years to figure out." In a panic, I began to press every one down the strip of colors. Once that failed,

I tried combinations. The entire time the roar neared with every second wasted.

"This is insane," Penelope said in frustration. She took out the knife, turned, and prepared herself for the coming attack.

"I'm not smart enough for this crap," I confessed.

She giggled. "Who is?" Her eyes locked with mine, and a flood of warmth pulsed in my body; blood rushed to my crotch. I tried to put the feeling down. At that moment, I wish I had a textbook with me.

I blushed and turned back to the strip of colors. My thoughts were consumed with panic and lust, colliding in a painful ache that sought to end my life. Then I wheeled around and spotted the alion corpse. A silver disk hung around its neck. A red orb glowed at its center. I examined the strip again, and below it, I found a small port that looked about the same size and shape of the disk.

I ran and detached it from its neck, then shoved it into the port. The entire disk lit up red. The door still didn't open.

I heard the roar booming down the hall towards us, a call of death, full of fury and hostility, all aimed at us. They were so fast, so incredibly fast. The alion approached on acrobatic paws, spread wide for perfect weight distribution.

Twitching, I punched the red button. The door slid to the side, withdrawing into a darkness meant only for lifeless objects. I grabbed the disk and yanked on Penelope's shoulder, bolting over the threshold. When I spun around, I saw the alion flying through the air, unmindful that I had a key to the door. I slammed the disk into the port with my right and pounded the red button again.

As quick as the OMP2 could fire a bullet, the door sealed shut. A PANG reverberated down the hall that we now stood in.

Penelope smiled at me as she panted. "I think it cracked its skull."

"I hope so," I said. I removed the disk from the port and slid it down into my pocket. "We'll probably need this."

She bent over, arms on her knees, breathing in quick bursts. "We need to go."

"We need to recover our breaths." I placed my hand on her back, and I thought about rubbing it, but then that sounded complicated in my head, so I just gently patted her. "Keep breathing."

We composed ourselves, slowly taking back control of our lungs.

I studied the room. It was identical to the one with our pods, except at the other end were two doors instead of one. One of the doors went off in a different direction. "You want to take this, see where it goes?" I asked.

She nodded. "Sure, dude. Sounds like a good plan." She stumbled forth, legs shaking. "I wish I had that shotgun."

I smiled. "You seem to be pretty good with the knife."

She laughed. "No, that was pure luck. It tripped on a wire, plunged right into the blade. I would have died . . . I should have died . . ." Her voice became dejected, full of burden and despair.

I gave her back another comforting pat, then stepped forward. The door connected to another similar room, which connected to another similar room, and it was the same after every new door, endless. We passed face after face, frozen, with calm eyes following our movements.

Finally, after several twists and turns, we crossed over a threshold into a room without pods. The shape of the hall resembled all the previous ones, but instead of pods along the sides, giant clear panes surrounded us.

Penelope gasped, stunned. "No," she whispered.

I cleared my throat. "Are we—are we really in space?" Before our eyes, bright and dim stars twinkled all around. I gazed downward. "Look." I pointed.

"No—no—no—no—no!" she cried. She collapsed to her knees. An eruption of tears followed.

I knelt down and rubbed her back. I thought the situation was appropriate. She needed the stronger form of comfort. I didn't say a word, for nothing that came to mind sounded right; no words existed that would make it better.

I stared down at the bright blue oceans of Earth. The shapes of the continents really did look like giant puzzle pieces from above. Brilliant white clouds blocked out sections of the globe. The planet looked so serene, so bright with the billions of lights in all the cities, expansive clusters of illumination.

Her tears stopped after a few moments lost in a world of devastation. We sat there in silence, observing the world and all its wonders.

"You see that?" Penelope said, pointing to an object traveling swiftly through space, a black dot on the backdrop of blue.

"Yeah, I do. It's coming this way."

The craft zoomed up, heading to an open bay across from us, hundreds of meters away. The strange crimson gas jetted out of the front of the craft as it decelerated, disappearing into the hard vacuum of outer space. The craft vanished behind a colossal gray wall.

"So they do have smaller ships docked," I remarked.

"We just have to get over there," she said, sighing. "It looks like a long, long way, impossible for us not to be spotted."

My nerves were trembling. "Yeah."

Collected, she eyed me with her bold brown eyes. "Then let us be well armed." The words brightened our mood. "We should search for a weapons depot along the way."

"I was just thinking that." I smiled at her. "Let's get moving."

We tiptoed along the clear walk, mesmerized by the view. I used the disk to get us through another secured door. An alion stood at the far end of the room, clicking buttons on a huge display with its human-like fingers.

"Here," Penelope whispered, yanking my shirt to the left. "Hurry, use the key."

I fumbled with the disk. My hands slippery, the object fell with a CLANG on the grating.

Penelope scooped it up and locked it into the port, pressed the red button, and snatched the disk, pushing me over the threshold. She shut the door. "Run," she commanded.

I ran for the door at the end of the hall. Five halls later, we stopped to catch our breath. We both needed inhalers, being on the verge of breaking down, mentally at least. Asthma was a hard thing to control with just mental exertion.

We eventually came to a square room, unlike all the rest, with a tall ceiling, and stacks of large white cases. Sidling through the towers, checking around corners for anything dangerous, I caught sight of an alion facing the opposite direction, at work pressing foreign icons on a small touch screen.

"Back," I whispered.

She caught my sleeve and tugged. She pointed to the cases near the alion. She gesticulated knocking over the towers onto the beast. With a wink, she turned, off to do the deed. She was fearless, utterly fearless, a big change from the night I had met her, when her cousin was torn from the duplex.

Picking up speed, she shouldered the white pile. Instantly the cases fell on top of the alion, crushing it under the weight of the mysterious containers. A feeble cry escaped the alion before it died. The sound almost made me feel sorry for the beast. One of the cases broke open by Penelope's feet. Thick, black polystyrene foam lined the inside, and set within ten perfect cutouts looked like weapons.

"Are those guns?" I asked. I squatted next to her.

She grasped one, jerking it from the foam, holding it up in front of us. They weren't fitted to our hands, and it didn't resemble our pistols exactly, more like two pistols glued together along the barrel, with horizontal triggers instead of vertical, like shooting gangsta style. The objects glowed blue in the bright lighting of the room.

I seized one for myself, gripping it with both hands crossed over each other, and one thumb on each trigger. "I think you hold it like this. They have two thumbs, remember."

"That makes sense." She tried it my way.

Each barrel ended in a canister that reminded me of a soda can. "Should we test them?" I asked, excited.

She shook her head. "What if they make a lot of noise, or blow a hole through the ship. We don't know what's on the other side of the walls."

"Good point. Well, how will we know if they work, or if they are even loaded?"

"Look for anything that looks like it would open a cartridge. If we find where the ammo is, then we'll know if they're loaded or not." She fiddled with hers for a while.

I played around with mine as well, but I couldn't find any buttons or switches, or anything that resembled such.

I looked up as I heard a click. From the middle of the object, a silver box popped out onto the grating. She snatched it up and inspected it.

I stared at her, amazed. "How did you do that?"

"Hold on, I'll show you in a second." At the ends of the box, she took out a small black globe. "It looks like a shotgun shot but *huge*." After her examination, she taught me how to eject the cartridge. "If it's not a weapon, then I'll be pretty surprised. But then again, they're aliens." She loaded up her cartridge.

I opened my mouth to correct her.

"Alions," she said abruptly. "I meant alions. Let's go through more of these cases, maybe there's other gear in here." With nimble fingers, she began to comb through the cases, piling the useless containers in the corner by the dead alion.

The cases were hard to open, for the latches didn't want to budge. Each one took a few minutes to finally snap open. When I unlatched my fourth case, my jaw dropped. "Come look at this."

Penelope rushed over. "Is it a harness?"

"Yeah, or an ammunition carrier. See, it has dozens of ports for spare ammo." I pointed to the globe-sized holes along the straps of the cross-section of the accessory. "There are two in the case, do you want one?"

"Looks too heavy for me," she replied.

Already holding one, I secured it around my chest and waist, tightening up the straps, made from a foreign material that wouldn't give when squeezed, but was flexible enough to bend through several buckles. "It's not heavy at all," I said. I danced around comically, flapping my arms up and down.

She smiled. "I wonder what an alion would think if it saw you. You're pretty goofy."

"Is that a good thing or a bad thing?" I asked, my heart pounding.

"I haven't decided quite yet," she answered. "Flap around some more, and I'll let you know the verdict." Her giggles were cheering up the moroseness that infiltrated my mind. It was nice to hear her laugh; it was sweet, high, and musical.

I flapped my arms out again, and on my way down, I hit a button on the belt portion of the accessory. A sharp pain zipped from my finger to my shoulder. I stopped. Penelope was looking at me, horror written across her face. I spun around. I expected to see an alion, crouching, waiting to pounce on us in its great stealth. But nothing was there. The pile of cases was the only thing I could see.

"What is it?"

"Darrel?"

"Yeah?"

"Darrel! Darrel!" She started cursing after that.

"What's wrong? Why are you yelling?"

She began searching the room, around towers, through piles, everywhere. She moved frantically. Cursing to herself, and every once in a while, she yelled out my name.

I tapped her on her shoulder.

She jumped three meters in the air, spinning. As she landed, she stuck out her alion weapon, aimed directly at me. "Whoa! What are you doing?" She scanned the room, still searching. Her eyes went right through me and on by, as if I weren't there. "Penelope, are you all right?"

She made no reply. Her arms shook and shook. I didn't know if I had ever seen someone so afraid. She backed up until she stood against the wall. Tears began to fall to the grating.

Then I thought about what I had done. I searched for the button I had accidentally struck, found it, and smacked it.

Startled, Penelope gasped. "Where the hell did you go?" she cried in a burst of breath. "I thought they had taken you away, just plucked you away from me like they did Mike." She collapsed. The weapon fell in a CLINK. "I thought—I—were—gone . . ."

I knelt beside her. "It's okay . . . it's okay. They didn't take me, I'm right here. I've been right here the whole time. I accidentally hit a button on the belt, and I guess it made me invisible to you. I'm sorry, I'm so sorry."

Her crying waned into sniffling. She stared at me, full of joy. She took my hand. "I don't think I could survive on this ship alone."

I gently squeezed her fingers. "You won't have to . . . we'll get out of here, together, and in one piece," I promised.

She laughed, irritated. "Why do people say things like that? In movies and TV shows, people always say things like that, but it's not true."

"In our case it is. The harnesses can make us invisible. Invisible, Penelope!"

It took a moment for the information to sink in. "Invisible? As in, nothing can see us?"

"That's right. You couldn't see me . . . I pressed this button." I repeated the action.

She jerked back.

I pressed the button and reappeared. "See. Invisible."

"We're going to make it . . . we're going to make it off of here, aren't we."

"Hell yes we are. Now put one on, and let's get to that hangar," I said, energized.

She fitted one of the harnesses around her, adjusting the straps. Tapping the button, she became invisible to me. I hit the button, and she appeared in full clarity. I nodded at her. We found a case with spare black globes and snapped them into the ports along the chest bands.

"Ready?" I asked.

"Ready."

"Remember, if we bump into things, things such as alions, they'll know we're there. So don't do it."

She smiled. "I think you are a little clumsier than I am, but I'll keep it in mind." Before we crossed the door's threshold, she halted. "They won't be able to hear us, right?"

"Could you hear me?"

"No."

"Then probably not. But they're catlike, so who knows what they can hear." I stepped into the hall and turned right.

"Wait!"

I stopped.

"Can we pick up stuff? We should test out what exactly we can do while invisible."

I whirled around on a heel. "All right, that's probably a better idea than wandering around the ship without a clue as to what we can do." After some tests, we learned that if we picked up objects with the cloak on, the object didn't cloak, unless we decloaked then recloaked. We had to cloak with anything we wanted to hide, which was a nice heads-up.

We crept down a few halls before our first assessment of the cloaks before the eyes of our enemies. An alion stood at a console, tapping the screen in a hurry. We stood motionless to the side of it, weapons up and primed to kill. At least we hoped. If it proved to have a safety, then our guts would probably be thrown all over the place, blood dripping through the grating. The image flashed in my mind: it was horrible. I wanted to puke. The fear of being heard kept the roiling of my stomach at bay.

The alion finished its work, turned to us, and walked past as we parted for the beast. It didn't notice we stood within an arm's reach.

I sighed. I cleared my throat a dozen times after the alion vanished out of sight.

"That went well," Penelope said. She saw my sick face. "It could have gone a lot worse."

I nodded at her. "I know. It's just . . . it walked right past us, you know?"

"Oh, I know. Come on, it's probably not a good idea to dawdle." She opened the next door with the access disk. An alion stared right through us, scanning from side to side, skeptical of its senses, as if expecting to see another alion on the other side of the shifting door. It crouched down, its head level with my crotch. Circumspect, it slinked by us. We jogged to the next hall, shaking.

"Every time I see one, I feel like I'm about to die," I told Penelope.

The disk in her hands was moving so fast I thought she was about to fling it right at me. "Well don't piss your pants yet, wait till we're out of here." She steadied her nerves.

She had a weird sense of humor, one that was growing on me.

In the few hours that we wandered around the ship, we passed numerous alions, some were dressed in light body armor of some kind. The black material had a nice sheen that caught the eye.

We finally stumbled into a storehouse with water supplies. I saw no food, but the water was inviting enough. Three alions typed at touch screens.

"How are we going to steal the water without them noticing?" I asked.

A stack of silver bottles lay next to the closest alion to us. Penelope eyed them with desire. "We'll just have to kill them all."

"Are you melted? What if they have sensors on the ship that can pick us up, we don't want to give them any more reasons to search for us; if we're lucky, it could be a while before they find out we killed any of them, let's just try to keep it that way."

She shrugged. "We need this water . . . what's your plan?"

"I'll create a diversion so that you can steal a bottle and run away. Once you're out of sight, cloak again with the bottle so that we can fill it without them noticing."

"That's actually a pretty good plan."

"Thanks. Sometimes I get them, sometimes I don't. I'll decloak outside the room and knock on the door."

"It will have to be a bigger diversion than that to get all three out," she said. "There's a terminal out there, smash it to the ground, you don't even have to decloak to do it."

"All right, I'll give it a try. Be ready." I jogged off around the corner. The giant display was much cooler than any of our displays, paper-thin with brilliant colors, and it looked like it could project holographic images. The screen was connected to the wall by a few thick silver poles, linked together by pivoting ball sockets, rotating in all directions. I grabbed the display with both hands and yanked. My back popped between my shoulder blades. I stumbled backwards. It didn't seem to have moved at all when I peered up at it. But Penelope was counting on me.

I pulled on the arm that attached at the back of the display and examined how it was secured. It was fused together as one piece. "Damn," I whispered. If I had the bag with all the saws in it . . .

I scrutinized the screen again. I lowered it, and on stable feet, I twirled, building momentum as I kicked it. A loud, sharp noise echoed in the hall, worse than glass shattering. I tottered to the grating. My ankle felt as if it were broken in ten places. I scooted out of the way, back against the empty wall across from the screen. The three alions rushed out to investigate the scene. Eyes scrunched, confusion shown plainly on their cat faces. One disappeared back into the other room. The other two trotted off in an unexplored direction.

Penelope emerged from the water room. She found me on the floor. "Nice work, dude. You okay?"

"I may have busted my ankle."

"Really?" She knelt down and handed me the container of water. "Can you move it?"

I attempted to rotate it. It popped in a blaze of pain. I cried out. "Oh man . . ." I breathed through the throbbing. Unexpectedly, I heard hard steps coming our way. "You know what, I can hop, it's all right." She helped me stand on one leg. Slowly lowering my foot to the ground, I put pressure on the ankle. It wasn't as bad as I had thought. "I think it was mostly shock."

She eyed me, worried. "If you say so. Come on." We hurried off in the opposite direction that the two alions had gone. Limping, the pace was slower than before.

More and more alions started to fill the halls, as if we were traveling to the heart of the operation. On the verge of hysteria, I swallowed my fears, clearing my throat every other second. Eventually we came to a pentagonal room bustling with alions. Consoles encircled a pit in the center of the room, where a low table stood, brimming with electronics. Bright, colorful buttons and switches and displays were everywhere in the room. The wall opposite from where we entered looked as if it were just one giant screen.

Dodging the massive alions, we crept across the room. The wall display was mostly black, with hundreds of tiny blue dots and tiny green dots near bigger multicolored dots. Almost all of the dots were on the right side of the wall. Foreign symbols marked the screen by the bigger dots.

Penelope's mouth dropped. "It's outer space," she observed. "The multicolored dots must be planets."

A cluster of blue and green dots surrounded a planet. An alion stepped forward and touched the planet. The screen changed, focusing on the cluster. Suddenly, feed from another ship appeared, as it was fired upon by other foreign ships. A face of an alion replaced the stream. A harsh growl came from the alion on the display. "Rark kak . . ." The screen cut out, then reappeared. "Roc . . ." The screen cut out and in several times, as the alion on the other side communicated with the alions on our ship.

From the pit below, a supremely large alion, with stripped fur patches displaying scarred battle wounds, pressed a button with a humanlike finger and replied to the figure on screen. The growl within its voice hurt my ears. The screen flashed black, then returned to the map of space. The blue dots retreated away from the planet where the two colors grouped.

"What do you think that was about?" Penelope whispered.

"I think they are at war, and those dots are ships. War maps usually have two colors for factions, at least in video games, you know, for the two opposing sides. There are so many dots though . . . so many ships . . ."

Puzzled, she watched the retreating blue dots. "If they're at war, why are they here?"

I shrugged. "I don't know." I appraised the alion down in the pit again. "That must be the admiral of the ship."

Penelope nodded. "Wouldn't surprise me, the ugly beast is huge."

I maneuvered out of the way of an alion in front of the wall screen, as it scurried over to a console. I assessed the map again, eyeing the upper left corner. A planet there rotated with two blue dots around it, one of which flashed continually. Several smaller, light-blue dots crossed over onto the planet itself, as if they were supposed to be on the planet. Penelope walked over.

I pointed up at the planet I was scrutinizing. "I think that planet up there is Earth, with the two blue dots and the mass of little dots. I think the big blue dots are the ships in space and the little ones are the ones under the atmosphere."

"What makes you think it is Earth?" she asked, squinting at the planet.

"That blue dot is the only one flashing, so I assume that's the ship were on." I reached up to tap it, but it was too high. "If we could touch it, I bet it would enlarge."

"Now who's the one with a melted brain?" She folded her arms across her chest. "You want to bring up Earth on the jumbotron right in front of them on their own bridge? That's completely stupid!"

"I just wanted to know," I responded. "I just wanted to know . . ." She was right, it was stupid, but my brain was addled by my haywire nerves.

Across the room, an alion bellowed. The Admiral in the pit

whipped its head towards the subordinate and roared a command. The wall map changed to a camera in the hall where we had escaped from our pods. Two alion bodies lay motionless on the ground. Another command was shouted from the pit, and the screen changed to show a picture of an alion's face, along with several lines of their untranslatable symbols and an orange bar. It reminded me of my driver's license. The image disappeared, replaced with a second face and a red bar.

I saw the furious displeasure of the Admiral down in the pit. The beast growled deep in its throat, then snapped an order. All the alions moved twice as fast as they had been going, their humanlike fingers touching displays like a computer hacker in a movie attempting to break into the U.S. Defense System in under a minute.

The silver disk hung from Penelope's invisibility belt. The glowing red orb flickered a few times, but then went out, as if it shut off. "The disk." I nodded at it.

Penelope detached it from her belt. "They must have disabled it. The alion with the red bar must have been the disk's owner."

"They're smart. Uhrm, too smart . . ." I dodged another alion as it ran by. "We need to find another one of those."

We scanned the room: all of the disks hung around the alion's necks. It would be impossible to steal them without notice. An alion trotted up to the map and pressed both humanlike hands to the screen. It shifted the top left corner down to its height, tapped the planet I thought was Earth, and immediately the image expanded. A big globe appeared with continents that matched Earth's. The alion hit all of the ships in the vicinity.

The screen suddenly split into fifty or more cat faces. At the center, a large section showed an alion that resembled the Admiral. The two chief figures discussed something, then all the rest of the alions in attendance roared, as if to answer commands given to them.

The map came back, and the alion returned to the console it had been working at.

The table before the Admiral unexpectedly came alive, shaping into a holographic image of a recognizable city. "That's Vancouver," I gasped. "They're even in Canada."

Above the city, a ship equal to the one above Seattle hovered in the cloud-laden sky. From it, dozens of fighters flew in formation, until they met resistance in the air. Canadian fighter jets blasted shots at the alion vessels. The aerial skirmish lasted under a minute. The Canadian jets were all blown to smithereens.

The holograph ceased, and the Admiral left his post, vanishing down a hall. "We should follow him," Penelope suggested.

"Uhrm. What?"

She tugged on my shirt. "Come on."

I stood my ground, but she was already gone, around the corner and into the same hall as the Admiral. I didn't have a choice but to follow. The alion sauntered along on the grating, as if it thought its body untouchable, invulnerable. We tailed a mere meter behind it, weapons raised. We could have killed it if we wanted, and from the look of anguish on Penelope's face, I knew she was on the edge of pulling the triggers. She resisted.

Across the ship we went, to the Admiral's quarters. The giant door closed behind us. The cat had a pillowy bed, shaped twice its size; it looked warm and inviting even to my eyes. The beast poured a glass of a clear amber liquid. It strolled over to a bench that sat between a desk and the bed. Using one humanlike hand to write on a screen, it fiddled with the disk around its neck with the other. The orb at the disk's center glowed yellow.

"What are we doing here?" I asked.

"We need that disk," she replied.

"Why that one?"

"Why not that one?" she snapped. I didn't have a good reason not to take it, except that the massive alion scared me senseless. "It will open all the doors, it will have the highest access. Who knows what we can do with it, maybe we'll need it to access the hangar bay."

"How are we going to get it from the alion?"

Penelope unzipped her jacket, unsheathing the knife. She crept towards it, blade ready for a piercing blow.

"No," I said.

She ignored me. At the alion's side, the Admiral shifted its head towards her, aware. It swiped the air as she jumped back a step. The long, deadly claws struck nothing but empty space. The alion growled, then returned its attention back to the screen.

On swift feet, she leapt, springing high, and as she came down, she stabbed the alion in its skull. She rolled over the beast. Flopping to the solid ground, she groaned.

The door to the chamber slid open. At the mechanical sound, I jumped in the air, spinning. A smaller alion entered. It studied the room and its commander, eyeing the blood draining around the knife, dripping from its face to the floor. It roared a monstrous, deep-throated cry that quaked my stomach. As the door shut, the beast ran to the dead alion.

Full of trepidation that the new alion would discover us, I aimed the foreign weapon, then squeezed both triggers with all the might I had left. The canisters at the end of the barrels started to rotate like a skill saw. The weapon pumped hundreds of black globes into the beast within a mere breath. I exhaled, letting go of the triggers. The force from each shot propelled it backwards, until it hit the wall, collapsing in a heap of burnt flesh. A black, oily liquid began to leak from each wound, mixing and pooling with crimson blood.

The shots from the weapon had been relatively quiet to the rate of fire, but it was still enough to draw attention to any alion walking by, maybe even farther; it was hard to guess with their cat ears what they could pick up. We didn't know how far away their sensitive hearing could detect our ruckus, if they could at all with the weapon cloaked under the invisibility shield.

We took no chances of waiting around to find out. I helped Penelope to her feet, then wrenched the yellow disk from around the Admiral's neck, popped it into the port on the door panel, hit the yellow bar twice to lock the door, and threw up a little when I finished. "I wasn't made for this work."

"Surviving?" Penelope asked after she swigged down some water.

She handed me the bottle. My throat was so dry that it scraped when I swallowed, and I swallowed a lot, to the point where it felt like blood-blisters were about to burst along my esophagus. "If that means killing alions, then yeah, surviving. I don't have the stomach to do the real thing."

"You've done the real thing already. You've got the stomach for it."

I took a drink and spied the puke in the corner of the room. "Not according to that." I pointed to the mess of stomach content.

"You're not the only person to throw up after taking a life. Come on, we have to get out of here." She climbed atop the desk, poking the paneled ceiling.

"What are you doing?"

She eyed me. "Trying to find a loose panel so we can get the hell out of here. They'll bust through that door eventually, and I don't want to be here when they do. We can still make it to a hangar." Done, she went back to her work.

I touched the screen of the Admiral's computer, or whatever it was. I couldn't read anything, which made it impossible to navigate. I quit when I realized it was utterly hopeless. We scooted the desk to the left, and Penelope tried lifting more panels. At the edge of the room, one popped up, unsecured.

"Can you boost me up?" she asked.

I nodded. The wide desk allowed for both of us to stand comfortably. I squatted and wrapped my arms around her legs. "Ready?"

She grabbed ahold of the edge of the ceiling. "Yep."

My arms and knees shaking, I hoisted her with all the strength left in me. She pulled herself into the duct, just as my knees buckled. I fell flat on my rear.

"You okay?"

I raised my eyes to her. "I don't know anymore."

"No time for talk like that. Get up here, and toss me the weapons."

I obeyed, no heart to argue or defy.

"All right, I'll help pull you up," she said. She offered me her slender hands. Huffing, she helped pull me up, squeezing my arms, as I climbed into the duct. Once far enough in, I collapsed, and she fell back, giggling.

"What's so funny?" I asked.

"I feel like a spy," she answered. "I never thought about being a spy . . . it's just crazy the paths that life takes you on."

"I guess it really is unpredictable." I smiled at her.

"We probably never would have met if the alions hadn't come," she mumbled.

My lustful eyes lingered on her butt as she turned around and planted herself against the left wall. "Well, you never know. I planned on going to U-Dub. What about you?" I slid forward and pushed up, situating my body next to her.

"Yeah, I did too. I wanted to go into graphic design, or computer science, or something interesting like those."

"Those are slick. I've thought about writing, maybe journalism. I guess it doesn't matter now . . ." I sighed and hung my head.

"You should put the panel back, so they won't suspect we're up here," she advised.

"Good idea." I reached over and slipped the panel into its place. The ducts, made for alions, spanned a meter high, if not taller, and a meter wide. I could move around easy enough. I returned to my spot next to her. We locked eyes for a moment. I cleared my throat.

She leaned closer, our shoulders touching.

Nervous, my mouth trembled. I had never kissed anyone before. I didn't want to disappoint her with my cracked and dehydrated lips, not to mention my fetid breath. She really was brave.

But then desire took hold. I leaned over until our dry lips grazed. *Magical* was all that came to mind, completely magical. No part of me believed the kiss was really happening.

She pressed harder upon me, and I slid against the wall. I threw out an arm to brace myself against the duct floor, but my hand didn't touch what I had expected.

Thick fur tickled my fingers.

At that moment, I knew my end had finally come.

6
Portland
Maggy

In my peripherals, I spied a flash of blue light in the main part of the store. "Did you see that?" I spun on my heels.

"The blue light?" Tortilla asked. He halted and turned back.

"Yeah. Where is Jelly? And Penelope, I thought they were right behind us."

"Guess not." He jogged over to the door leading to the front room.

I followed. Two alion corpses lay on the floor in smelly heaps. I waved a hand in front of my nose. "Wow, they stink." We surveyed the room. There was no sign of either one. "They're not here."

"Darrel? Penelope?" Tortilla yelled. "Where are you guys?" He crept from bed to bed, throwing up sheets as he searched under the frames. Soon he was frantically tossing bedding towards the back of the store as he made his way to the front, shouting their names the entire time.

When Tortilla checked under the last bed, I stopped beside him. "They're not here, Tortilla." I spotted tears rolling down his flushed face.

"I don't understand . . ." He plopped down on the bed. "They killed the alions. Where did they go?"

"I don't know. Penelope wouldn't just leave her sisters behind, so they didn't run off together, that's certain. Maybe they were taken the same way everyone else was taken. We still don't know how they do it." I sat beside him and placed a gentle arm around him. "They're probably up on the ship above Seattle."

His surge of tears quit as abruptly as a fleeting rainstorm. "Then that's where we have to go."

"How?" I asked.

"What's going on? What happened?" Amanda's serious voice echoed in the open expanse.

The sweet voice of Jane followed. "Where is Penny?" The two rushed to us, eyes seeking their sister as they ran. Without a trace of Penelope, Jane started to sob uncontrollably, devastated by her sister's absence.

Jelly had been good at comforting them. I on the other hand had no inherent motherly or sisterly tenderness; it was hard for me to console them. Surprisingly, Jacob pushed Jane into his stomach, her tears soaking his shirt. He patted her on the back. "It will be okay, Jane." His voice was not as soothing as Jelly's, but it lightened her despondent, sorrowful heart. It was easy to see that Jane needed Penelope most of all, and she was broken without her guidance and loving hand.

"We should leave," I urged. "No telling how many alions are here."

Jacob lowered his eyes to me. "Not very good with children, are you?"

"She's right," Tortilla spoke up. "If more are roaming around, it will not take long for them to find us."

I smiled at Tortilla for defending me. "I'm sorry that my words do not always comfort. I'll try to be a little gentler in tone, but right now, we have to get moving."

Jacob clenched his jaw. He gazed down on the crying twin. "Jane, we have to go now. We'll find your sister, I promise, but right now we have to go." He picked her up with trembling arms and shuffled off towards the back. Amanda strode behind him, as Tortilla ran ahead, and I tailed them all.

Tortilla held the back exit door open for us by the time we caught up. Dark rainclouds frowned upon us in the sky, promising to weep beside Jane for the day.

I stopped at the edge of the curb and scanned the parking lot for viable rigs. "There's a bus." I pointed south to a bus with a large banner for Intercity Transit spanning from front to rear. As we sprinted forward, I stopped them every few meters to scope out the area. When Tortilla reached the bus, he pried open the doors, wedging a knife between the rubber.

Once loaded, I took to the driver's seat. I found the key in a combination box under the dash. My first seven tries were failures, but then

I saw the bus number on the right-hand console and entered them. The lock clicked and the lid popped up. I started the engine and slammed the GO pedal to the floor.

Tortilla hovered over my shoulder, nervous. "We still going south?"

"I don't know of a better plan. We have no way to get to the ship, but Jacob's father was working on unmanned fighters, so maybe we can use one of those to get aboard."

"Why don't we try an airport?"

"You want to take the twins up to the ship? Come on, bromigo, that's a bad plan." I steered left onto a main road.

He sighed and sat down in the seat behind the stairs to the bus. "That's a long time for them to be up there, alone. What if—"

"We don't know what they do to the taken, let's not assume anything right now. I just want to focus on getting us down to Pasadena."

"We both know it's not anything pleasant. More than likely . . ."

"I know, Tortilla. I know. Just let me drive, okay?" I found the on-ramp for I-5 and cruised along for a while, until we hit congestion, and I had to bump several cars out of the way.

Tortilla brooded, gazing out the window.

In the back, Jacob comforted Jane and Amanda, giving them water and some chocolate bars that we had found in the Apocalypse Room. I couldn't hear all that he was saying, but a compassionate sweetness resided in his tone.

When night struck, I didn't pull off into a city, as that hadn't worked so well the last few times. I shut down the bus in the far left lane.

I glanced back at Jacob. He was sitting up, staring at the lights outside, shivering. The twins slept, huddled together in the seats across from him.

I nodded back at Jacob. "You think he's all right?" I asked Tortilla.

He studied Jacob. "His skin is pretty pale. It looks like he's getting sick."

"That's what I was thinking." I grabbed a granola bar from a food pack. The wrapper was noisy as I peeled away the artificial skin. "I hope it doesn't get bad."

He sighed. "And if it does?"

"We find a hospital."

"And pray that someone is still there who knows about medicine?"

I nodded. I had no words. The rest of the night went by without any disturbances, though I did not sleep as well as I had on the bed.

Tortilla wrapped his arm around me as I leaned against his shoulder. I stared out the window in long gaps, periodically drifting with heavy, heavy eyes.

The sun crawled over the Cascades in the east. I could see Mount Rainier, clear and snowcapped, and dazzling in the morning light.

Tortilla twitched awake. "Sorry. I didn't mean to jerk like that."

I smiled up at him. "We all twitch these days. I'm sorry I jabbed your stomach during the night." I had really elbowed him in the gut.

"Forgiven. Are you hungry?" He stood up and stretched.

"As a bear fresh out of hibernation."

He laughed. "I don't know if we have enough food to appease that kind of appetite. Turkey Jerky?" He offered me the bag after he plucked a few pieces for himself.

"What else could I want? I certainly don't want nice warm pancakes."

"Who would when turkey jerky is on the table," he said, smiling.

I wanted to kiss him for lifting my spirits, but the others shifted awake. The twins ran over and seized their own breakfast, munching down peanut butter chocolate bars. Jacob didn't move; he just stared at us, sweating and shivering.

I walked back to give him water and jerky. "Hey, you okay?"

He gently rocked back and forth. "I think I'm getting sick. It feels like I'm getting bronchitis. I've had it before, the doctor said it was Asthma-induced bronchitis."

"Yeah, I've had that before, too. You need steroids," I told him.

"Guess I'll just have to tough it out. I'll be fine in a few days, no problem." He gave a sliver of a smile. He accepted the water but shunned away the food. "I'll eat something later. I'm not in the mood right now."

"All right, but you have to eat," I pressed him. "Even if you don't want to."

He nodded. "Yeah, yeah. Don't worry about me."

I went back to the front and started up the engine. The day crept by irritatingly slow. I bumped hundreds of cars out of our path, breaking small bits of the front of the bus with each impact. In the afternoon, Jacob began coughing, softly at first, but then it morphed into a hacking, lung-puncturing cough.

We hit Vancouver by four. It was the last major Washington city before the border into Oregon. All the lanes were packed, dense and unyielding. At one point, I was pushing six cars at once, until they separated and a gap appeared. The bus was old, retrofitted with new technology, including the rectenna that constantly collected energy from an electrical relay plant. We would never have to stop off I-5 if the batteries didn't die, and new batteries lasted ten years or more before they went out. The bus still made noise, since Jacob never fiddled with the wiring, but I had turned the knob to its lowest setting, barely a rumble, though the grating of vehicle on vehicle did nothing to hide our position.

I could see lights on for kilometers and kilometers, all around us, and as the sun drifted lower, more popped into view. Without warning, the lights all around started to flicker.

"What's going on out there?" Tortilla asked.

An alarm belled from the bus speakers. Then a woman followed: "Power failure. Connection to electrical relay plants severed. Batteries switched to primary power source. Check dash for charge levels."

"Look!" Tortilla pointed out the window to the right. The city's skyscrapers became massive black towers of portending doom. Within a blink, all the lights vanished, and we were drowned in a sea of darkness.

"They must have shut down the solar stations," I said, slamming on the breaks before we crashed into two white SUVs. "I don't know if the bus can make it all the way down to Pasadena." We sat, idling.

"What are the battery levels?"

"In total it says 96%, but hitting these cars puts a lot of strain on the engine and the batteries." I searched for hope in his burnt eyes, but there wasn't any to be found, only misery and ache.

"We'll probably have to switch again."

I nodded my concurrence.

Amanda strode up to the front. "What happened out there?" Her saddened eyes possessed confidence beyond any of us. A hope also glimmered in them; hope that her sister would be rescued, if not by all of us, then by her boldness alone. Yet, reliance was also present, a reliance on us as adults, or at least the closest people to adults around.

"The solar stations were probably shut down," I told her.

Amanda eyed me intensely. "Does this mean we have to abandon the bus?"

"At some point, yes," Tortilla spoke up.

She glanced out the window into the world of shadow; it was beyond creepy to see. "Jacob is getting worse, I think," she reported.

"Make sure he drinks a lot of water," I said. "Give him some food and the green pain relievers to lower his fever." I smiled, but I doubted it was as cheerful as I meant it to be.

Amanda nodded and returned to her sister and the coughing, shivering Jacob.

"You want me to take over driving?" Tortilla asked.

"Sure," I said. "My butt is cramping and my legs are stiff."

We swapped seats. Tortilla drove until the sunlight escaped our side of the world.

"We shouldn't drive at night anymore," I told Tortilla. "We'll be a million times easier to spot."

"You don't have to tell me," Tortilla snapped.

I glared at him. "You okay, bromigo?"

He shook his head. "Just exhausted. Sorry. But you don't have to tell me obvious things like not driving at night with all the other lights off." He pulled over to the left lane and powered down the engine.

"I'll go check on Jacob."

He yawned. "Sounds good, bramiga."

I offered Jacob a green pill and he took it with some water and a quarter bag of jerky. "You doing any better?"

His eyes were sunken in and discolored. "No."

"I didn't even know you were sick, what happened?"

Jacob continued to shake as he talked. "I've had a cold the whole time, I'm just pretty good at hiding it. Not getting much sleep isn't helping at all."

"We need to get you some medication tomorrow. Do you remember what you took the last time you had it?"

"Something romycin . . . and pradnisone, or something close to that. They gave me steroids and antibiotics. Which is which, I don't remember."

"The romycin is the antibiotic," I said confidently. "I'll leave you alone so you can try and get some sleep."

He smiled, then broke out a sharp cough. "Yeah, thanks."

I peeked over at the twins. Jane had cried herself to sleep in the late afternoon, and Amanda slowly trailed her sister into dreamland. They were slumped against each other, warmer than the rest of us.

I sat next to Tortilla. He was staring out into the blackness that swallowed the globe. "So do you want to look for a pharmacy?" he asked.

I locked my hands in his. "They'll be too hard to find. We should just go to a hospital. I know there's that one on the hill in Portland, that monstrous one."

He squeezed my hands. "All right, but it might be hard to get to." A yawn struck him. "I can't keep my eyes open."

I glanced up at him. His lids were shut, and in the darkness, he was soon out. "Goodnight," I said softly.

"Goodnight," he whispered.

When morning broke upon my swimming eyes, I crawled out of Tortilla's comforting embrace, and stretched out my legs, scanning the Vancouver skyline. So many buildings just sat there, cold and monotonous, as if all the color had been stolen during the long night. The green solar panels didn't seem so green and alive, but more charcoal and dead, dead without their function to perform for the world.

"The days are growing grayer, or maybe it's just our moods," Tortilla commented. He stroked my back in a gentle massage.

"The world doesn't look right without lights . . . without electricity."

"The world doesn't look right without people," he responded. His hand froze in the middle of my back. "Are we going to make it?"

I shuddered at the fear in his voice. "We have to protect those girls." My shoes squeaked as I spun around.

"You didn't answer my question." He stared at me, still tired even after a night of rest.

"As long as we have guns in our hands, we'll survive," I told him.

Tortilla hung his head. "Darrel and Penelope had guns." His voice quavered, full of despair. "They had guns . . ."

"What do you want me to say? I don't know what answer you're looking to find, but I tell you we'll survive, and that's what I think." I grabbed a hold of his fingertips. "We have to protect those girls, you understand?"

He nodded. "But what about Darrel and Penelope . . ."

"They're not dead," I whispered, tearing. "We both know that." I swallowed back words.

He pulled me close to his chest, tears dropping onto my hair.

Neither of us said another word until Jacob woke up from a painful, bursting cough. His coughs were intensifying, increasing in both harshness and rapidity. At times, he even fell over, clutching the seat in front of him, yellow phlegm exploding out his mouth.

We ate breakfast together, gathering around Jacob. No one spoke. Hungry bellies growled fiercely. Done with breakfast, I climbed into the driver's seat and started smashing bumpers. For all the fun that it had been the first few hundred times, it was terribly boring the few thousand times after and it was really starting to take its toll on the bus once we lost the front bumper. Not to mention the toll on my nerves.

By the time Portland came into view, the batteries were in the red, almost completely drained. My back ached from all the impacts, and my jaw was so tight and sore from clenching my teeth every time I rammed a car out of the way. But no one complained.

We crossed the I-5 bridge over the Columbia River. I sighed in relief when I noticed how empty the bridge was compared to the rest of the interstate.

Portland: a city of bridges. Bridges spanned rivers and roadways everywhere within sight. It was nothing like Seattle or Vancouver, both the Canadian and American cities. The glassy green of the skyscrapers reflected off in the sun, blinding glares of warmth. At first glance, it appeared that all of the city's buildings remained intact, which couldn't be said for Seattle. But I didn't know the city skyline at all, and numerous buildings could have been scattered as rubble, out of eyeshot.

The Hill, a slope brimming with medical buildings, lay close to I-5, beacons of hope and promise, something we desperately needed. As I studied the view, the clouds hovering above the city drifted, parting for a second to show a glimpse of an alion ship.

"They're here," I reported.

Tortilla spotted the ship just before a cloud cloaked it again in a gray blanket. "Figures. Darrel and Penelope could have been taken there instead . . ."

I didn't reply. It was too much to think about.

The batteries died before we reached the nearest off-ramp to the hill of hospitals. I had always hated that about batteries, they never told the truth when they were in the red, always half the time they approximated.

"Can you carry anything, Jacob?" I asked.

He nodded. "I'm not dead."

"But you look pretty tired," Tortilla responded.

"We need this stuff, all of it." He bent over and grabbed the backpack with inhalers and other medical supplies. He had been sucking on them like cough drops, puffing a mist into his mouth every half hour, or so it seemed.

He was right though; we needed all of it. We had left so many bags in different places, on the run and out the door in a hurry. "We'll have to consolidate again." I started placing the bags we absolutely needed on the right side of the bus, and digging through others to make sure nothing essential was left behind. We had four duffels and three backpacks full of supplies. Tortilla handed Jane the duffel with blankets, and I gave Amanda the backpack with food. Jacob and I exchanged the pack with inhalers for the duffel of food, so he would only have to carry one bag. After I adjusted the backpack, I picked up the duffel of water bottles, which left a backpack of cooking supplies and the duffel with guns for Tortilla.

With everything sorted, we planted our feet on the road, heading south for an exit sign. We found one, continuing onto I-405, pointed towards the Oregon Health and Science University. Taking the first off-ramp, we hooked around under an overpass until we reached the foot of the hill. Cars were parked up and down the road, littering the streets at angles, almost as if the people had been frantic to escape before they were taken.

Jacob coughed, wheezing with the duffel bag strapped around his shoulder, across his chest and back. He clutched an inhaler in his left. "I'm okay," he answered in a weak voice when I asked him how he fared.

"Let's rest here," I said, pointing to a group of chairs surrounding a table outside a café. Jacob said he didn't need it, but no one else argued, so we stopped. The buildings of the hospital campus were close now, viewable above the tall trees that surrounded the hill.

Jacob sat down and hacked up a glob of yellow.

"That's gross," Jane said.

"You're gross," Amanda taunted.

They started quarreling, poking at each other. "Enough," I said in a tone too harsh for the dismal mood. They were only having fun.

They ceased their game and sat in silence.

When Jacob's breathing slowed, we started up the hill again, leaving behind buildings for a long tree-tunnel road. Walking underneath dozens of sky bridges, we found a small entrance at the north end of the campus. "Look for anything that says pharmaceuticals, that will be our best bet at finding something."

Tortilla ran to a desk and began searching through drawers. "Found a directory." I scrambled over to him from a desk across the walkway. "Looks like there are pharmaceutical storage rooms on the third, tenth, and twenty-fifth floors in this tower. There is a pharmaceutical lab on the nineteenth floor in tower J, which is pretty far from here. There are others—"

"Let's try the third floor first," I cut in. "You guys can stay down here; we'll be back in a few minutes."

Jacob was resting in a lobby chair, next to Jane. Amanda watched for movement outside through the long rectangular window in the door. "I'll keep them safe," Jacob said.

"So will I," Amanda added. In the last few days, she had taken a liking to carrying around a pistol. She clinked the muzzle against the door, winking.

Tortilla and I headed up the stairs, cautious, with every nerve on edge. My heart didn't want me to explore, but Jacob required the drugs. I tried thinking positive, happy thoughts, but I kept coming back to Mike being pulled from the window. It was so gruesome. They could take us at any moment without alerting our ears in the slightest. Their steps were more than deathly quiet.

The third floor was as quiet as the first. Guns raised, we crept down a long tiled hall, its white reflective floor shining in the daylight. "Here." Tortilla pointed his gun at the room numbered 377. A blue Pharmaceutical Lab sign hung by the door, directing traffic to the pain relieving contents inside, and a glimmer of hope burst in me as the door swung open.

I started shuffling through white containers. "Look for something that has romycin at the end of its name, and another drug called prednisone." The bottles that still sat on the shelves were empty. Every lid I popped off revealed the bottom of the plastic.

Tortilla jerked up, throwing a bottle high, whipping around to the back. "Did you hear that?" His voice shook. "Did you? Did you?"

My gun was up in an instant. "I didn't hear a thing, bromigo." The room had a dozen shelves three meters tall. With my back against the first shelf, I sidled along until I came to the end. Breathing heavily, I twirled around the edge, expecting to see an alion. I let out a long, long sigh. "Nothing here. Come on, let's try the tenth floor."

He fell in behind me as we ran for the staircase. The spacious Pharmaceutical Lab on the tenth floor stored twenty times more bottles of pills. "This is going to take forever," Tortilla remarked, staring at the rows upon rows that seemed to never end. The floors were layered in empty bottles and scattered pills of all different colors and shapes.

I picked up a bottle and read the label. "He could develop pneumonia if we don't find those pills."

Tortilla reluctantly gave in. We piled the inapplicable bottles and pills in the corners, away from the door. Mounds became hills and hills became mountains. "Time?"

"We've been at it for over an hour," Tortilla said, checking his wristwatch.

I started whispering romycin to remind myself what I was looking for, as all the labels jumbled together in my head after a while. Ten minutes later, I threw up my arms with glee. "Found it!"

Tortilla looked up. "Found what?"

"Er-Ery–thro–my–cin. Erythromycin. I don't know if that's right, but who cares, probably no one alive knows how to say it." The words hurt us both. They reminded us of the situation of survival more than creeping around the empty hospital campus did. They reminded us that we were on the brink of extinction. "There are tons in here, though, so it should be enough." The label had directions concerning dosage. "Now we just need prednisone." Hesitation layered my voice. Slowly, we worked through the remaining bottles.

Near the end of the last row, Tortilla found a bottle labeled prednisone, but it only contained four pills. "Look." He pointed at the ground to a pile of soft pink pills. "Those are the same pills." He bent down and examined the numbers to see if they matched. "Yep, same pill."

I knelt down beside him and shoveled the pills into the bottle.

A crunch sounded by the door.

"Shh!" I threw out my arms and stopped Tortilla. We crouched in silence for a minute, listening with sharp ears, focused on the possibility of crushing steps.

Tortilla stood up. "Goddamn, this is getting old, bramiga. If they don't kill us, fear will."

I rose, wiped exhaustion away from my eyes, and stared. "Fear might be a better death, though," I said.

"An alion's claws would be faster," he joked.

As we approached the door, Tortilla scanned out the large windows to our left. He grabbed my elbow. "Maggy, down below."

When I peeped out the window, down on the street in front of the facility, I spotted an alion rushing away with something green clutched in its mouth, bleeding from one end, round like a ham with a white bone at its center. "Is that . . . a leg?"

"Looks like it's from an army soldier," he said.

The alion galloped off out of sight.

I turned for the door. "We have to get back to I-5."

"No argument here." Tortilla fell in behind me, at a dead sprint.

We were huffing by the time we planted a foot on the first floor. Jacob sat hunched over, elbows on knees, guns against his cheeks, and his eyes dozing. Jane rested against his back, eyes closed.

"We have to go! Get up, we have to go!" I shouted.

They jolted awake, puzzled and woozy. "You find anything?" Jacob asked, squinting at us. Jane slid off the chair to help Jacob to his feet, but she was small, and her strength did little.

"Yeah, bromigo. We found what you need." Tortilla rattled the bottles. "We also found what you don't need, an alion outside, running with a human leg in its mouth. We have to get out of here, now." His severe voice carried a weight to it that bordered on eerie. Tortilla didn't have much heart for taking charge. Yet, no one could help but comply.

Jacob took the recommended dosage, though who was the standard it was set to, we didn't know. "If it kills me, it kills me," he said as we ran through the halls, heading towards the northwest entrance. "It seems like everything wants to kill me these days . . ."

It did seem that way. There were no breaks for the living, no comfort to be found, no assurances of a better tomorrow, just more fear, running, sweating, puking, and exhaustion waiting at the next sunrise. Sleep was the one thing I wanted to do most, but it was also the one thing I wanted to do least, out of terror that we would be caught off guard.

Jane's feet became tangled as her worn out legs clashed. She tumbled elbows first to the white-tiled floor.

Amanda offered her sister a steady hand. "No time for weakness now," she whispered to Jane.

"I'm not tough like you . . . I'm tired," Jane whined.

"We share blood, so you're tough enough. Come on!" Amanda yanked her sister up with a sore arm.

We had stopped to catch our breath as the sisters regrouped. Jane was growing paler as Amanda was turning as gray as steel, shiny, resistant, and sturdy. The entrance doors fought against our ten arms when we tried to push them apart, but they would not slide.

"Should we break them?" Jacob asked.

"Too loud," Tortilla responded.

I stared at them. "There's no power, they should be easier to open . . . I don't understand."

Amanda went up to the seam where the doors met. "It's locked." From her pocket, she pulled out a switchblade with a bright blue handle, jamming it between the doors underneath the lock. Pushing up, the lock unlatched with a click. "See, no problem." Her black hair swished as she heaved the doors open.

The muggy air outside closed in around us as we swept by the doors and out into a parking lot. The sweat pouring down my back made me even more uncomfortable and tense. If only something would go right . . . just one thing. We found the main road again and ran down the hill, resting at a bistro midway, after the tree-tunnel.

Sounds of digging claws echoed in an alley.

"Amanda," Jane cried, nervous. She clutched her sister's arm in tortuous, eye-blurring, heart-bursting fear. Her trepidation coiled in the rest of us, ready to spring in an explosion of screams, tears, and spit.

An alion jumped from a balcony three stories up. The beast landed nimbly on four burly legs of corded muscle, coated in silky fur, armored in a thick hide of anger. A roar churned our stomachs, the acid promising to eject in full force.

Jacob fired his OMP2s. The bullets barreled towards the alion in an implacable stream.

Jane shrieked, on the verge of deafening.

A second alion sprung over a fence to the side of the bistro, finding the ground near Tortilla. He squeezed the triggers in rapid pulses. The beast was a hard target, but finally Amanda and I added a few rounds.

Both of the alions collapsed in an ugly mess of dark blood. A third sprinted down the street, full bore. The alion differed from the others. Reflective green armor protected its chest and back region. A green helmet covered its head, with a yellow and red visor across the eyes. In its humanlike hands, it carried two objects that resembled guns, but with large soda cans for barrels. Suddenly, black dots peppered the concrete in front of us.

Jacob retaliated with bullets of his own. Yet, we were forced to retreat behind a dead car to shield the incoming fire. Black bullets sprayed the area, penetrating everything but our skins, almost as if it meant to scare more than kill us. We huddled together. I couldn't bring myself to shoot under such heavy fire.

Down the hill, an explosion boomed, and more gunfire echoed in the street. Without warning, the alion burst apart in an array of blood, guts, and metal. I peeked over and saw nothing where it had stood.

Voices carried past, voices of men and women yelling curses. The clatter of boots filled my ears. Military soldiers, clad in camouflage and nifty black sunglasses, rushed by us.

"Secure those two points!" a woman shouted. Four soldiers ran off.

I was studying them when, with a start, I whipped to my left and saw a woman standing tall before us. She had medium-length caramel hair tucked back in a ponytail.

"You kids okay?" she asked, gazing down at us with brilliant blue eyes. Her smooth, milky skin was attractive, but toughness emanated from her austere appearance, with a straight back and chiseled jaw.

No one answered.

She knelt down. "Are you okay?" Her speech was directed more at Jane and Amanda.

Amanda nodded. "Are you here to save us?"

"That's right, kiddo. I am. We have to move, there are more of those things in the city. Can you run?" She stood, hefting up a long rifle.

The woman who had shouted orders ran up beside us. "Private Burnhammer, are we ready to move out?"

Burnhammer nodded. "Yes, sir. All civvies are capable."

A man bolted up the hill and halted at the commander's side. "Sir, we have multiple targets heading this way."

She nodded. "Assistant, move the squad out, we'll head up the hill and cross west at Gibbs Street." The man took his leave, ordering others to their positions. As we stood up, she examined us. "I see that you're armed, that's good. If you need new weapons, just ask someone in the squad and we'll do our best to give you one."

Amanda stuck out her hand. "I'm Amanda."

The woman smiled and took Amanda's hand in hers. "Hello, Amanda. I'm Staff Sergeant Henderson. It's nice to meet you all, but we have to get you out of here. If I seem harsh, I apologize in advance; it's just how we were trained. I want all of you to stick to Burnhammer here. She'll protect you and get you to where you need to be." She locked eyes with Burnhammer. "Private, congratulations, you've been field promoted to corporal. Keep them in sight at all times. Got it?"

"Yes, sir!" Burnhammer said. "Thank you, sir."

"Let's get the hell out of here." At that, Henderson went to the head of the squad as we started up the hill again. Two men filed in after us. They glanced back constantly. One of them almost seemed to run backwards, and he did it as well as running forwards.

The road leveled out. An excited voice shouted over the radio attached to Burhammer's arm. "Three tangos on approach. Check your six." Then static.

"Inside! Inside!" Burnhammer shoved us into a medical building to our right.

Six soldiers took up positions within. More set up outside. I scanned and counted four. Then a fifth ran up behind an SUV.

Henderson spied the hill and grabbed her radio. "Engage, engage." Her voice was twice as sharp as it had been a few minutes ago.

The soldiers outside let loose a shower of death. The guns kicked out bullets at amazing speeds. A soldier hand signaled to Henderson, who replied by making a loop with her index. The man dashed inside, breathing heavily, almost gasping. He whisked an inhaler from one of his many pockets. After, he reloaded his rifle.

The firing ceased and the rest joined us in the building. "They retreated, sir," a man reported.

Henderson gave him a pleased smile. "So they have some sense after all. All right, let's get our legs going, mine are getting stiff just looking at your idle asses. Move, move, move."

As Burnhammer pushed us out the door, I turned to Jacob, who was plodding along, with a face even more exhausted than he had shown over the last few days. "We're gonna make it, see. Those pills will kick in and you'll feel better," I encouraged him.

He gave me the weakest smile. His lungs struggled to suck in air as he wheezed and wheezed. "I might faint."

I gave him the inhaler from my pocket. "Use it."

He complied.

The road curved left and finally we hit Gibbs Street. "Hold!" Henderson ordered as we came to a cross street. "The Connor Trail is at the end of this road, we can sweep back to the city through the woods."

North we went, along SW 9th Street.

My legs grew tighter with every step, but the sergeant wouldn't let us rest. These soldiers had more endurance than the ones I pretended to be online. I was astonished by how they worked as a team, moving around, positioning themselves without voice commands. At the end of the road a narrow dirt path continued on, part of a giant maze of trails. Dense clusters of trees protected our sides, or so I hoped.

Yelling came over the radios: "Requesting backup—dentist—high—Terrance Drive." Static overtook the line.

Henderson pressed a button on the side of her radio. "Repeat transmission. I say again, repeat transmission." She released the button and a beep followed.

"This is Sergeant Loritz requesting backup from anyone near SW

Terrace Drive. We are pinned down in a dentist office. Crossroad is SW High Street. We have civilians. Repeat, we have civilians." A beep came a second later.

"Sergeant Loritz, this is Sergeant Henderson, we're a few klicks south of there. Hold on tight, we're coming for ya." She released the button. "Let's move."

"Candy bar waiting," Sergeant Loritz said, static cutting out most of his words.

"God only knows what that means," Burnhammer commented.

The trail was soggy, too slippery for my shoes to do much for stability.

The wide, thick-treaded boots of the soldiers dug into the wet earth, giving them superior traction and maneuverability.

They kept us going at a quick pace, even after Jane fell several times. She hadn't said a word since the soldiers' arrival. Her eyes seemed distant. She fell again. Burnhammer clutched Jane by her arms and yanked to her feet, guiding her forward.

The quiet of the woodland disturbed me even more than the quiet of the city. Complete, overwhelming silence that engulfed my senses. Fear kept me from focusing on anything in particular. My head swam.

"You all right?" Tortilla touched my hand. "You're not looking so hot."

"Are you dizzy?" I asked him, sucking in a huge breath. The axe across my back was starting to weigh me down, as if it were all of the sudden made of steel.

"A little," he replied. "We're just tired. These *real* soldiers will get us to safety, and we'll sleep tonight."

I nodded. "You hear Jacob?" Jacob slogged along at the rear, panting violently.

"How could I not?" Tortilla glanced over his shoulder and eyed Jacob's stumbling steps. "Are you worried about him?"

"Aren't you? He's on the verge of collapse." I focused harder on the trail. Large rocks occasionally rocked my ankles if I didn't keep a close eye on the ground.

"He'll be all right, we got him the medicine. Everything will be okay now."

His words sounded awful in my head. A threatening shadow lay hidden in them, one that worried my nerves and scared my heart. I swallowed, my throat dry and roasting. I trudged on, reflecting on the long journey from Bellingham, such a short distance expanded into a few lengthy, miserable days. My mind wandered and my thoughts fell upon Jelly. My gut twisted in agonizing concern.

A couple of the soldiers talked amongst themselves in hushed voices as we slowed for a breather. I walked up to Burnhammer. "Hi, my name is Maggy." I stuck out my hand. I had never met a soldier, though I had imitated them enough from movie scenes.

"Hi, Maggy." She gripped my hand and shook. "I'm Burnhammer." She let go and smirked. "That's quite an axe you have there. You must be pretty strong to lug that around."

"It's made from neo-plastic," I explained. "Though often it's a weight I don't care to support."

"Neo-plastic, that must have cost an arm and a leg," she replied.

"It was a birthday gift, and I imagine it was two legs."

Burnhammer laughed.

"Can I ask you a question?" I said.

She nodded. "Go for it."

"Who are you guys and what are you doing here?"

"We are 3rd squad of the 2nd platoon, most often called Shadow Stalkers. Our blood runs in the Charlie Company, 909th Infantry Regiment, 2nd Brigade Combat Team of the 56th Infantry Division."

I gawked at her. "That's a mouthful."

"Don't worry, I write it more than I say it. But that's who we are, the Shadow Stalkers. Right, Stalkers?"

"HOOAH," the squad said in unison, keeping their voices under control. Even Henderson, the Squad Leader, had responded to the call.

"Been thinking of renaming ourselves the Cat Killers, though," a tall, barrel-chested man said, whose skin was as dark as night. He grinned wide, displaying luminous white teeth. "I'm going for the record. I'm guessing I'll have a million by the time the war is over." His voice was the lowest bass I had ever heard before, rattling my body.

"We'll see about that, Park," Burnhammer said, laughing.

"Were you out to rescue us?" I asked. I found their presence welcoming and overwhelming, glad to be surrounded by them, but also nervous. I didn't want them to think of me as just a defenseless child, though that's probably what I was.

"We were ordered to collect medical supplies, and to bring back any civilians. You're lucky we found you when we did; twenty of those monsters were advancing up that hill."

My eyes grew. "Twenty?" My voice cracked. I contemplated the outcome of twenty alions encircling us. It was not a pretty scene.

"You'll be all right now. 5,000 of the 56th are waiting for us back across Skyline, secured at the White Water Tower. We'll get ya there before the sun goes down," Burnhammer promised. Something about her voice made me believe her, made me trust her. "We'll kill every last one of these aliens."

"Alions," I corrected, as if she were Jacob.

"What was that?"

"We've been calling them alions because they look like lions," I explained.

"Slick," Park chimed in, his voice shaking my chest. "We should report that to command. You'll be as famous as me for that one." He grinned again.

"It is a pretty clever name," Burnhammer said. "Alions." She repeated the word a few times to let it ring in our ears.

"Toughen your tongues," Henderson ordered.

I looked up at Burnhammer, not knowing what their commander meant.

"She means we have to shut up and listen."

I nodded, focusing on the silence that encompassed us.

The noise of our feet grew. The heavy breathing of tired bodies was loud and noticeable, even at a good distance.

My eyes fell upon Tortilla. He still looked lively despite the dark circles around his eyes. I had always thought him determined, and now it showed in his thin body, trudging on the squishy soil. He would keep me safe, and I would protect him at all costs. For an instant, I thought about life after the alions, a life with just the two of us living on the coast, reading books as we listened to the crashing waves. But the daydream disappeared as the squad ducked down.

We halted.

A roar flew through the trees. Immediately Jane began shaking. Several more of the gut-wrenching roars hit our ears.

The soldiers were hunkered down, scanning every angle.

From atop a rock cliff above, an alion pounced, claws out and jaws wide with the intent to kill. A woman jerked her rifle up and launched a stream of destruction that tore the beast apart. With the soldiers distracted, another beast sprung out of the trees, grabbing hold of a man in a tumble. He fired into the woods as they rolled off the path. Henderson took aim and blasted a hole right through the alion's ear. The soldier pushed the soon-to-be corpse away, the body twitching as it slumped down into a thicket of bushes.

Ahead of the column, another alion attacked, firing black bullets. A soldier went down, pierced a dozen times. It ran right for me. I lifted my pistol and braced with my hand around my knuckles. PAP. The bullet shattered a tooth as it sunk into the back of its throat and out its neck. Afraid, I pulled the trigger again. PAP. Its body failed at my feet, buckling to the mud, which splattered all over my already dirty clothes.

"Well goddamn, she can shoot," a woman near the end of the column said. "I think we found another soldier to enlist."

Henderson and Burnhammer ran to the corpse of their fallen comrade. Henderson cursed. "Oh, Deter. Goddamn you." She tore off one of his dog tags hanging around his neck, sticking the other paper-thin tag between his front teeth and slammed his jaw shut. She scanned the vicinity, cautious. "Specialist Deter is the last to die today, is that understood?"

"Yes, sir!" the squad returned in unison.

"Good. Now move your butts."

Amanda had a hand wrapped around Jane's stomach, and another across her mouth to mute her screaming. "It's okay . . . it's okay," Amanda soothed her sister. "They're dead now."

Jane struggled against her sister's strength, yelling furiously into Amanda's hand until she calmed.

Amanda let go. "I'm here for you."

Jane nodded, streams of tears wetting her clothes.

The soldiers moved us on. The path wound back and forth, meandering like a river. Soon our path met up with the Shelter Loop Trail, where we took a right, which then led us to the Sunnyside Trail.

"Nice aiming back there," a woman told me. "I'm Corporal Emma Fox."

I smiled at her, but I was too tired to talk.

"We're gonna need your ability," Fox said. With a pat on the back, she sped up and left me alone.

Tortilla grinned at me.

The minutes slowly passed. Finally, the trail ended and we emptied onto SW Broadway Drive. Henderson ordered the squad to head left until we found an alley and cut across to SW Gerald Avenue. "The dentist office should be up just a few blocks." She regarded us with stern eyes. "Whatever you do, don't panic. Stay close to Burnhammer."

We halted at the bend in the road. Henderson snatched her radio. "Sergeant Loritz, state your situation."

"Roadway clear along Terrace. No tangos in sight."

"We're coming in from the west on Gerald. Repeat: Golf, echo, romeo, alfa, lima, delta."

"Copy position, sergeant. Soldiers are holding ground."

"All right, we're clear. Move out." Henderson began hand signaling.

Four soldiers crossed the road to the north side. Burnhammer pointed to where she wanted us to cross Terrace Drive. "Go fast and low to the ground. Make yourself a small target."

Tortilla and I helped Jacob, and Amanda pulled Jane along, ducking, shielding their faces in fear.

I glanced up and saw a yellow ball glowing like a million sparks glued together. The top of the three-story building exploded in a burst of yellow flame. Old red brick particles flew through the air, little comets of death that sought to pierce a thousand holes in our skin. Sections of the front broke off, falling to the sidewalk and road.

In the sky, five alion ships buzzed past, yellow balls destroying buildings, cars, trees, everything and anything. All I could see was set afire. In the distance, skyscrapers—pillars of achievement that stood as a testament to the ends humans could engineer—crumbled, collapsing to dust and debris. One after the other, as if the alions were playing dominos with some of the greatest architectural designs in the world, the buildings were bombed into ruins. The ground shook as if an earthquake. Plumes of debris gathered together to create one massive cloud that expanded in all directions.

Burnhammer yelled for us to stop as men poured out of the building.

"Back, back, back!" someone boomed, but I could barely understand the words as they became lost in the pollution of noise that swept by in an ear-penetrating rumble. Burnhammer yanked hard at my elbow. She threw Tortilla and I back towards Gerald. Within moments, the debris cloud surrounded us like the shocking desert sandstorms that occasionally showed up on the news.

Someone pushed me into the building across from where the dentist office had stood. A hand put a cloth across my mouth. I took hold of the cloth and gasped in air. At times, when the dust parted enough, I could see a dozen or more bodies, all crowded around me. I think Tortilla bumped me, but I couldn't see him, and I made no notion to acknowledge whoever did it.

A thunderous boom echoed all around. Boom after boom sounded off, louder than the cannon fired during Bellingham's Fourth of July celebration. I sat and waited, listening to the horrific noise, frozen in the most excruciating fear I had ever known.

Hours passed. A wind slowly stole away the debris. Eventually I could see again, and Henderson made sure everyone was okay and accounted for. The 3rd squad huddled around us, and encircling them were the survivors of the 1st squad and the other civilians, all packed together as tightly as we could manage.

Henderson saluted a man with an austere face, sharp-jawed and stone-eyed. "Sergeant Loritz."

"Sergeant Henderson," Loritz replied. "We have three civilians. I've lost six soldiers to get this far, only four of us remain."

"We have to get back across Skyline," she told him. "And we've gotta move quickly. Wounded?"

Henderson's assistant walked up. "Nothing too serious, sir. No broken bones. We're good to move."

The Leaders discussed routes and their advantages and disadvantages. At Henderson's command, the squad made ready, prepared to defend each other to their graves. There was no time to talk to Tortilla or any of the others, as Burnhammer hustled us out the building, motioning to the left.

My mouth gaped when I saw the empty skyline. Instead of cloud-reaching towers, mounds of rubble lay before my eyes, and a mist of finer particles.

Tortilla rubbed my back. "Do you think we'll live through today?"

I didn't want to answer that question: there was nothing positive left in me. Burnhammer ordered us along. Tortilla jogged beside me. I turned to him, reaching for his hand. "I hope so." My faint, weak voice barely carried to his ears.

He squeezed my hand, a comforting squeeze that I thought I could have been all right dying in. I glanced around at the soldiers. They were tough, their faces afire with determination, almost as if unaffected by the annihilation of the city. But deep, deep in their eyes, I saw that it did get to them: they were human. Yet, they put it aside, composed themselves, summoned up strength and courage, and they carried on with perseverance written on their trained faces.

I whirled around and saw Jacob laboring to keep stride, inhaler in hand. The next time Burnhammer motioned us down, while soldiers secured the area ahead, I tugged on her arm and got her attention. "How much farther? My friend." I pointed at Jacob. "He's not doing so well."

"I've noticed. It's about two klicks until Skyline with the route we're taking. I'll keep him alive, don't you worry." She ran back and gave Jacob a water bottle. A minute later, an order sounded, and we ran on.

Broadway came under our feet once more, a wide eight-lane road. At an intersection, Burnhammer motioned us up SW Humphrey. The streets were silent again, undisturbed by the racket of living creatures. I couldn't hear the footsteps of the soldiers. I couldn't even hear my own steps, and for a moment I thought I might have gone deaf, but when I asked Tortilla, his voice assured me I hadn't.

A highway stood to our right as we ran, still intact, but dead and motionless. It chilled my blood to look at it, though I'm not sure why it frightened me so much.

Then I noticed light-brown dots running along the road. "Alions!" I cried.

Burnhammer regarded the highway and spotted the beasts. She radioed Henderson, who was ahead of the column, out of earshot, unless she wanted to yell.

An army barricade came into view, standing between a massive intersection, where on and off-ramps connected to the highway. Tanks, jeeps, and other vehicles waited behind the barricade. The highway curved towards Broadway, and on mighty legs, alions sprang from the raised road.

Both squads open fired on the beasts. More jumped. They just kept coming. Enough of them survived the rain of bullets, regrouping, forming a line between the barricade and us. A scream informed the squads that more advanced at the rear.

We were trapped.

Tortilla and the twins huddled close to me. Jacob crouched a few meters down from us.

Soldiers open fired on the alions in front of us. I wasn't sure, but I thought I heard gunfire from behind the barricade, and I hoped reinforcements saw our situation.

Burnhammer waved us on. I took Jane's hand, and Tortilla grabbed Amanda, who despite her fearlessness, was on the verge of tears. The soldiers pressed towards the barricade. Alions and soldiers died all around. Blood sprayed and splattered everything.

Small bright yellow balls burst forth from alion tube-weapons. Buildings and soldiers exploded. Cars erupted in fire.

From behind the barricade, soldiers approached, and crossfire became a threat. Within seconds, all of the beasts that blocked our way had perished.

"Go, go, go!" Burnhammer shouted.

I pulled on Jane but her legs were frozen. A car near us exploded in yellow fire, and I yanked so hard on Jane's arm that I thought it might break off from her scrawny body. Tortilla and Amanda raced beside us.

As we neared the barricade, I glimpsed behind as soldiers fired from behind whatever cover they could manage to come by.

Jacob had fallen even farther behind, close to where we had run from, ducking at the center of a group of soldiers. All of the soldiers had refocused their attention on to the alions advancing up Humphrey. A soldier to the right of Jacob fell over, blood misting Jacob's clothes.

I yelled for Jacob to run, but he couldn't hear me: the gunfire drowned out my feeble voice.

A soldier motioned Jacob to make for the barricade. Three soldiers covered him as he struggled to run.

When the twins were safely beyond the barricade, I turned again to watch the battle. Dozens upon dozens of alions charged up the road. Roars quaked the earth. The first alion with a mane, resembling a male lion, galloped forth, holding a sleek silver tube above its head with its humanlike hands. It reminded me of a bazooka. Taller and wider, the alion instilled a deep fear in my trembling body. It shot a blue orb from the tube, one that resembled the yellow balls, sparkling as it flew.

In an instant, the blue orb struck Jacob. He froze as a field of brilliant blue light encircled him. He stood motionless. Veins of light blue crept towards his body from the surface of the barrier. The veins pulsed, as if shocking him, keeping him in place. Blue orbs hit the three soldiers defending Jacob. All of them paused in suspension, as if frozen in time.

In a burst of speed, other alions bolted for the four. As the beasts came within striking distance, the field vanished, returning Jacob to his normal state. By then, a paw clobbered his back, and five sharp claws pierced through his chest.

A soldier swept me up in strong arms, carrying me away. Screaming, I ordered to be put down.

The soldier handed me off to a burly man, tall and solid. He held me against his chest as I fought, wriggling, struggling against his might.

"Put me down! Put me down!"

He ignored me.

Another soldier ran up and gave the burly man his instructions. He took me to a jeep far behind the barricade; Tortilla and the twins sat in the back of it. He set me down.

I took the axe from my back. "I'll cut you down." My voice, a furious stream of defiance, broke upon a stolid face and resistant ears.

"I'm not the enemy, girl. Now get your ass in the jeep."

"Maggy, what are you doing?" Tortilla jumped up to the edge of the jeep's bed. "Stop! Stop!"

"Jacob's dead, Tortilla. Murdered. We have to go back."

"What can we do that the soldiers can't," he said.

The soldier stared at me. "Revenge will come for us all, girl. Store your anger for when the time comes, and lash out then. Now is not the time."

His words struck me down. I fell to my knees, dropping my axe. I couldn't stop the tears.

The next thing I knew, I was in the bed of the jeep, and we were driving away. I looked up with blurry eyes. Jeeps and tanks were following. Hundreds of soldiers walked behind the column.

Tortilla wrapped an arm around me. I leaned into his chest, and his tears fell away, soaking my hair.

I had never felt so fragile, so weak, so helpless.

At that moment, all hope vanished within me, and darkness swept my mind away in a tide of agony.

7
Bones as Sweet as Candy
Darrel

My hand slipped over an alion paw.

I spied Penelope's eyes grow wide with terror.

Pushing me down, she snagged the alion gun resting against her left thigh. Awkwardly, she pulled down on one of the triggers and let loose the deadly black globes.

The alion had nowhere to go. Trapped, its blood splattered the duct walls, ceiling, and floor, along with both of us. Red touched everything within sight.

I shuddered, dripping blood onto the floor. It ran down into my eyes and stung. The taste of iron filled my mouth. The foul tang mixed with foul thoughts of what swam between my teeth. I spat.

Shaking, Penelope dropped the gun. "Everywhere . . ." Her faint and broken whisper barely reached my ears.

The alion twitched, struggling to breathe. A moment later, it lay dead, eyes open and staring intentionally at me. My stomach disliked the eerie gaze, so I crawled away, down to the end of the duct, where it branched off in a T. "Come on," I choked. I cleared my throat. I really needed an inhaler, but since we didn't have one, I knew my only option to calm my breathing was to get far, far away from the beast.

Penelope grabbed our gear and followed. "That was unpleasant."

"You can say that again," I replied. I took the right at the T, and the section of duct went on out of sight, straight.

We crawled and crawled and crawled.

Scratches on my hands started to bleed. We finally stopped when I thought I was about to keel over.

I rested my back against the duct wall. Penelope sat across from me, drinking. "We should get some sleep," she said.

"I'm not sure that I can sleep," I responded. "I'm not sure, that I want to even try." I looked over at her; she was covered in blood, now dry and peeling. "I think I'll keep watch while you sleep."

She laughed. "You won't last five more minutes."

I was panting, my eyelids were drooping, and my head was as heavy as a sack of potatoes. I knew she was right. "We'll see," was all I said.

I jerked awake. My own snoring startled me. I didn't know when I finally passed out, but Penelope probably had been pretty close in her estimate. With blurry eyes, I straitened up, squinting at her as she slept away, undisturbed by my roaring snores. My stomach growled. For a brief second I thought about going back to cut a flank from the dead alion, but I knew I would get lost along the way, and after some thought, just the idea of the rotting carcass churned my stomach.

I eyed my fingers, my mouth salivating. My stomach growled again and a burp exploded up my throat and into the close-quarters of the duct. I needed to find food, and fast, as I didn't see myself lasting too much longer, staring at each digit of my hand.

I cleared my throat and snapped out of the trance that had taken hold of me.

Penelope raised her head. "What?" she said abruptly.

I tucked my hands between my thighs. "Uhrm. I didn't say anything." We made eye contact. Her oak-colored irises swept me away into a different land and time, but only for a second, when they first locked together.

She smiled. "You were snoring. Did you know that?"

I returned her cheerful grin. "Yeah, I know." I shifted to my knees. "We need to find some food before I die."

"Oh, don't be so dramatic. It's only been a day or so."

I stared at her. "Dramatic? When was the last time you went without food for a day? I don't think I ever have."

"I'm not saying I have, I'm just saying we're far from dead."

"Maybe . . . and maybe not. It could be just around the corner." I pointed to the T ahead of us. "That's not very far."

"Well then, hold your gun up and make sure to give 'em hell." She giggled. When we made it to the T, she decided to go right, and her shoe caught my wrist.

I barely saved myself, dropping the alion gun in a CLANG that resounded throughout the entire duct system.

"Sorry," Penelope said.

"It's not your fault. I was too close." I picked up the gun and we moved on.

Once we passed the next fork, she chose to take a peek into a room, quietly removing a panel. "Looks like another quarters. Should we go down and search for food?"

I nodded. "I'm hungry enough to try anything. Uhrm. I might even wait for the alion to return, just so I can roast it."

"Roast it, eh? Well, I think you would find that troublesome without an oven." She dipped her head down into the room again. "Ready?"

"Yep."

She turned around and hung her feet over the edge of the hole. "Lower me down."

I gripped her forearms, then dropped her as gently as I could, but my arms shook out of control, and by the time her feet touched the ground, they had turned to jelly.

"I'm going to rest a second. Go ahead and look without me."

"Are you that scared?" she asked.

I showed her my trembling hands. "I'm not that strong. Just hold on a second and I'll be down." I recuperated with my feet dangling in the hole.

"All right," she said. Shuffling items around on a desk, she began to scour the quarters for any evidence of food. Finding nothing in the desk, she scooted it underneath the open panel.

I hopped down. "Thanks."

"No problem," she said with a smirk.

Turning over the room, I finally found some dried meat wrapped in a salt-laden towel. I bit into the tender strip.

"What's it taste like?" Penelope asked when she spied me chewing it down in a gulp.

I offered her a long, thick slab. "Venison, I think," I replied. "But it mostly tastes like salt. The most delicious salt I've ever had."

She munched down a morsel of her own. "That's certain." A huge smile of relief crossed her lips. "Maybe a day is longer than I realized."

I accepted the water bottle when she offered it. The salt hurt my dry lips and mouth, and had made me incredibly thirsty. I almost drank the whole bottle.

"Whoa, dude. We have to conserve the water. We don't know when we'll find another water depot."

I gave her back the bottle. "Sorry. I'm just used to drinking as much as I need, or don't need." I wiped my mouth clean.

Penelope stored the meat in a pocket. She decloaked and cloaked again, so that the meat would become shielded from watchful, hostile eyes. "Let's go," she said. She hopped onto the desk and climbed up with a boost from my weak arms.

She helped me as I struggled to lift myself back into the duct. "Thanks," I said, coughing. "Uhrm. I need a breather."

Nodding, she replaced the panel, then sat down beside me.

My heart skipped as our arms grazed. This was the last thing I needed. My heart couldn't take the blood pumping through it. I cleared my throat again. I scooted away, just so our skin wouldn't touch again, I couldn't risk it; my heart would explode if it happened a second time.

She looked over at me, calm. "You ready?"

"I guess so," I said. My breathing was still shallow and fast, but I had managed to compose myself a little. I followed behind her; she was a good leader, and I didn't mind the view.

We crawled and crawled and crawled.

My stomach grumbled again, not satisfied with the tiny portion I had fed it. I shook my head and focused on crawling, ignoring my cravings as best I could. Our pace slowed, and I could barely move, with sore arms and legs, and everything else.

I savored our breaks, which were few and spread out, with great long gaps of bleeding and crawling between them.

"Are you ready to try another panel?"

I shook my head. "Nah. There's only so much you can stomach in a day, and who knows what we'll stumble across, though it's likely to be something I don't want to see."

"And it may be a cache of macaroni and cheese," she said.

"Macaroni and cheese?"

"I don't know. I was just saying . . . it could be worthwhile." She slid a panel onto the duct, whether I wanted her to or not didn't matter much, and she lowered her head inside the room to get a look at what doom awaited us. She came back up. "I don't know what kind of room it is; it's weird, with bright lights and big tables. You should take a look."

Against my better judgment, I did take a peek. "It reminds me of a hospital," I told her.

"I was thinking the same thing, but it's so foreign . . . did you see the huge tables?" she asked.

I nodded. "Well they're big animals."

"Let's get a closer look," she urged.

Reluctantly, I gave in. "All right, but if I can't get my ass back up here, it's on you."

She laughed. "I've been working out, don't worry. Haven't you noticed that it's already on me to get you up here?"

I blushed and hid my eyes from her. She was right; I was weaker than her, and I didn't possess a tenth of her perseverance or willpower.

"I didn't mean it like that," she said, trying to comfort me.

"What way did you mean it?" I asked, my voice cracking. I couldn't even make myself sound bold, and I knew it was easy to see through my feeble attempt to appear manly.

"It's a lot easier to pull someone up, you know that. I was just kidding. I wouldn't make it if you didn't boost me." She put a hand on my shoulder, then slid it down my arm. "It was just a joke . . . nothing more." With a smile, she jumped through the hole onto a cushioned bed, piled with blue-green blankets. "You're good to go," she said.

Though her words hurt, I brushed them off and descended to the bed. Penelope was out of sight. "Penelope?" I called.

"Around the corner," she said. She was poking her head around another corner, spying.

I came up behind her, and as she twirled to meet me, her soft hair slapped me across the face. The long strands of copper smelled like citrus and sweat. "What are you doing?"

"Watching," she replied. "I saw one, lying on a bed around the corner. It looks sick."

"I hope we gave it to the beast," I spat.

She nodded. "Come on, it can't see us." She sidled past the corner and along the warm wall, turning down another corridor. Five more beds sat spaced out evenly along the hall, one of them occupied. An alion rocked side-to-side, calling in a sickly tone. In the next hall, rooms branched off, and we glanced inside. A mother and her newborn cub lay sleeping, curled up together.

I walked out and down the hall, where it ended in a T, and a large room with a huge glass windowpane. I stopped at the window. Dozens of warm blankets clumped together in mounds. Little fur balls slept, interwoven with each other and the blankets.

Penelope brushed up against me. "A maternity ward," she whispered when she spotted all the little critters.

"Guess so," I responded. "They don't seem so evil when they're small."

She pressed a hand against the glass, spreading her fingers wide. "That's certain. Maybe we should ransom one of them, a trade: our lives for the cub's life." Her quiet steps stopped at the door's threshold. "What do you think?"

"I think I wouldn't know how to go about communicating that to the alions." I stepped back from the window. I spotted a reflection in the glass and flinched to the left. Whirling, I fell, backing away from a gigantic alion. The beast stared through the window, observing the sleeping young. It seemed to smile in serenity. The alion pressed its nose up to the glass as another alion crept to its side.

Penelope walked around them, and joined my gaze in utter bemusement and apprehension. One of the alions entered the room for newborns and nuzzled a cub, then it nestled down and fell asleep. She turned to me and offered a hand.

I took it. Once on my feet, we ran down the corridor, without a word spoken. After a few more twists and turns, we entered a massive room with hundreds of beds, all fit to the size of the biggest alions. At the opposite end of the room, a line of alions waited, communicating in low cat voices. Their soft speech was unlike anything I could reproduce. The line went hundreds back, and as we drew closer, it became apparent as to their task.

At the head of the queue an alion stood, holding a silver gun in one of its humanlike hands. It grabbed hold of an alion patient nearest to it, tapped one of its humanlike elbows, and injected something into a bulging vein. The alion patient growled. The doctor nodded for the patient to leave, and it scooted out of line and went back to its duties, grumbling as it disappeared down a lengthy hallway.

One after the other, alion patients stepped up to the doctor to receive a shot in their humanlike arms. Each one growled, then plodded off, annoyed. The line did not seem to dwindle at all, as a replacement filed in the moment one left it.

"What do you think they are doing?" I asked Penelope, to see if she had an answer. My mind drew a blank.

"Did you ever play the old video game *War of the Worlds?*" she said, returning my question with a question of her own.

I shook my head. "I don't think so. At least it doesn't sound familiar. What about it?"

"In the game, at the end, the aliens died because of diseases, bacteria attacked them that we had grown immune to over time. It was devastating to them, like smallpox to the Native Americans."

"Never thought of an end like that," I said.

A cheerful grin spread wide, and with it, her dimples grew deep and beautiful. "Yeah, it was pretty profound, ingenious, and simple all wrapped into one."

"So, what does that have to do with anything?"

"These alions are smart, *very* smart . . . twenty bucks says those are inoculations." Her voice overflowed with confidence. "You want to get a closer look?"

"I want to find a craft to fly us off this piece of shit," I said, irritated. "Come on, let's get out of here."

Her eyes showed the intrigue that captivated her into staring at the alion doctor. "Fine, fine. Wouldn't mind getting one of those shots, though."

"We have no idea what's in it, might kill you. Better not risk it." I turned back to the corridor we had entered from, navigating down several halls, twisting and turning again, until we realized we had made a mistake along the way. "All right, let's just get back up into the duct. We can use one of these empty rooms."

She sighed. "Our trail is becoming easier to track. They'll know we're using the duct system the more we leave open panels with desks and beds underneath them."

"You have a better idea?"

She grabbed my arm and stopped me. "They can't see us, we don't need to use the ducts."

"Uhrm. Well I feel a lot safer up there, don't you?"

"Okay, fine." She used the yellow disk to open a locked door. Jumping atop the bed, she began poking the panels again. POP. The panel at the head of the mattress flew into the duct. "Boost me."

I wrapped my arms around her knees, touching her warm legs, so close to her thighs. I almost dropped her as I cleared my throat, slightly dizzy. Once I was safely in the duct, we took a breather. I drank some water. She didn't want any.

Then we crawled and crawled and crawled until I was bone-tired. I collapsed, my chin planted into the duct. A curse escaped.

"Yeah, it's probably time we rest."

"Probably a few hours past the time," I said, smiling a soft, sleepy smile. I closed my eyes and found dreamland welcoming me with caressing warmth.

I woke up as my stomach rumbled. It ached. I wasn't as hungry as I had been the last time I awoke; my fingers weren't quite as appetizing, but I definitely needed the salted meat, worried that those thoughts might return. Penelope had the meat hidden away in a pocket, and I didn't want to wake her, but my fingers were twice as big as her pockets, and her jeans were so tight, I knew I would have to squeeze a finger into them just to get a centimeter. I gave up and shook her shoulder. "Hey wake up."

"Why?" she asked, drowsy. "I'm not ready."

"I'm hungry and you have the meat," I explained.

She reached into her pocket and tossed it to me, along with some lint. She said no more and nodded off again.

I tried to conserve the meat, taking small bites at a time, but each small bite led to another and another, until it was almost all gone. I cursed myself for my weakness. I swished around the water, listening; less than a quarter remained. I didn't think she would be kissing me any time soon. I waited for her to wake, anxious. I feared her reaction to the situation. I feared her disappointment in me. I played out the scene in my head a hundred times, and every time it ended with me getting slapped, or punched, or kneed, or some kind of physical abuse.

My stomach growled again.

When she woke and saw the leftover portion, a sigh left her, but that was all. "It wasn't going to last anyway. We better find some more."

I nodded and sighed in relief. "Lead the way."

We gathered up our things and began to crawl. "Can I ask you a question," she said a short while after we had started our trek.

"If I say no, will you not ask it?"

"Probably not," she replied.

I laughed. "Well, then, I guess I don't have much of a choice but to say yes."

"That's certain." She laughed. "Why do you let Maggy call you Jelly?"

An awkward silence crept in. It was easy to tell Jacob off, he was a guy; I didn't know what to say to a girl. "It's just what she calls me," I finally said.

"That's not really a reason," she argued.

I suppressed a laugh. "No. No, I suppose it's not. You think it's mean that she calls me Jelly?"

"A little offensive, yeah," she said.

"Because I'm fat?"

"Because you're *not* fat," she threw out quickly. "You don't have nearly enough kilogramage to be ol' Saint Nick."

"I guess I should be thankful for that," I said, laughing. "I've gotten used to it; it's not a big deal." We turned left at a T. My knees ached, red and sore. Regardless, I followed on.

"I just think the nickname is insulting. I'd call you Tyro." She glanced back at me and smiled.

"Why Tyro?"

"Because I like the way it sounds . . . it means novice, and compared to me, you're a novice at Death Squad." A giggle filled the duct.

"Is that so?" I laughed.

"It's certain."

"Well after we get off this dismal ship, we'll have to go a few rounds," I challenged her.

"We'll have to find the game and some computers first." She plopped her butt down and rested. "Let's take another breather. How are your knees?"

"No worse than my back, I suppose," I said. "Yours?"

"They feel raw, like they might be bleeding, but every time I check, there's nothing on them." She pulled up her pant leg and showed me.

"Ouch." I rolled up my pant legs and examined my own knees. Spots of thin skin promised to break soon, but there was nothing to be done about it, we had nothing to pad them.

"Yours look worse," she said, cringing.

"Maybe we should just hack them off and be done with it," I joked.

She grinned, then suddenly changed subjects. "You know, you never really kissed me. It was too short to call a *real* kiss."

I flushed. "Uhrm. Didn't seem right with the alion there and all."

"Oh, is that the reason? Well, I don't see any alions around now." To my eyes, her soft lips seemed to pucker up, dry and splitting, but still alluring and desirable. "Do you?"

I cleared my throat. I shifted uncomfortably, scanning the duct left and right. My cheeks grew hot to the point that I thought someone had set them ablaze. I opened my mouth to say something, but only a squeak escaped. I sat frozen.

"You've never kissed anyone before, have you?" she asked in a sympathetic tone.

I shook my head.

"I think you'll enjoy a *real* one." Her smile grew and grew until it swallowed her face. Then she advanced, her eyes excited.

My heart pounded so hard I was afraid I would faint, or just drop dead after it exploded.

The kiss lasted a quick second. It was a closed-mouth peck that made my head swim.

Penelope bit her lip as she slowly pulled back. "Let's do that again," she said, exhilarated and beaming.

"Why?" I asked.

She stared at me, curious as to why I would ask that.

My nerves ate away at my stomach and it growled, so noisy and fierce.

"Because it was too quick, and I want another," she replied.

I leaned in, and this time our lips locked, moist despite our dehydration. When we parted, I was smiling so wide, I thought my mouth would split apart; luckily, it didn't. "You were right." My words were rushed and screechish.

"That's certain. Now you can say that you've had a *true* kiss." She chewed on her lip and grinned. "You ready to find some food?"

I looked at her, mystified. She was an utter mystery to me: one minute she wanted to kiss, and the next, find food. I couldn't argue with my stomach, though. "Uhrm. Yeah," I said, nodding.

After a few more turns, Penelope stopped and pried off a panel with her nails and poked her head through the hole. When she came back up, she shrugged. "Looks like an engine room or something like that. No food."

She repeated the process a few more times, each with the same result.

Finally, I took a turn, hoping my luck was better. I slid off the panel and a blue cloud engulfed us. I couldn't see Penelope for a second, until the cloud dissipated in the duct, though a trace lingered around us like a disconcerting mist.

"Spooky," she said, half-joking, half-afraid.

"It's cold," I said, feeling the air. I put an arm through the hole, lying on my stomach. "I think it's a freezer."

"A freezer could be promising." She scooted up beside me and waved a hand around in the blue mist. "Shall we take a look inside?"

"What if we freeze to death?" I shrieked.

"Then it'll feel better than a gash through the belly." Pushing herself up by the elbows, she turned around and held on to the ledge, easing down. "It's not a far drop. Maybe a meter and some change."

My legs kicked in a flutter as I gripped the ledge. Penelope found my feet, calmed them, and helped me down. My teeth instantly chattered, my skin bit by the extreme cold. "This is insane," I reminded her.

"Maybe. Look for a door, we're not getting back up to the panel." We groped around for a door handle. Nothing. The blue mist swirled about, as if frolicking.

I bumped into something hard, hard enough to bruise my shoulder. Jerking back, I raised my gun, primed. The mist cleared the closer we walked to the center of the room. Large chunks of red and white hung from the ceiling. Long stringy fibers as solid as rock stared back at us.

"It's a cow," Penelope gasped. The cow-shaped meat was perfect, almost as if it had been pristinely skinned. Behind the butchered carcass of the cow, more hung in a row that went far on out of sight. We walked on and another animal dangled beside the cow. The big slab of icy meat matched a horse, and next to it, an elk. Animal after animal appeared, all different, and behind each one were thousands more of the same species. We passed elephants, dogs, turkeys, rats, deer, bears, bison, lizards, fish, whales, alligators, kangaroos, rhinoceros, goats, rabbits, toads, and walruses, and hundreds of other animals. The ceiling shaped to each one, as high as needed for the largest, and for the small animals the ceiling spanned the same height as where we had entered down from the panel.

It felt as though we walked for hours, and we gasped at each new species, surprised to see the red muscle that existed beneath the skin. Then at last I could see the end: a shape dwelled there that horrified my eyes and churned my stomach in revulsion.

Penelope stopped, gaping at the human hanging like all the rest of the animals. Skinned just the same, with frozen muscle and fat exposed, yet it was different to gaze upon our own kind, so much worse, the butchery seemed. But in the end, the alions gave us no special treatment. We were animals just the same as all the rest.

Dizzy, I fell back on my butt, then rolled over, facing the wall.

Shivering, Penelope stepped away, her back against the wall, allow-ing the blue mist to hide the suspended corpses. She slid down and sat next to me.

"Now we know," she whispered. She grabbed her knees and shook in the cold.

Nauseated, I couldn't see straight, and my mind worked in scram-bled flashes. Incoherent thoughts popped in and out, as if I had lost control, melted in a freezer.

Then I noticed my arm lifted up, and my body glided across the slick floor. A pressurized door opened. Warmth invaded my skin, lungs, and blood. The blue faded. I peered up and saw Penelope with unclouded vision. The fuzziness that had attacked my head vanished.

"You all right, dude?" she asked me.

I shook my head. "No, are you?"

"No," she choked on the word, then cleared her throat. "No, I'm not either." She flopped down beside me.

I rolled over and sat. "It's so much worse to know . . . to see it . . ." I mumbled.

She gave no reply as she stared at the tiled floor.

I closed my eyes and dreamed of my parents. Their faces were al-ready hard to see clearly, distorted from the terrible days and nights, and the traumatic events that never seemed to stop. When I opened my eyes, I saw the giant room for the first time, with rows upon rows stocked full of all the foods and snacks that I most desired. My stomach bellowed a song of joy and anticipation. My mouth watered and my eyes grew as wide as bowling balls.

Skeptical, I blinked. All the food still sat idle on hundreds of shelves, so I shut them again, counting to five. I braced myself for the reality of my melted brain as I opened them again. Yet, bags of tortilla chips and boxes of fig bars awaited the return of my vision, speaking to my stomach as much as my eyes. They pulled me toward them, as if they had shot a grappling hook around my back and the rope retracted, drawing me within a centimeter of their wrappings.

My outstretched arms grazed the box of fig bars. "Penelope!" I yelled.

She jumped awake, instantly on her feet. "Run," she spoke to her-self, now an automatic motivational tool.

I smiled at her and tossed the box.

It slipped through her fingers as she tried catching it with one hand. She rested her alion gun on the floor and examined the box. "Fig bars?" she said, doubting her eyes. Furiously, she tore the box apart, throwing the paperboard in all directions. Six individually wrapped bars awaited her desperate fingers. Once the wrapper was peeled, she bit into the fig bar, realizing that she wasn't dreaming. "It's real!" she said with a mouthful.

I snatched a bag of tortilla chips and popped it open. Each chip was perfectly crunchy and salty. "If we're sharing the same dream, I may have to kill myself when we wake," I told her. I wouldn't have been able to handle that reality.

She studied the room with care. "It's like a hundred grocery stores."

"Like a thousand grocery stores," I said. "The biggest stockpile that anyone could ever see. This must be what they were after, our food supplies."

"More like Earth's food supplies," she corrected me. "Don't forget what we saw in the other room."

"That wasn't a dream?" I stacked five chips in my mouth at once, sucking them down like a vacuum hose sucking up feathers.

"No, that wasn't a dream." She pointed to the freezer door.

I stared at it for a while. I kept up pace, crunching yellow triangle after yellow triangle. "I really wish it had been."

"Me too . . ." she replied. "Let's see what else we can find." Tossing the fig remains aside, she walked off along the wide aisle.

I followed close behind. We passed all the chips I had ever known, and then some foreign chips of rice, corn, pita, and more beyond naming. It was a different world of food. I found a box of cheese fish and one of graham cracker bunnies. I ate as we walked. My stomach was approaching maximum load, but I didn't want to stop, just in case this was my last meal.

We came upon a huge mountain of sport drinks in a different row. They were unrefrigerated but appeasing. I drank two or three one-liter bottles stamped with a foreign language. The pink one was the best, I thought it was watermelon, but I was just happy it was sweet.

Soon though, the liquid ran to my bladder. "I have to pee," I told Penelope.

She nodded. "I've been holding mine in for a long time."

"So have I, but the tank is bursting." I was shaking my hands to distract my mind from my bladder's urgent calls. "I've only gone twice since we've been here."

She giggled. "Well you beat me, I've gone three times. I'll wait here for you."

I half-grinned. "I won't go far, just around the corner." I rushed around the corner of a shelf. Empty, I ambled back. "Relief at last."

"But now it's my turn. Watch our stuff." She pointed to our pile of reserves, then walked around a different corner. Returning, she smiled. "Ready to return to Earth?"

"Since I got here." I trailed behind her quick steps. The aisles were long and unending. At the end, I glanced behind us. Quickly, I pushed Penelope out of the aisle, behind a corner, jumping as I did.

"What is it?" she asked.

I peeked around the shelf. "Alion," I informed her of the peril. "It's sniffing around where we peed like it's not invisible."

"Dammit that was fast." She bent low, poking her head around the corner, just enough for her to glimpse the alion as it sucked in long whiffs of our scent.

I trembled in fear. I knew it would find us by its powerful nose. No matter how hard I shook, there was always a trace of urine left after I went, a trace that would lead that nose right to my crotch. "We have to run," I whispered. "If it can smell the urine on the floor, I bet it will be able to smell any that might have leaked onto our clothes."

She nodded. Without a reply, she turned and sprinted off.

I huffed after her. Running was so much worse on my lungs than crawling, and even that had nearly killed me. Running now shot sharp pains through my gut, back, and sides, not to mention my sore knees and aching feet. I doubled over a couple of times, hunching as I continued on. Pain stabbed me everywhere.

Quick footed, Penelope wound this way and that way, dodging shelf corners, pivoting in a blink. I wondered if she was a basketball player, but I didn't have the breath to ask her. She held open a door as I whirled around a shelf a few steps behind.

The door pressurized as it closed. The room was a long hallway filled with electronics. Using the yellow disk, she opened the door to the left at the end of the hall. We entered an empty square room. The walls were padded with a foam material, as if to dampen collisions. A door across from us led to another square room with a table covered in weapons. We brushed the weapons aside and climbed on top of it. The ceiling was much taller, too high for Penelope to reach, so I punched the first panel and up it shot. I caught it with a hand and slid it to the side.

In a hurry and without thinking, I pulled myself up first, stronger now than when worry had a grip on me. Fear motivated me much more.

Before I could turn my body around, alions burst into the room from three separate doors.

Penelope threw up the yellow disk, spun around and started spraying black globes, until a blue orb broke on her skin and enveloped her. Tiny, light blue tubes that resembled little lightning flashes crept down from the edge of the ball, drawing near her skin until they pierced her fragile body. She didn't move. She looked stuck in time.

I retreated and watched with only a fraction of my eyes able to see.

A group of alions approached her. One pressed a button on a bazooka weapon. The blue ball that encapsulated Penelope vanished. An alion patted around her belt, finding the decloak button. Her body now revealed, another alion injected something into her elbow with the medical gun we had seen earlier. Her eyes closed as her body collapsed.

A light growl burst forth from an alion, and several looked up in my direction. I crawled back in a hurry. I rolled over and put my feet to the duct floor, crouch-walking away. I stopped, hesitant. I couldn't just leave her behind. I went back to the hole. All but one of the alions had disappeared. The alion was sniffing every centimeter of the room, searching.

I cleared my throat, staring at the beast. If I didn't follow now, I wouldn't ever find her. I undid my pants and tossed my underwear aside with the hope that most of my scent was concentrated on the article. My nerves twitching, I slipped back down into the room, gun up and firing. One of the doors was open, so I took a chance, wishing it were the correct one.

My wish came true. A dozen or so alions surrounded Penelope's body; one carried her over its furry shoulder. None of them stopped to smell the air. If they could smell me, they pretended not to.

I stayed back, lingering at a safer distance than if I trailed at their heels. Their languid pace melted my brain, and drove my nerves haywire. My blood zipped up and down my arms and legs, swelling in my brain, then deserting the area in a rush of blackness that threatened a loss of consciousness. Despite my out of control body, I continued to follow, gun raised to their hindquarters.

After what seemed like a hundred turns, they finally stopped in a giant room; its walls were adorned with blue slabs of reflective metal.

Strapped to the slabs, a few people struggled to get free, while others lay limp and lifeless. Three tables lay in the center of the room where they secured Penelope. A corpse rested on one of them, its chest open, a heart showing, and when I passed, I saw it pump once with life.

The room spun. Swooning, I ran to the edge of the room. I choked on air as I struggled to breathe. The air turned to fire, and my vision left me, lying alone in the calm darkness.

A second later, I rolled over, gasping. I fought off the swirling shadows. At last, I won, staring at the high dome ceiling of the alion room.

As I raised my upper body off the floor, bending at the waist, I saw a yellow line flying at me. It looked like a detection laser that protected museums and other high security places. Not knowing what else to do, I jumped to my feet and fled. The line stopped at the end of the door. It turned aside and scanned along the walls.

Afraid, I turned back to regroup. None of my thoughts were clear and I didn't think I was doing Penelope any favors as woozy as I was. I found a long hall with more pods, most of them vacant.

I sat and collected my thoughts.

If the yellow line were a scanner, I wouldn't make it far enough into the room to free Penelope. I had to disable it somehow. Several plans shot through my mind. I didn't think I could pull off a single one.

I got to my feet and wandered through a few halls, memorizing the path back to the torture room, or whatever it was. I entered into a massive room lined with rows of short tables, no more than a few centimeters from the ground. Hundreds of alions feasted. Not one peered my way, so I thought I was safe, still invisible and without a strong scent.

I studied the alions. They ate at their leisure, tearing meat from bone, some cooked, some raw. Along the tables, bodies of birds, rabbits, deer, and humans overflowed, bones tossed about, plucked clean of tissue.

Two of the nearest alions finished off the flesh sticking to a long, thick bone. When all the meat sunk to the pit of their stomachs, the bigger one stole the bone away and bit at an edge, breaking apart the end. Holding the bone with a humanlike hand, it swung back its head and sucked down the marrow within, seeming to enjoy it as if it were candy.

The sickening sight made my stomach gurgle in abhorrence.

I turned and ran back to the hall.

Now I knew that if I tripped the alarm, hundreds of bone-sucking alions would be there within moments, long before I could make an escape.

I made my way back to the room where they held Penelope. She still lay unconscious on one of the three center tables. An alion examined the body with the slow pumping heart, experimenting. The short-haired man made no gut-wrenching screams as I had expected; he just rested with a tranquil, drugged face, slightly curved up in a smile.

I scrutinized the yellow line's pattern, but after a while I figured out it scanned around the room at random. I looked about the room, searching for its origination point, yet it didn't appear to have one, as it glided along the room without a trace of the source from where it was emitted.

Another alion walked into the room and pressed a combination of keys on a translucent screen. One of the slabs along the wall to my right moved forth. The slab, controlled by a computerized arm, reached the alion within a second, rotating the table so that it was horizontal like the other three.

The alion took a cutting tool and began to open the chest cavity of the woman.

She screamed in agony.

I crushed my ears with my hands. It was no use; the horrific sound penetrated my attempt to muffle the screaming, shooting right down into my stomach. I backed out of the room again.

For all my effort to sit and watch the room, I couldn't stand by the door for longer than a minute, but when my stomach settled, I went back to study the layout once again. I went back and forth a hundred times or more, adding on to the picture I was building in my head.

I searched all the rooms circling the torture room. Three were hallways, one a square room with padding, and the fifth was pitch-black and smelled of decay, so I did not linger. For hours, I walked back and forth through the connecting halls, scouting out the entire area, looking for an opportunity. As my body slowed in exhaustion, I realized I had to make my own opportunity, but I couldn't fathom how.

Using a pod, I climbed up into the duct system to clear my head. I visualized the torture room. Nothing came. Hungry, I took out a chocolate bar I had found in the stockroom of food.

I didn't know how long I had sat there, but soon a horrible itch came over me, pushing me back to the torture room. Stashing what little water I had in the duct, I went back and stared at Penelope. They hadn't touched her yet. But how long would it be before they did? A minute? An hour? A day? How long could I stand outside and do nothing?

Anger flooded my veins. Helplessness followed.

Hungry again, I went searching for food. I found a smaller storage unit brimming with food, not far from the massive dining hall. I also found the kitchen, watching alions prepare plates crowded with meat and thick flat breads.

I stuffed my face with cheese crackers, unable to control my appetite. I felt sicker and sicker by the minute, but I couldn't stop eating.

Then suddenly I looked up and an alion stood in the doorway, gaping down at a floating box of crackers that I had forgotten to cloak. Dropping the box, I grabbed the gun that lay between my legs. The black globes pierced the beast's skull. I hurtled over the carcass and out into a short hall. Another alion caught sight of its dead companion and chased after me. I whipped around frantically, shooting but never hitting. The bazooka tube was strapped across its back. Unfastening the buckles with its humanlike fingers, the alion lifted the weapon above its head and aimed in the direction of my fleeing body.

I zigzagged as I crossed into another, lengthier hallway. When I came to the door at the end, it was locked, and I had no time to use the yellow disk.

I whirled around to face the alion.

It shot the blue orb at my invisible face as I launched a stream of black globes. The blue cloud immobilized me. I felt the blue lightning strikes pierce my vulnerable pink skin in a thousand different places. With every pulse came a stabbing pain.

Suspended, I gazed out of the semi-transparent cloud, watching as the claws that promised my death approached.

I waited with open eyes.

8
The Truth
Maggy

No one spoke as we drove south. The thrumming of gas engines surrounded us. Most of the vehicles were electric, powered by high-absorbent solar panels, but they were also old and the batteries did not last when darkness came. I was told that we had entered California a short while ago, but it didn't look any different than southern Oregon. What road our wheels rode on, no one knew, and I received the same answer from all of the soldiers: "We'll be there soon."

But soon wasn't soon. Alions ambushed us over and over, and the column of heavy vehicles stopped a hundred times to fight off the small groups of attackers. Once, an alion tore a soldier from the edge of the jeep, just stole him away in the daylight. It was even more horrific than when they took Mike.

Tortilla and I, along with the twins, huddled at the front of the jeep's bed, shivering under a single blanket. Tortilla continuously comforted both girls, even though Amanda insisted she didn't need it. Jane dug her head into his chest and squeezed his body, terrified. She clung to him for a better part of the journey.

As dawn broke on the next morning, Burnhammer appeared at the tailgate for the first time since our departure. "How are you four doing?" she asked. Her camouflage uniform already looked normal to my eyes. She hopped up into the bed and took a seat across from us on the long benches.

"We're hungry," I answered. "They haven't really been giving us rations."

She cursed. "Hold on, I'll go get you some." She returned with four quick meals, wrapped and preserved; two were turkey subs and the others were ham.

"Thanks," I said, unwrapping the package.

"I'll tell the ones looking after you to keep you better fed, but I have to go," she spoke softly. "Duties to be done."

"Can't you look after us?" Jane asked.

"Wish I could, but I have orders to watch our six. We can't let them sneak up behind us anymore." She smiled and hefted her rifle over her shoulder. "Your guns still working?"

Tortilla and I nodded.

"Good. Ask one of the soldiers to show you how to clean them. Keeping a clean gun will keep you alive." She nodded and left.

The sandwich tasted much better than the jerky at this point, a relief from the same foods we had been eating for what seemed like a year. I tried to count the days, but when I did, Jacob and his house and his death wish always popped into mind, so I quit counting after the second day. I know it couldn't have been more than nine or ten days max. A sick taste filled my mouth when my thoughts drifted to Jacob. Watching his death now ate away at my nerves. I replayed the scene over and over. I wasn't even sure I had any nerves left.

Even though we were surrounded by hundreds of soldiers, who were trained and packing heavy-duty weapons, I felt more vulnerable now than when I woke up alone in my house. After losing Jacob, the soldiers did not promise safety as I once thought they had. None of us were safe . . . none of us.

As the sun awoke, dark, unfriendly clouds blocked out its warmth, pouring rain to muddy up the ground off the road. It rained into the afternoon, until we had either passed the clouds, or they had been swept away. By three, the clear blue sky smiled again.

I walked to the edge of the jeep, bouncing around as the driver failed to miss potholes. I stared up at the sun. The warmth bathed me and I absorbed as much as I could. I closed my eyes from the harsh light.

Then a mass blocked out the rays for a second.

I opened my eyes and spotted the alion craft. Balls of yellow exploded at the rear of the column, sending giant plumes of red and yellow flames skyward. Thick black smoke engulfed what I could see of the convoy's tail. The boom generated from the tanks deafened. Huge mounted machineguns added to the chorus of blasts.

The jeep sped up.

Out of the smoke, an alion craft flew low, zooming over the tops of vehicles. The triangular ship fired a wave of yellow dots. The jeep at our backs exploded; its flames reached for my face, like a hand grabbing blindly for food to consume. I fell back.

One of the soldiers inside our jeep radioed his superior. No response came. The large black man called over and over, but it was futile, no one was going to respond.

"Give it up, Charles," the Asian woman said, who sat next to him. "Just protect the civvies, that's our duty."

A broad, pale man with a bushy mustache and thick eyebrows took guard at the tailgate. He helped me to my feet, then turned his attention to the sky, searching for alion crafts. One approached, flying even faster than its last pass over. The man aimed an anti-air rocket at the front tip of the craft. Waiting until it zipped over a tank four vehicles behind, he pulled the trigger, and with gray smoke filling our mouths, the rocket raced towards its target.

I coughed, hunching over. I shifted my squinting eyes to the alion craft. The rocket found its mark and detonated upon impact. In seconds the entire craft burned, afire from front to back to wings. The crimson gas emitted by the alion vessel combusted, adding to the chaos. The ball of fire whooshed over us, drifting to the left. In a crash, the wet trees and foliage burst into fire as the craft blew apart into flaming shards.

"Got one," the soldier who had shot it down said. His Slavic accent sounded odd, as I had only heard it in movies and video games, but never in person, never in real life.

The other soldiers whooped and hollered their delight. When the celebration died down an hour had passed. The soldiers took every kill as a victory, and they relished in it, as if the end of the war—or whatever we were in—drew near. The only end I could see, the only future I imagined awaited us all, was death: flesh torn apart and sliding down the throat of an alion, digesting in acid.

"You look grim," Tortilla told me.

"I feel like my heart is growing cold, bromigo." My heart hadn't leapt at his touch the last few days, and my skin didn't care what poked it; it was all the same now: metal, neo-plastic, food, soil . . . it all felt ten times harder than my skin.

He hugged me, kissed a cheek, and smiled. "They're taking us to a safe place."

I laughed. "There are no safe places left."

My mood irritated him, I could see, but he hid it, pushing my words aside. "There's still a fight . . . still a chance. We're soldiers now, whether we ever wanted to become what we played or not, that's us now. You better put all that pain some place deep, and save it for later, it's not doing you any good right now."

"Tortilla, we're not sol—"

He put a finger up to my mouth. "We're tough, our skin is thick, and our muscles only know endurance, just like in Death Squad. If it wasn't true before, it's true today." He nodded at me.

My heart pounded for a second, alive. I nodded at him. He needed me to be strong. I hugged him tightly. We sat motionless for a while, our warm bodies pressed together, a sweet embrace that both of us desperately needed.

The trees of middle California rolled by as night came.

At night, the convoy stopped, and the soldiers assigned to us walked around to see buddies. A low-ranking soldier ran up to the jeep, visiting Charles, spreading news as he did every few hours. "San Francisco, Sacramento, Oakland, the whole Bay Area wiped out. Nothin' left but debris, same as Portland. They're everywhere, taking out the major cities . . ." His voice trailed off as the two walked away. They left the four of us alone again.

Tortilla seized my hand. "Thick skin," he said.

"Do I have thick skin?" Jane asked. "It feels the same as before."

"It's the thickest, toughest skin around," Tortilla lied. "An alion would have to be melted to come after you again. But if they do, we're all here, standing guard."

Burnhammer checked in again a short while later. "They tell me the ride is almost done. We're going up into the hills, to a secret base under Mount Baldy. Never been there, but apparently it's one of the ten last resort bases. I guess it's like a small city, places for civvies."

Jane grew excited. "We'll be safe there?"

"You betcha, kiddo," Burnhammer replied, smiling. "I've been told survivors can settle in until we exterminate the infestation."

"Can I help . . . with the extermination?" Amanda asked.

"I think your days having to use your weapons are over, kiddo. You won't have to until you're old enough and choose to enlist. When we get to Mount Baldy, you can relax again."

Amanda frowned at that; I could tell she detested being treated like a little girl. Her angered cheeks puffed, and she scooted to the back of the jeep, lying down on the bench in a sullen pout. Jane followed her.

I slipped down from the jeep to stand next to Burnhammer. "Corporal Burnhammer, can I ask you something?"

"If it's not classified, I'll answer." She situated her assault rifle to rest across her stomach, hanging from a shoulder strap.

"How did your entire brigade survive?"

"The entire brigade didn't survive, but most of us were underground when the alions—" She smiled when she said the silly word— "Started taking the masses. The complex was designed with aluminum built in the walls, and intelligence thinks that's one of the tricks that saved us, but they don't really know for sure."

Tortilla and I smiled at each other, probably with the biggest grins anyone could ever have. "We had aluminum foil above our beds. We thought that's why we survived," Tortilla informed the corporal.

Burnhammer laughed. "Well I'll be damned. Maybe it's true then."

"I guess so," I said, laughing.

"Well anyway, our brigade was stationed at Tooga's Training Facility, a military base outside Rockcreek." She must have seen the confusion written on my face. "Rockcreek lies about twenty klicks west of Portland, so that's why we were able to rescue survivors in the area. We survived because we got lucky, just like you."

"That's certain," Tortilla said. "Do you think we can exterminate them like you said?"

"So far it's been a losing battle, but once we regroup, organize, and make some plans of attack, yes, I think we'll have a chance. The problem was when they started taking people, we didn't know what was going on, it was all done so fast . . . the alions made sure our reactions were panic and confusion, and because of that, we didn't regroup to strategize our next moves." Her voice was sad and mournful, yet a hope traced her heavy words.

"Do you know anything about other countries, what they are doing to combat the alions?"

"I haven't heard anything as of yet. I suppose they are scrambling like us."

Suddenly, loud, thick roars boomed through the convoy and drowned out her voice. They came from all directions, a circle of calls, instilling fear. The alions had us surrounded with what sounded like thousands of soldiers.

Burnhammer spun around, searching the tree line. The grass grew tall before the trees, tall enough to hide a crouching alion. The unending roars never faltered. Deep, powerful, and shocking, they rattled my body, shaking the ground beneath my feet.

Voices yelled down and up the column. Most were commands, but screams of panic mixed in, shrills thick with fear. The roaring was unimaginable: it was a sea of horrific calls that knelled our death sentence. I had watched animal shows about lions before, groups of 30 or 40, all crying to each other, singing songs in the night. But this was different. These roars were filled with pure malice. And they were crawling toward us, creeping upon our position, slow and threatening. They wanted us to piss our pants, and I did. I soaked my thighs. The warmth quickly turned cool.

Burnhammer grabbed my shirt collar and threw me into the back of the jeep. I had no idea she possessed such strength. She handled my body like a toy. She jumped onto the bed and opened up a weapon case stacked against the middle right wall of the box-bed. She threw out the foam padding and jerked out a sleek black and tan submachine gun. She punched it against my chest.

I took it with both my hands. "What is it?" I yelled, trembling from the constant roars.

"The KRISS VP55. It's the best submachine gun on the planet, slower than the OMP2, but there's no recoil and no muzzle climb; it shoots straight and true every time, even on full auto." She picked up four magazines and placed them in my pockets. "You'll need these." She leaned in close to my ear so that no one else could overhear. "I think this will be our last stand, Maggy. You protect the little ones with every ounce you have left, you hear me?"

I stared up at her, tears oozing from my eyes. I nodded slowly.

She rushed back to the case and found another one for Tortilla. He accepted it with a bruise to his chest. She stooped down and snatched up her assault rifle resting against the jeep's bed. Floodlights flashed on, shining across the grass, scanning the border where the tall evergreens stood. I peeked out into the darkness and saw nothing but grass and trees.

The roars continued to quake the Earth. Gunfire exploded down the convoy. Rockets ignited by the trees. The forest lit up in a giant blaze. An alion swooshed out of the grass and ran past a soldier who carried the rocket launcher, snapping its jaws around the soldier's ankle, hauling him off into the grass on the other side of the road.

It all happened in a bat of the eye. The man screamed and pulled the trigger. A spray of saltwater jetted out the back of the launcher. The rocket burst from the tube, zoomed through the air, then exploded as it impacted a nearby tank. A single soldier jumped out of the burning tank, afire and running wildly into the grass, until death found the soldier in the forest.

Another alion zipped through the convoy. Soldiers shot their heavy assault rounds, huge shotgun cartridges, and speeding machinegun bullets. For all the projectiles of death thrown at the alions, I didn't see one dying or dead.

An ear-splitting scream rent the air to the side of the jeep. Burnhammer poked her head around in a flash. Her breathing remained calm. "Ready?" she asked us. Amanda had her gun raised, sitting on the bench, hunched over Jane.

Tortilla nodded.

My vision remained glued to the square view of the jeep's tail. I kept my finger off the trigger; I didn't want to accidentally shoot a friendly if they rushed by, and I knew I would clamp the trigger the moment I saw anything. My fingers twitched and twitched.

A man ran by, another civilian, screaming: "THE END! THE END!" He ran into the grass where streams of bullets sought to kill the advancing alions.

When I glanced around the corner, I didn't see any alions coming, just grass. Gunfire and alion roars rattled my head.

"They're toying with us," Burnhammer yelled. She knelt down on one knee. Fear was starting to shake her. The longer we waited, the more our nerves broke down: it was inevitable.

In a blink, an alion sprung from the tank behind us, landing before the jeep's bed. A roar washed over me, a wave so intense that I dropped the submachine gun, and I stood there unarmed and unhinged.

It pounced up at us, claws out, ready to tear us to shreds.

"DIE! DIE! DIE!" I heard Burnhammer holler. Her bullets punctured the alion's skull and chest, flying through its body and into the tank behind. The carcass slipped from the jeep's bed. She stepped to the edge and sunk a dozen deathly rounds into the body. Blood gushed out.

Tortilla had dropped his gun as well. Amanda stood there quivering, unable to shoot.

The corporal jumped down, alive with adrenaline, a murderous glint in her hungry eyes. She joined the mindless firing into the woods, seeking to find an enemy target, hoping that the bullets hit a furry mark. A world of bloodlust swept in. Soldiers all around bore the same glint in their eyes.

The scene lasted for an hour or so, bullets and roars crossing, but not more visible deaths. The forest fire burned for long hours after, but there was nothing to be done about it, except hope that it didn't spread near the road, and thanks to the good graces of the wind, it stayed far from us.

Early light powered up the solar panels. Soldiers went out searching for carcasses, to see the damage they had inflicted in the blind night.

Burnhammer approached, bearing an armload of sandwiches. She sat down on a bench. "Five, five carcasses . . . that's all we found. It sounded like thousands, but they had these." She dropped a box that resembled a speaker. "They really were playing with us . . . vile tricks." She ground her teeth in anger. "All those roars, made from these. So far, we've found dozens of them scattered all over, in bushes and trees, some of them melted down to a pile of whatever it's made of, some plastic it feels like." She stopped and caught a whiff of the sickening smell. Instantly she recognized the scent. "I'll have someone bring you all a change of clothes. Hopefully we can find some spares for the young ones."

At that, the corporal left us, and another guard took over. Corporal Gardner, a thin, short black woman, talked us through the traumatizing events of last night. She had been training as a counselor before the alions came. Her hair was matted and unwashed, but so was mine. She spoke with a gentle voice, soothing, repairing our shattered spirits. She helped Jane most of all, who took a strong liking to Gardner the instant she stepped foot onto the jeep's bed.

A sour, grim-faced man brought us a change of clothes, dropping them off and almost running away, as if afraid of children.

By midmorning, the convoy started up their engines and pressed on. The day passed without horrors or atrocities. We reached Mount Baldy at twilight. The compound was heavily fortified, with guards posted everywhere. The walls that surrounded the mountain entrance were three meters thick at least. Automatic turrets shifted atop the walls in a row, with the smallest gap between each to allow them to move around; otherwise, they stood side by side. Remote-controlled toy helicopters patrolled the area close to the perimeter walls, circling the woods.

We stopped at checkpoints until we finally rolled into a garage the size of three of four football fields. The building was crawling with soldiers, mechanics, and other personnel, along with tanks, jeeps, four-wheelers, and several vehicles I had never seen before. They gathered us up with other civilians at the far right end of the space. Officers barked orders for all to remain calm.

I counted up all the civilians: 47. That was all they had rescued from Portland. 47. Four of us weren't even from Portland, and at that moment, I wondered if the others were from different areas too. Before I could ask anybody, they scooted us off into several elevators. Down and down and down we shot. The elevator stopped at level 41. A woman soldier with bright red hair asked us to go left, so we did, walking through a long corridor into a big open room like a gym, with yellow hardwood floors. Five white booths were set up with banners hanging above them displaying groups of letters: A-E, F-K, L-P, Q-U, and V-Z.

"I think they were expecting a bigger crowd," I said to Tortilla.

"Yeah . . ." he rasped, his voice weak and grating.

We walked over to the L-P line; three people stood in front of us. Jane and Amanda followed our heels. "What are your last names?" I asked Jane.

"Whitestone," Amanda blurted out.

"She asked me, not you." Jane pinched her sister.

"Not here," I commanded.

They ceased immediately. Amanda slipped between Tortilla and I.

"We'll get you signed in once we're done," I promised. I could see the impatience growing in their eyes. Their bodies became antsy and squirmy, fidgeting with their hands as they stood.

The civilian man speaking with the soldier behind the table moved out of line and we took a step forward. Tortilla went first when our turn came. He answered the woman's questions in a shy, reserved voice. "Félix Portillo. Seventeen. Bellingham, Washington. It's by the border of Canada. Single child. Both were taken . . ."

After they were done, I stepped forward.

The woman eyed me with distaste. It was evident the soldier hated her menial task. "Your name?"

"Maggy Li."

"Age?"

"Sixteen. No wait, what day is it?"

"It's April Fool's Day, hon," she answered.

I gawked at her for a second. I turned around and found Tortilla's eyes. "Today is my birthday. I completely forgot . . ."

He frowned. "I did too. I'm sorry."

The soldier hustled me along. "So you're 17 then?"

I nodded at her. "Yes. What a birthday, huh?"

"Better than if you had it a week ago," she replied curtly. "City and State of origin?"

I answered the rest of her questions, and she gave me a temporary I.D. card, so that I could move around the facility, otherwise we were restricted to our quarters. Jane and Amanda received their I.D. cards, and then they shuffled us off to another level, where apartments lined the corridor. I estimated two hundred or more. A soldier led us to our apartment: 49. It was a three bedroom: one for the twins, one for me, and one for Tortilla. Tortilla and I were each given a key. We unlocked the door and it swung wide.

"Thanks," I said to the soldier as he walked away.

He turned. "Someone will be by shortly to see that you're all settled." With a smile, he spun on his heels and left us.

The walls around felt sturdy, as if they could withstand a massive blast. A furnished living room was all set up with a TV and movies to watch. A kitchenette lay to the right of the entrance, stocked with cookware, silverware, and everything else we needed. With all the electricity flowing through the compound, it was evident that the base did not rely on the solar stations for energy.

Jane ran to the couch and switched on the TV. A network of old shows came up, an archive of 90 years or more.

A young soldier stopped in to check on how we fared a short while later. "You look like you're adjusting to the apartment," she commented.

"I guess so," I replied. Though I'm not sure how she gauged her observation; we had only been there a few hours, and we didn't have much to put away.

"I brought some fresh clothes, based on the sizes you gave us when you signed in. I hope they all fit well enough."

I nodded at her. "Do you know how I can contact Corporal Burnhammer?"

"Who was that?"

"Corporal Burnhammer. She's in the 56th Infantry Division."

"Hon, almost everyone here is in the 56th. I'm sure I can track her down, though. Is there a message you want relayed?" She placed the bag full of clothes on the dining table.

"Just tell her our apartment number, and ask her to stop by when she can," I said.

She wrinkled her brow. "Sure, I can do that, but I can't make any promises she'll come. Most likely she's got her hands full, as you can probably guess from the chaos above."

"All right, well I'd appreciate it anyway," I said with a courteous smile.

She nodded as she walked towards the door. "Yeah, you folks have a nice night. Try to get some nice long hours in; I'm sure you need it after what you've been through," she said, as if she knew the details of our horrific journey.

I waved a hand as I closed the door.

"That was strange . . . the way she looked at you when you told her to ask Burnhammer to stop by."

"That's certain. You think she'll tell Burnhammer?" I asked him.

"I don't know why she wouldn't," he responded, yawning.

Jane and Amanda were already rifling through the bag of clothes, tossing aside the articles too big for them. They began to argue over who got what, pinching each other all over. Once all the disputes were settled, and the clothes distributed, it didn't take long for them to pass out on the couch, watching *The Mansion On Mouse Hill*, a big animated movie released two years ago.

Tortilla and I closed the door to the room I had chosen. "Should we sleep together with them here?" I raised the question.

He adjusted his spectacles. "Why not, we slept on the bus together, and at the mall."

"Yeah, but this is private, there's a door between us now. They might think . . ."

"If you don't want to, I'm okay with that. I'll sleep in the other room."

"I think it's best until we really settle in," I told him.

"Settle in? So we're staying here? What about Darrel?"

"We have no idea where Jelly is . . . how do we find something when we don't know where to look?"

"We start at the JPL . . . we'll find something to fly."

"The two of us? The two of us against spaceships loaded with alions, how is that going to work out?" I whispered. "We have to face reality, bromigo, we can't find him on our own. Maybe from here we can learn more and come up with a better plan."

"And we're really not going to stay together tonight?" he said, changing subjects.

"No. Not tonight."

He nodded. "All right. Well, I'll see you in the morning then." His face bore his disappointment and irritation. He had really gotten used to sleeping with his body next to mine. When he left, I turned off the light, and slipped under the covers. The only light in the room came from an alarm clock, a soft red glow projected on to the ceiling.

After a few hours of tossing and turning, I got up and walked out into the living area. The TV flashed white, then blue, then green, as the scenes changed from a new movie. I crept into Tortilla's room and climbed between the covers. I wrapped an arm around him as the big spoon.

"Can't sleep either?" he asked.

"Nope," I replied. We rolled together so that he was now the big spoon.

He gently squeezed me and whispered, "Goodnight."

"Goodnight," I replied.

It was 72 degrees and cozy. I fell asleep instantly.

I heard a knock. Then a second. Then a third. Realizing that it wasn't my dream, I slipped out of Tortilla's arm, and went out to the living area. Another knock came from the door. When I opened it, Burn-hammer stood outside, ready to knock again.

She smiled at me. "I was beginning to think they told me the wrong apartment and level."

"I thought I was dreaming," I told her.

"How are you adjusting?" She nodded at the accommodations of the apartment, as it tried to emulate normal life, but we both saw that it was false. We were untold meters below the surface. It wasn't a life anyone of us would have chosen.

"It was nice to sleep without so much fear. I had a few nightmares, but I had a few good dreams too."

"There will be a time when all the good dreams come back," she said. "I came to tell you that General Kramer and Senator Stowitz are going to speak in the general auditorium in an hour. Apparently, they have some answers to the invasion, and to what exactly is happening out there, which I'll be glad to learn. It's open to everyone, even civvies. I sent you the directions, you can check the PocketPad, and you might want to bring it anyway, to record what they say. Good or bad, it will be monumental."

"In an hour?" I asked.

"In an hour," she answered. "I'll be sitting with the Shadow Stalkers to the left when you walk in to the door I mapped out."

"All right, I'll be there." I waved goodbye as she left. The twins were still asleep, the TV voices gave comfort, and it didn't look like they would be waking any time soon. I shuffled into Tortilla's room and nudged his shoulder. He didn't stir, so I shook him awake, then told him about the speech.

The hot water of the shower was revitalizing. I had forgotten its magical properties, its ability to refresh the body, as if it made me a completely new person, ready to take on new challenges. I still had to deal with old ones though, but now I wanted to, as hope bloomed anew within my mind.

In 45 minutes, we had showered, dressed, and eaten. PocketPad in hand, we navigated the many levels of the compound. Most of the floors were restricted to civilians; the elevator simply would not open, flashing RESTRICTED on the digital display above the doors. The higher we climbed, the more packed it became, until floor three, where people rushed out in droves. The auditorium spanned a few levels, and we walked up a flight of stairs to level two, to the door pointed out by Corporal Burnhammer. To the left, a dozen or so Shadow Stalkers sat, waiting for the event to begin. The rest must have been on duty.

Burnhammer saved us two seats near the end of the row. She nodded as we sat down in the red velvet padded chairs. They were soft and contoured to our specific shapes. "Made it in time."

I nodded back at her. "There are a lot of restricted levels," I commented. "Yet we're supposed to feel at home . . ." My voice trailed off, as a man in a solid-black, three-piece suit took to the stage 50 to 60 rows down below us.

"It's the same way for the lot of us. Only scientists and officers are granted access to most of the levels. A real short end, if you ask me." She hushed up when the man on stage cleared his throat.

"Thank you . . . thank you all for coming. This morning, Senator Stowitz, along with General Kramer will explain what they know about our situation, and will try to answer any questions as best they can. I kindly ask for no comments or commotions during their initial speeches, and that you reserve any words for the end. I also ask you to be polite and respectful when forming your questions; this is a delicate hour, and no one wants haste, anger, or frustration to cloud the room.

Thank you. With that said, I would like to introduce Senator Stowitz and General Kramer."

General Kramer stepped forward from behind a black curtain to the left of the stage. His matte blue uniform bore a single star on each shoulder. He forewent the standard beret, displaying a proudly shaven sunburnt head, wrinkled and lumpy, and as shiny as the new stars designating his authority.

Behind the general, Senator Stowitz, dressed in a slim-fitting blue suit and red necktie, walked onto the stage as applause sang a song of approval. He waved left and right and left again.

As the noise died, General Kramer stepped up to the podium centered on the stage and gave a salute. In seconds all sounds stopped. Soldiers and civilians resisted their urges to talk, and suppressed any heavy breathing. The auditorium grew dead silent. "Life as we know it is at an end." His voice rang in the auditorium. "We are at war with an enemy never before seen on Earth . . . with technology surpassing our own . . . and untold numbers of soldiers, more than likely a great many beyond all the remaining survivors. We enter into a new era, where we must marshal new strength, new life, new determination, and a new unity, one the likes our race has never known. We have had loved ones taken from us . . . seen our homes marked by strange symbols . . . and had to defend ourselves with the most basic of weapons." A long pause came over the general. "What I am going to say next is virtually unprecedented in the United States of America." He emphasized his last words, giving them a quality that inspired the heart.

"What I mean to do today, is give every willing and able man, woman, and child over the age of thirteen, a weapon to defend themselves with, which many of you brave souls have had to wield during the absence of your protectors, your leaders and law officers, your military strength and scientific vigilance, those that have made us feel safe since the birth of our Great Nation. I ask for volunteers to step forward to fight for our freedom . . . for our land . . . for our very survival.

"To those who will take up arms, a crash training course will be given. To those who wish not to participate in field engagement, we ask that you contribute in any way that you can. We have need for teachers, custodians, miners, computer technicians, engineers . . . I am afraid to say this, but if ever it were truly appropriate, it is today . . . Uncle Sam wants you . . . he wants all of you.

"I would not say these words unless our cause was desperate, and believe me, I do not speak them without a heavy heart, for I know what

I am asking, especially of those many who feel too young to be included, but without hands to hold our guns, we are few and defenseless. To elaborate on our dire situation, I will turn the floor over to Senator Stowitz, who will give you the details that we know." The general stepped back.

I looked around: mouths gaped, people gasped—soldiers and civilians alike—and no one sat without attentive ears, listening to take in every last word. Despite the shock that had just hit the audience, no one spoke, waiting on the edge of their seats.

Senator Stowitz stepped forward so that the room had eyes only for him. "As far as we know, the entire western and eastern seaboards have been devastated. Seattle is gone. Portland is gone. San Francisco, Sacramento, San Diego, Los Angeles . . . all decimated. Boston, Philadelphia, New York, New Jersey, Dover, Norfolk, Charleston, Miami . . . the list goes on and on. Washington has been leveled. As far as we know, the president and her next fourteen successors have been taken. I have been told that the Secretary of Energy, Leo Sterling, is being held down in a complex like this one, outside of Fort Worth, Texas.

"As for the world outside our borders, reports suggest that half of Mexico City has been destroyed. Shanghai, Tokyo, Seoul, Delhi, São Paulo, Moscow, Hong Kong, London, Cairo, Berlin—what I'm trying to say is that the world has been devastated, but not beyond the point of recuperation. We can rebuild. We can renew. We can bring ourselves out of the darkness, but it is going to take every one of us, we cannot afford the laws and ethics of the past to infiltrate and fog our future. What we are asking our children to do is unsettling, atrocious, and compromising of old standards. But if we do not ask our children to join the military ranks, we very well may not have a future on this Earth.

"They are our last line."

Shouts from the crowd pierced the silence. Voices spoke against the extremely young fighting in combat, against training child soldiers.

An image of Amanda flashed in my mind: she held her pistol, rapidly pulling the trigger, killing alions left and right. I knew she could handle it. Killing an alion wasn't the same as killing a man, and Amanda had nearly done that. If she could, the older ones could too.

Tortilla leaned into me. "Do you think this is wise?"

"If it's not wise, it's necessary," I replied.

He looked astonished by my words. "13-year-olds?"

"Amanda is eleven."

By his reaction, I could tell he had forgotten that fact. "Eleven," he repeated to himself.

A few of the Shadow Stalkers made comments to each other, accepting what needed to be done. Burnhammer leaned over the armrest. "Are you going to volunteer?" she asked Tortilla and I.

I looked at him to confirm my assumption. "Of course," I told her. "We have some vengeance to fulfill."

"I'm glad to hear it," she said. "You two would make fine Shadow Stalkers."

A man near the front yelled out: "Why are they here? How did they get past our space defenses?" Others grew bold once the first voice had put forth their thoughts. It was something I wanted to know as well.

Stowitz raised a hand to silence the crowd. "Please . . . please." His words were lost in the clamor of growing voices.

"SILENCE!" General Kramer screamed. The crowd obeyed, beaten down by his powerful presence and commanding tone.

The senator nodded at the general for his support. "I know that is the prevailing, dominant question: how did these aliens slip past our defenses . . . To all of you, it is a mystery, and it shames me that I know the truth.

"I will tell you, but you must listen, and judge me not until the very end of what I have to say." He waited until nods were requesting that he continue. "Two years ago, Earth's population was approaching 37 billion. Water supplies, even with advances in seawater desalination, were still declining considerably. Food supplies were on the brink of collapse. Unemployment was peaking. Even the very space with which to live was dramatically affected by soaring numbers. Society has been living on the edge these last few years, and we, your government officials, along with all the other government officials, decided a drastic plan was called for.

"That same year, at the World Summit, we met to discuss what actions could be taken. That's when a scientist from Japan played us a recording. It was a message sent to our planet from space over fifty years ago, and ever since, the Japanese had been working on translating it. They succeeded. The translation called for aid, food, and water, anything we were willing to spare. Their species was at war with another species, and they couldn't produce enough supplies to keep up the war effort. A description of their diet was included in the message."

Everyone in the audience, including myself, tensed; as if all could sense what the senator was about to say. I didn't want him to, but I knew it was coming . . . the words were on the edge of his tongue, about to roll off.

"Animals fit their needs. Humans fit their needs."

Shock and horror rang out in the audience. General Kramer looked appalled, possibly even stunned, as if he had been kept in the dark. When the uproar of the crowd became too much, the general stepped forward and yelled for silence.

"We believed the situation dire, and so was that of these aliens . . . it was never supposed to be like this," he cried. The senator scrambled in front of the podium and kneed. "The deal we made with them was only for one percent . . . only one percent of the population. We powered down our auto defenses when they arrived, the entire Planetary Defense Network . . . and then there was nothing we could . . . we never imagined."

The crowd could no longer sit and listen to the abominable words the senator was saying. Angry cries were called out: "You killed us! Extinction bringer!" As the seconds advanced, the calls evolved into a single word: "Murderer!"

"Please—please—please. I beg your forgiveness. We didn't know! We didn't know. The aliens weren't supposed to take so many; it wasn't the agreement. We didn't know." He sobbed in front of us all. He turned into a heap of emotion, tears spilling from his red eyes, his body trembling.

The general shook his head. Eyes open and staring into nothingness, he just shook his head. He looked as if he didn't know what to do next.

An officer in the front row drew the pistol holstered at his hip. BANG . . . BANG. BANG.

The senator hit the imitation-wood flooring.

People screamed in panic, until they realized what had happened, then cheers rent the enclosed space. Their cries of retribution rattled the auditorium.

General Kramer peered at the senator's corpse with disgust.

I could feel the hatred in the air from all the bodies of the living. We had all been betrayed. I gazed at Tortilla.

His eyes met mine, full of streaming tears. He shook his head as well. "How could this have happened like this . . . our own leaders . . . our own . . ."

"I don't know," I said, my voice cracking. I shuddered. "I don't—" I started to say when my eyes sighted a soldier running down the steps of the lower level. He leapt up the stage and whispered into the general's ear.

General Kramer nodded and dismissed the man. Walking up to the podium he asked for silence. No one listened. Then he demanded silence. Everyone obeyed. "Private Locke has just informed me that a strange mark has been discovered on top of the buildings that surround the complex. It is a single bar coming out of a horizontal line. The last of the three marks." He paused and sucked in a deep breath. "We now know they are coming for us and most likely soon. I want volunteers to line up at the right end of the auditorium, down in the staging area. Soldiers, return to your superiors for orders." His words were rushed and his movements frantic.

"This could be our last stand." His words echoed. "We now know why they are here, we are food to them, and we can guess why they are still here, using our planet as a training ground, while they weed out those of us who remain. I ask you . . . I ask you to remember, remember those who you are fighting for, remember those who have been taken, and those who have died. Remember our strength, our perseverance, and our intelligence; and the very thing that makes us human, the core of our species . . . remember our love.

"Remember these things in the coming darkness, and know that we stand united: a unit of anger fueled by the will to survive. Stand strong, stand composed, stand as one."

A wave of HOOAH thundered in the auditorium. The end of his speech penetrated the very hearts of his soldiers. Blood boiling, the soldiers were moved to a state of charged preparation, awaiting the enclosing noose with determination in their eyes.

His speech moved me too, somehow, some way unbeknownst to my mind, as my blood was charged with energy, and I was ready to unleash my fury at the alions.

The room became busy with movement, with soldiers running out, and civilians running down to the staging area.

I turned to Burnhammer. "You should go enlist," she said. "Both of you."

"We need to get to Pasadena," I blurted.

She eyed me curiously. "Pasadena, why Pasadena?"

"We need to get to NASA's Jet Propulsion Lab." A plan formulated in my head. If the end was near for all, then it didn't matter if we died aboard an alion ship; all that mattered was that we gave it a shot. "We know that they were working on unmanned space fighters there, and we could try to use them to board the International Space Station to fire up the Planetary Defense Network. The whole system is offline."

"We would also have to power up a Solar Station," she remarked. "And how do you know they were working on space fighters there?"

"Jacob, the one we lost in Portland, he told us his father was on the project. And no, the Space Station has its own solar panels, remember?"

She paused and hung her head, searching her mind. "I'll bring the plan to my commander, this has to be taken to the general."

I grabbed her arm as she jumped to her feet. "There's no time."

"If you want this plan to succeed, then there's time," she replied. "Go back to your quarters for now. I'll come for you as soon as I have word."

I frowned. Tortilla and I left the auditorium, but before we rounded the corner of the door, I saw the line of volunteers; it wound around to the back, and back down an aisle. Hundreds wanted to fight. I gauged 4/5 of the civilians that had sat in the audience now waited to enlist.

Knocks rapped our apartment door thirty minutes later. Burnhammer smiled as I swung it open. "Approved," she said. "They didn't want you two to come at first, but I argued in your favor since it was your plan. You can take the little ones to the care center, they will be safer there."

I nodded. I had already explained the situation to the twins. Amanda ardently protested being left out. Jane didn't want to part ways either, but she also didn't want us to leave the facility. "Lead the way," I said. We had everything packed and ready to go. I brought nothing for a long journey, as I hoped they would give us transportation.

We dropped the twins off at the care center. Jane sobbed helplessly. Amanda screamed for us not to exclude her, yelling, "I'm old enough! I'm old enough!" A bulky guard stopped them at the door.

"Since we do not know if the unmanned fighters have room for passengers, the plan has been altered; instead, we are going to use them to strike at the ship above L.A.," Burnhammer informed us of the modification.

"Jacob seemed to think that a person could fit in one," Tortilla, who hadn't spoken much since the meeting, chimed in. "If they can fit people, what then?"

"Then we are to proceed with your original plan," she said. "But that's a big *if*."

We raced down a long corridor to an elevator. Up we went. Burn-hammer brought us to an armory three times the size of the apartment they had given us. Several different types of guns were neatly racked along the walls, and on tall, wide shelves on wheels in the middle of the room. All of it was orderly. She found Tortilla a shotgun and spare bullets. "400 RPMs and no recoil," she boasted. Then she asked if I had liked the submachine gun she had given me before. I nodded, and she handed me two. For her own hands, she grabbed an assault rifle with Barrett M968 imprinted above the magazine clip. She also grabbed a shorter gun similar to her assault rifle. "It's called a Personal Defense Weapon, shorter and lighter than a standard assault rifle, but it keeps up the range. Good for cramped situations."

After we loaded up on weapons, which outnumbered people ten to one, if not by more, she led us to a crate stocked full of military cloth-ing: Vests, jackets, pants, boots, belts, and everything else. "These are part of the DS45 uniform, adopted three years ago. It's called Dragon Scale. Trust me, it will save your life."

"From 25-centimeter teeth that can exert a few thousand kilograms of pressure?" Tortilla asked, guessing about the power of the alions' jaws.

Burnhammer chuckled. "No, probably not from that. But maybe a few of those black bullets they shoot."

We nodded, then dressed, covering ourselves in the lightweight armored-clothing. The clothes fit over our regular clothes, still light and somewhat breathable with both sets on. Burnhammer led us to another hangar, where the entire 2nd platoon geared up and assembled by three jeeps. The head of the platoon, Lieutenant Laffrado, greeted us when Burnhammer scooted us in his direction.

"I've heard you two have made quite the addition to Henderson's squad," Laffrado said. "Well, good, in these times we need capable ad-ditions. We have no time to train you, just do as you're told, and for God's sakes, don't shoot any of my soldiers. Are we clear?"

I looked up at the lieutenant. He was a tall, wiry man. He looked strong, but not as crazy hulky as some of the other soldiers we had seen. "Yes, sir," I replied. Tortilla followed up with a yes sir of his own.

"Good, good." Laffrado smiled and waved some laggers over. "Burnhammer will keep you informed and under her guard. She's one of the finest young corporals I've seen, so know that you're in good hands."

Henderson, along with Loritz and another squad leader, joined

Laffrado, discussing the route we should take to the JPL. "Shadow Stalkers!" Laffrado yelled. "Gather round." He waved his men in close. "You know the mission by now, we have to get to NASA's JPL. We'll be taking two scientists with us, and two 17-year-olds, who have fought with the 3rd squad already. Our route is simple, a straight shot down the main road to 210, and we'll find our exit about 48 klicks west after we hit the highway. We're ten down from our usual 31, but we're strong and determined, so let's get the job done. HOOAH!"

The platoon thundered HOOAH back at Laffrado.

As the platoon loaded up the jeeps, two women strolled up with computer gear and other gadgets. The taller one with long black hair walked up to us with a smile. "You're not soldiers," she observed. "You must be the two that devised the plan. It is nice to meet you. I am Doctor Strafford, and this is my associate, Doctor Sutton." She offered her slim hand to us.

I shook and released. Dr. Sutton made her way over, but did not offer her hand, and she spoke nothing to us. Her shorter brown hair curled in a frizzy mane. Her eyes were cold and tired, as if only awake because of the graces of the coffee bean. The two were loaded up in the first jeep a second later.

Suddenly a siren broke our silence. "They're here," Laffrado shouted. "Goddammit. Hold on." He ran off into the main yard. He returned a moment later. "An army of the alien bastards has been sighted making their way up the main road, so we can't go that way. We'll have to take the back roads that connect to highway 2, then make our way west from there. It joins back up with 210 near the JPL exit." He explained the rest of the details to his platoon, then dismissed them to their vehicles.

Tortilla and I followed Burnhammer into the second jeep. The vehicles ran without making a sound; their fake engine noises must have been disabled. The platoon rolled out into the main yard. Giant howitzers were lined up a few meters from the compound wall. Missile launchers were parted behind the howitzers. Everywhere massive guns were prepped for the coming onslaught. Soldiers gathered civilians in an empty hangar across the yard. I could see the fear in their trembling bodies. They looked just like me.

The remote-controlled helicopters flew in and out of the compound. Soldiers ran from one building to another, out into the main yard, and around the giant guns; they were hurrying back and forth in every direction, near chaotic, as they primed all possible weapons and secured all possible vulnerable points.

We turned left, heading towards the northeast section of the compound, around the mountain entrance. We stopped as the driver of the first jeep handed a soldier guarding the gate a green slip of paper. They saluted each other and we were on our way as the gate parted.

Trees began to blur as we zipped down the rugged road. I was bouncing all over the place, using my seatbelt and the door to brace my movements.

Then I saw a yellow ball drop from the sky.

An instant later, the first jeep was blown from the road in a ball of fire. The trees around us ignited in a sea of red and yellow. The heat pressed upon us as yellow bombs exploded all around.

Tortilla grabbed my arm. Our eyes locked. "I love you," he yelled above the crackling flames. "I love you."

The words scared me, scared me more than I had ever been scared in my entire life. It meant it was the end. I could barely see him with my blurry vision, but I reached out and touched his face. "I love you."

The front of the jeep caught fire and exploded, sending the vehicle to its side. As the red and yellow that pierced my vision turned to black, I heard the screams of soldiers, and the repeated cry of, "NO!"

Then I heard nothing but the crackle of death.

9
Go Engines, Go
Darrel

As the swiping claws plunged at me, I watched the last black globe I had fired, now trapped within the blue suspension field. No lightning bolts struck the bullet. Unstopped, it approached the edge of the cloud at almost a crawl.

The globe penetrated the barrier.

The world of blue shattered, evaporating into nothing. Bullets resumed launching from the alion gun.

Black globes suddenly riddled the alion. Blood sprayed everywhere. My faced dripped with the horrific crimson, mixing with my sweat. My stomach wanted to shoot out my mouth, but I battled it back down, calming my nerves. I swallowed. The metallic taste of iron engulfed my tongue. I spat. A few coughs rattled my chest, and I spat a couple more times, clearing my throat afterward.

I didn't want to faint, so I slapped myself, but that didn't help at all. My heavy eyes closed, and I was swimming in summer's warmth. When I opened them, the walls blurred, and were too fuzzy to make out with any distinctions. I reached, but there was nothing within grasp, and I collapsed to the grating.

I rolled over.

Hours passed before my vision cleared. Or maybe it had only been minutes. I sat up, holding my knees, breathing deep and slow. The dead alion lay a meter or two away. Its blood had pooled, now motionless and shiny, reflecting my face back to my eyes. I hated what I saw.

Everything about me now screamed of enervation. If the alions didn't kill me soon, my own weariness would.

My stomach rumbled.

I clutched the sides of my gut. Those cheese crackers had done nothing to ease my hunger pangs. I ran back to the stockroom and grabbed a few supplies, uncloaking and cloaking again. Returning to the torture room proved much more difficult than the last time I navigated from the dining hall. The halls looked different, with my memories faded instead of fresh, and I stumbled around each corner, surprised by every terrible sight reminding me I was on an alion spaceship.

Finally, I chanced upon the room. Penelope lay in the same place. Three alions now worked, fiddling with bodies, using strange instruments, touching screens to input calculations and adjust the angle of dozens of mechanical arms hanging from the ceiling.

Every other minute a bold nerve struck, and I was centimeters from jumping into action, on the verge of dashing into the room to scoop Penelope off the table and make a break for the exit at the other side of the room. But then another nerve pulsed within, a cowardly nerve, and I stood stock-still, staring.

If only I could freeze the ever-shifting laser that monitored the room. If I could put it in stasis like the people in the pods . . . or . . . the blue cloud . . .

I spun around and headed back to the dead alions. I left a trail of cheese crackers off to the side of each hall. Whether or not any alions could see them, I didn't know, and I pushed the consequences out of my mind of what would happen if they did.

I found the stockroom, unwashed and unnoticed by any alions. I ran for the second alion and its bazooka. Strapping it across my back, adjusting it tight, I uncloaked and cloaked, sprinting to rescue Penelope.

The cheese cracker trail made it ten times faster on the way back. I passed a few alions, but they paid me no heed, as if I didn't exist. I went to the room where I had climbed up a pod to stash the water in the duct. I left everything behind in the duct, carrying only the bazooka to the torture room.

The alions used both of their humanlike hands to fire the blue stasis-orbs, so I hunkered down to a knee, bracing myself by tightening all my muscles. I placed three fingers on the giant trigger. Courage waited for its moment to burst through my veins; it waited a good long while, as my eyes tracked the yellow line.

I pulled back.

A stasis-orb launched at the scanner. Within a blink, it was trapped in suspension. I adjusted my aim to the closest alion and fired. The second and third alion were snared an instant later, blue lightning bolts striking into their furry bodies. I swung the bazooka to my back, using the soft straps. I tightened the straps until they pinched my skin.

When I ran for Penelope, no sensor gave away my position, or alerted the dining hall full of alions to my presence. The buckles that held her down were difficult to undo, and the faster I tried to go, the longer it took, as the uncooperative buckles fought against my trembling fingers. The eyes of the alions seemed to stare directly at me. I had no idea how long the stasis cloud lasted, but with every passing second, my nerves told me they would fail soon. The straps released after a dozen CLICKS, and I snatched her up, huffing as I raced out of the room.

My muscles were too fatigued, and too weak at that, to push her into the duct. I searched for one of the square, padded rooms with a table, coming upon one three hallways later.

I laid her on the table. Her closed eyes darted all around underneath her lids. She looked as if she were dreaming about something pleasant. I waited as time passed at a rate slower than my mind could take. Agitated, paranoid, and afraid, I twitched while I paced from wall to wall.

My gaze never left Penelope.

Then suddenly, she coughed, bringing herself upright at the waist. She gasped. "What the—"

"It's okay, it's okay," I said, running to her side. "You're okay now."

She swung her feet over the table. "Darrel?"

"I'm here," I said. "I'm here for you . . . Oh, right." I realized she couldn't hear or see me, so I pressed the button to uncloak. "See me now?"

"I can't believe . . ." she started.

I threw my arms around her in an embrace, squeezing. "I got you out. You're okay." My words were more for me than for her. I needed comforting.

"There was a cloud . . . I was trapped." She stuck out her hands. "I couldn't move."

Our eyes met. "I know. I was in one too. But we're okay now. Can you walk?"

She hopped down and took a few steps. "I feel pretty drained. Do you have any water or food?"

I nodded. "Yeah, I stashed some supplies in the duct." I grabbed ahold of her hand. "Do you think you can climb?"

"Maybe," she said. Her voice sounded worried. "I'll have to try."

I led her to the corridor where I had marked the pod I used to climb into the duct system. "The supplies aren't far from here," I said. "I'll push you when you're ready."

She nodded, though her eyes looked sedated, as though she were about to collapse. She gripped the thick plugs that attached to the pod, climbing up until she met the ceiling panels. I had jumped and popped up a panel before she began her struggle ascending the pod. Once her fingers clutched the panel's frame, I boosted her the rest of the way, grunting and panting.

I slipped as her legs left my hold.

She peeped over the edge. "You all right?"

"Yeah," I said, staring up at her. "I'm fine. Loss my balance is all . . . I'll be up in a minute. You should see the food to your right."

She smiled and retreated into the duct.

I gathered my breath. The effort had winded me after all the running and walking, all the pacing and worrying. It all took its toll. I clambered to my feet and headed up the pod when I figured enough of my strength had returned. Replacing the panel and tossing the bazooka aside, I lay down on my back, recuperating again.

"You need some sleep," she said. Her lips smacked as she chewed down a piece of salted meat.

I hoped it wasn't human muscle, but I didn't say anything; I knew she would throw it away at the thought, and we desperately needed it to survive. "Yeah, that's certain." I groaned, rolling over and pushing myself up on my knees. "Could you hand me the water?"

She offered me the bottle. "What happened? You said you rescued me . . . what did you rescue me from? Did they put me back in a pod?"

Taking the bottle, I shook my head. "Nope. They laid you out on a slab to experiment. They were torturing people in the room . . . but I got you out." I nodded, my body rocking. "I got you out."

"You all right, Darrel?"

"Probably not. I don't think too many people, if any at all, have seen what my eyes have taken in over the last few days." I set the bottle down with a CLINK. "There was a monitoring laser in the room, to detect intruders, at least I guessed as much. I killed an alion with one of those bazookas." I pointed to the silver tube. "It was all luck, but I did it, somehow . . . anyway, I froze the laser, along with a few alions. That's how I got you out . . ."

She stared at the bazooka. "Wow . . . just wow," she said. "I can't believe you did all that for me. You didn't—"

"It was my fault," I cut her off. "It was all my fault. I went up into the duct first. You went first all the other times, but not that time . . . it was my fault, I'm a coward."

She crawled over to me, wiped away the tears that had started to moisten my cheeks, and smiled at me. "You're not a coward, Darrel," she spoke softly. "You saved me, remember? Would a coward risk their life like that?"

I sniveled. My nose filled with globs of snot.

"No," she answered her own question. "No, they wouldn't." She held me, laying me back to the floor. "You need to rest. Take it easy." Behind me, she curled up, becoming the big spoon.

Penelope rolled over. Her hand slipped from my stomach and pinched my side.

Startled, I jumped awake. I turned and looked at her. Her eyes were still closed, and her slack mouth hung open, exhaling long, deep breaths. I slid down the grating until I could crawl without disturbing her body. I ate some of the meat. The salt bit at my lips and the inside of my mouth, while increasing my desire for a drink by tenfold.

Bottle in hand, I sipped twice and set it down, painfully aware of the amount remaining. I wasn't going to repeat what I had done before. My fingers shook in self-control; thirst gnawed at my nerves. "I don't need it," I whispered. "I don't . . ."

"You don't need what?" Penelope asked.

"I don't need to drink all the water," I explained. "I want to, but I don't need to."

"If you need more—"

"No. No, I'll survive. I think you need it more." I handed her the bottle.

She accepted it and drank her fill. "So, is getting the hell off this ship still on the agenda for today?" She smiled at me.

It was great to see her smile; it filled me with warmth that tingled all throughout my body. "I hope so." I smiled back.

"They took everything I had, including my cloaking device," she said. "What are we going to do about that?" She dug a hand into the box of cheese crackers.

"I could scout the ship by myself," I said, but before I could finish, she was already shaking her head.

"No, they know we're using the cloaks. They might have scanners that can detect us."

"They might not," I blurted. "You never know."

"Too dangerous."

"No more dangerous than you walking around without one," I said.

"Without one, you're cautious," she said. "And with one, you might get too comfortable, you know, your guard drops."

"So, what do we do?"

She chomped down on the golden crackers. "We should just go together," she suggested. "If they don't detect you, at least you'll get away."

"In that case, you should wear it." I loosened the straps to the device. "You should get rid of your . . . your . . ."

"My what?" Her brow furrowed. "Oh, right. My underwear."

I blushed. My face grew so hot; it was almost as if I had eaten a habanero.

She grinned at me. "I take it you've never talked about a girl's panties before. They're the same as yours, I'll bet. Only a lot smaller."

"Okay," I stuttered. I cleared my throat.

"You all right? They're just words."

"Uhrm. Fine . . . I'm fine."

She laughed. "Well, okay then. I'm going to go around the corner, I'll be right back."

I nodded. As she left, I breathed in deep, letting out a lengthy exhale. I finished stripping the cloaking device off my body.

"Hopefully that's good enough," she said, appearing from around the corner.

I smiled a red-cheeked smile. "Uhrm. We should just crawl in the ducts until we find a hangar bay." I definitely could have used my inhaler right then, but I had to rely on keeping control of my breathing.

"Yeah, that's what I was thinking, too."

I handed her the alion gun when she neared, grabbing the bazooka for myself. Penelope strapped on the invisibility harness, but forwent cloaking since I couldn't see her if she did. We started another long journey on our hands and knees. In every new duct we entered, we stopped and scoped out what lay beneath us, but all of the rooms were either living quarters or rooms with pods.

When my knees became good and sore, we stumbled upon a room storing water supplies. I lowered Penelope down—cloaked—and she filled up the bottle. The guards paid her no mind, though one of the two stopped for a second to take in a long sniff, but after it assessed its quality, it continued pressing images on a display.

The ceiling was low enough that she could jump and catch my arm. It took all I had, but I hoisted her up, heaving with a thousand puffs. We rested awhile and I dozed off.

"Hey," she whispered, poking my shoulder.

I heard her muffled speech, dulled in my head, as if it were coming from across a ballroom.

She poked me again. "Hey."

I sat up straight, my heart pumping, shocked. Gasping, I stared at her.

"It's all right, it's just me," she said reassuringly. "Sorry to wake you, but we should get going. I'm itching to leave."

I nodded. "Oh, I know. I'm just so tired all the time. This place is draining my life."

"All the more reason to hurry up and make our escape." She smiled as she handed me the water bottle. "Ready?" she asked when I capped the bottle.

I cleared my throat. "Yeah," I lied. My vision was blurring, and my arms and legs were shaking, but I didn't want her to get frustrated by waiting for me.

Our pace had slowed when we started off again. My motivation to escape was fought by fatigue, and it was becoming a losing battle.

"Your eyes are pretty droopy," Penelope observed a while later. "You sure you're okay to keep going?" Worry lines attacked her forehead.

"For a little bit longer, yeah. I think we're getting close. We have to be getting close . . ." Unconcealed desperation carried in my voice.

She frowned but kept going. On the third panel after our discussion, a cloud of steam hit our faces, like a refreshing sauna, though the warmth made me even sleepier. We waved the steam away, glad that it wasn't the blue mist that had been in the freezer room.

When the steam cleared, a sight like I had never seen before mesmerized my eyes. The room spanned a hundred stories or better, tiny lights shined in long rows everywhere, and ships buzzed in all directions.

"Wow," Penelope gasped.

"Wow," I duplicated.

She turned to me and grinned so wide I thought her lips might split. "We're going home."

"Or die trying," I declared.

She giggled. "Or die trying. Come on, we can't get down from here, we have to find another room to enter from."

I replaced the panel and followed as she crawled away. A few passages down, we happened on an empty square room. No convenient table awaited our feet, so I lowered myself first, falling to the grating. Groaning, I hopped to my feet and helped Penelope down, wrapping my arms below her knees.

The top floor of the hangar bay greeted us with a dejected tone of disuse.

"It's a scrapyard," she remarked. "These ships don't look flyable."

"Well let's not give up so easily. If it is a scrapyard, then the alions are unlikely to visit it often, which is a plus for us. There might be something here. Look how far it goes on." I pointed down the narrow walkway. To our sides, piles of abandoned junk piled high like mosaic towers. Gaps of open space were left between each pile, allowing for a view of the lower levels, though I couldn't distinguish much beyond the lights, walkways, and spaceships. If alions stalked the paths below us, I couldn't detect them.

"I guess it's worth a shot," she said. "But I will say I told you so when we find nothing but discarded alion parts." She headed off down the walkway.

We passed ship after ship, all with huge holes scattered throughout their hulls, as if a devastating weapon had shot them down. Mixed about the ships were rusting fragments of various metals, most I had never seen before, I just knew the feel when I touched them. I could have been wrong though.

"That looks like a microwave." Penelope pointed at a box with a panel of electronic buttons down one side of its front. "You think they cook using microwaves?"

I laughed. "A cat using a microwave, now that's a picture I never imagined."

"Did you imagine walking through an alion scrapyard, searching to steal a ship, all so that you could get back to an Earth where everyone has been taken?"

I shook my head. "I just imagined blowing up a spaceship," I said.

"I don't even know why, I just wanted to blow up a spaceship, you know, like in a movie."

"Well now's your chance for real," she replied.

"My chance? How?" I shook my head again. "We can't with all those people on board . . ."

"We can't rescue those people," she said. "But we might be able to help the survivors on Earth." She bent over and picked up a green canister that looked like an outdated muzzle of the gun she carried.

"Even if that's true, we don't have a way to blow up the ship, unless you have some explosives stashed in your back pocket. Though judging from their tightness, I don't think anything could fit in them." I stared at her, blushing after I realized what I had said. The words echoed in my ears.

She giggled, this time much louder than before, traveling out into the open expanse of the hangar. "You're right, they're useless. You're also right that we don't have a way to blow up the ship. I was just saying to say, I guess. I just wish we could." She tossed the broken part back into a pile, then continued on down the walkway.

We neared a bend in the walk when I heard a chinking ahead. "To that ship!" I whispered. "Go!"

She dashed for the open entrance of a damaged ship. I hurried after her. Inside, only darkness smiled upon us, a foreboding darkness that welcomed our end.

I peeked through a hole in the ship's frame. Three alions strode sluggishly along the walk. Their claws clinked as their feet dragged. Their ears were perked up, listening.

"What are they doing?" I whispered.

She put a finger to my mouth. Then she moved her hand down to my chest, over my heart, and tapped me, as if to tell me something. My heart beat faster.

The alions stopped at once.

She waved her finger back and forth, breathing slowly, trying to get me to imitate her.

Panic pulsed in my veins, escalating with every quick breath.

She rolled her hands, breathing in and out, slow and controlled. Our eyes locked.

It started to work. I copied her, slowing down my near puffing attack. When I was able to close my mouth, I shut my eyes too, relaxing. I focused on nothing else, just breathing, slow and controlled, synchronizing with Penelope.

"They're gone," she said a minute later. "It's a good thing you calmed that heart down, they could hear it, but I guess it wasn't enough for them to inspect."

I was still doing the breathing routine. "So they do come up here . . . I guess we have to be a little more careful."

She nodded. "And keep our voices hushed. Come on, let's move."

We walked, side by side, shoulders grazing every so often, which did little to help my rushing heartbeat.

Three bends later, we spotted a ship that appeared to have no exterior damage. "There must be some faulty wiring or something," Penelope predicted.

"Or something," I said, grinning. "You want to check it out anyway? It could be that it was just old and slow. Things are always trashed when a newer model comes out."

"I think that was four models ago for this pile of crap."

"Why do you say that?" I asked. I put out a hand to the hard metal door. "Feels pretty sturdy to me."

"I'm just guessing by the paint." She indicated to a line of faded foreign symbols that had once meant something. But now most of the blue coloring gave way to broken white spots, or sheer blocks of the white metal underneath, leaving behind only traces of blue. "But yeah, we should check it out anyway." With a large stride, she crossed into the pitch-black beyond the door.

Trembling, I followed, the stasis gun supported on my shoulder.

"Shut the door," she called back to me.

"Are you melted? I'm not closing the door."

"Close the damn door, Darrel," she whispered. "If it works, we'll need it sealed shut."

"Uhrm. All right, fine. Jeez." I found the handle to the door and pulled, but nothing happened. I pushed it to the left and it slid in a track. "It didn't seal."

"There's no power," she said sharply, as if I should have known.

"Right." I stretched out my arms, feeling my way around. There was no light in the compartment we were in. "Dammit," I said, when I bumped into something sharp. "It's dangerous in here."

"I found a door," she exclaimed. "Help me, I can't push it open on my own."

"Keep talking so I can find you." She started to sing a quiet song, and for a second, I stopped to listen, captivated by her unique voice: it was beautiful and light, elegant and soft, completely enchanting.

She ceased. "I can't hear you moving towards me."

"Oh, sorry," I said. "Keep singing. I'm coming." She began again, until I finally jammed my fingers into her shoulder. A curse escaped.

"Stop your whining and help me." She guided my hands in the dark to the door.

We yanked on the door and it budged a centimeter. A shaft of light flooded the darkness. I squinted, momentarily blinded. Once our eyes adjusted, we went back to work, heaving with heavy grunts. Centimeter by centimeter, the door gave, until it hid inside the space between compartments.

Three large windowpanes formed the front of the flight deck. Two benches were positioned before a console of dead buttons, along with two flat displays, black without power. Four pads were built into the floor at the corners of each bench.

"You think that's how they fly this, with those pads?" I asked.

"Look for a big on switch and we might find out . . ." She scanned the console, touching every button as she went.

I examined the buttons along the wall to the right. None of them did a thing, and some of them were too rusted to move at all.

When Penelope reached the middle of the console, she flipped a big blue switch. The ship lit up with life. Sounds of pressurizing reverberated throughout the hull. The entire console flashed a couple of times, then ceased, as the flash continued only at a port for a disk.

I took out the yellow disk from my pocket and fitted it into the port.

From the console, a voice greeted us in the alion language, and the lights began to dance all around, until only one button remained lit.

"I think it wants us to press the button," she said. "Should we?"

"Let's think this through for a second." I sat down on the right bench.

She took a seat on the left bench. "They might notice that the lights are on in here. We shouldn't delay too long."

"All right, fine, press the button," I told her. "I just thought you might want to think for a moment."

"Time for thinking is gone. Time for doing is right now. Ready?" She rested her hand over the button.

I cleared my throat. "No."

She pushed down hard.

An alion appeared on the left display, speaking to us with a courtesy in its voice. Then it squinted at us. Its jaw dropped in surprise.

Penelope pushed the button again but nothing happened.

The alion twirled its head and called out. All of a sudden, an alarm rang in the hangar bay, alerting each and every alion to our presence.

She cursed. "Well there's nothing for it, put your hands and feet on the pads," she ordered, as she flopped down on her bench.

I pressed down with my hands. Nothing. "Press down at the same time," I suggested.

She nodded. When we did, the engines fired up. I could feel the power behind us. I pressed my feet down and the ship jumped a meter, grinding its bottom on the grating that supported it.

"Press your right foot down," I said.

The ship took off, flying from the grating, out into the open hangar.

My leg started to shake, and it twitched off the pad.

The ship nosedived.

I replaced my foot on the pad. The ship leveled out. "So we have to keep our right foot on the pad," I said.

She exhaled a long sigh. "What does the left foot do?" She tapped her left foot on the pad.

The ship jolted left.

"These definitely weren't made with us in mind," I screamed. My leg was shaking violently now. "I can't keep my foot on the pad, it's too awkward and too far away."

"Too far way? Try being my size. My tiptoe can barely reach."

I glanced back at her foot. It was shaking more than mine, scarcely connecting with the pad.

"We can make it," she asserted. "You see the opening?"

"Yeah, to the right."

"To the right. Tap the right footpad when I say go . . . GO!"

We tapped the pads in unison. The ship shifted right, jerking.

"What about all these buttons. We haven't even done anything, we don't know if it can go into space."

"We'll find out soon enough, I guess." She laughed, grinning.

Within a second, my leg began convulsing, and the ship dropped, lurching as my foot connected and disconnected from the pad. Cramping, I couldn't extend my leg anymore, and I rolled off the bench, howling in pain.

The ship plummeted straight for the bottom of the hangar.

I rolled towards the console and smashed into it.

"Darrel!" Penelope called out. "Darrel, get up!" She looked over at me. Our eyes met. She noticed my leg and gasped. Finally, her leg no longer reached, tightening up. Her body shaking, her grip waned to nothing, and she hit the console.

Neither of us could see out the windows. I didn't know how long we had until the end, but I gauged we had only seconds left. "You're beautiful," I shouted.

She stared at me.

I had always wanted to tell a girl what I really thought, with confidence, and this was my last chance. "I just wanted you to know."

She smiled at me. "You're—"

The windows shattered. An explosion followed; it was a boom that ruptured my eardrums. I saw a flash of red before engulfed in blackness.

I came to when I felt a tug on my leg. I gazed up at the blurry contour of Penelope. A stabbing pain attacked my ribs. My shoulders seemed disconnected from my body. Spasms plagued my muscles.

I noticed a red outline around her body, around our bodies, protecting us as if a force field.

The ceiling shifted as she hauled me away, until we were out in the hangar, and lights infiltrated my eyes from all directions. The red force field faded. Heat pressed upon my skin, burning. Suddenly, my leg smacked the floor.

Blue stasis-orbs flew over my head. Penelope was cursing furiously. Then I was sliding along the grating again.

The open expanse of the hangar was replaced by a short ceiling of a corridor. She lifted my back and scooted me to the wall, handing me the alion gun. "If you see something, shoot it," she advised.

"What's happening?"

"We crashed," she panted. "Now we're running." She held up the bazooka, glancing between doors.

"Everything hurts," I informed her. My head was swimming. "We made it?"

"Yeah, we made it. Just rest a moment." She counted to ten aloud. "Can you walk?"

"How did we survive?" I asked.

"I'm not sure, but I would guess it had something to due with the red field that surrounded us. I think it was a safety mechanism for when they crash. Can you walk?"

I shook my head in disbelief. "We should be dead, a nosedive from

100 meters or more . . . we should be dead."

"Try walking." She clutched my arm and helped me to my feet. "Easy now," she said in a gentle tone.

I wobbled. "My legs feel dead." I attempted a step forward. My foot landed with a CLOMP. "Yeah, I think I can walk."

"We'll take it slow, we just have to get out of here." She took my arm and placed it around her shoulder. "Lean on me if you need to."

In a fog, I must have leaned on her pretty hard, as she groaned under my weight. I wasn't brave enough to walk on my own. I limped through a doorway, into another empty corridor, then into a pod-filled corridor. We climbed up into the duct system and rested.

"I must have frozen twenty of them. They were coming at us from everywhere. I wonder if this bazooka-thing has a limit . . ."

Her voice trailed off as my hearing went in and out. Everything was dulled, except for the aches terrorizing my body. "What do we do now?" I asked her, my voice cracking and strained.

"We find a way to blow the ship up . . . we can't escape, so we blow it up." She gave a sliver of a grin, but it wasn't as pleasant as it had been when we found the hangar. Now it was dark and full of despair.

I nodded at her. "Okay . . . we blow it up," I agreed.

"When you're ready, let's find us some explosives," she said, her smile expanding.

We rested, listening to dozens of alions pass underneath us, roaring and calling; it sounded like we had created quite a mess in the hangar. Once I recuperated enough strength, we began another tiresome trek, crawling like infants about to collapse for a nap.

Eventually we found a room brimming with electrical equipment, advanced beyond anything I had ever seen, including the flight deck with its giant wall map.

Penelope lowered herself down to a flat space atop a console. She helped me ease myself down next to her. We slipped off the side where no electronics decorated the panel. "What is this place?" she asked.

I shrugged. "A control room . . . or maybe some kind of communications room? I don't know; your guess is as good as mine." I touched an unlit button, feeling its smoothness.

"Look, on the wall, the chips." She pointed to a rack of objects hanging on a wall, as she walked to the far side of the room. "The chips that were in us." With delicate fingers, she slid the chip off the rack and tossed it to me. She grabbed a second one to inspect for herself.

"You still thinking they're locator beacons?" I asked.

"Aren't you?" She flipped the chip over and showed me a little red button. "I think this is how they activate it."

"I'm just glad to be rid of it." I tossed mine to the floor; it skidded into a dull silver console. I studied the unit for a moment. "Hey." I poked her shoulder to get her attention. "Does that look like a radio transceiver?"

"You mean because it has a dial?"

I walked up to it. "Yeah, I don't know. It just looks like one to me. Maybe we could send a message to Earth."

She stepped beside me. "Send a message . . . so far, we haven't had very much success working their electronics. Even their guns are difficult to fire."

"It's worth a try, don't you think?"

She shrugged and waved her hands. "I'd rather look for explosives."

"Just give me a few minutes to fiddle with it," I said. I started adjusting a big orange knob.

"Are you any good with our own electronics?" she asked.

"No, not really," I answered. "But just give me a minute to try. If I fail, I fail . . . and if I don't, you'll kiss me later."

"Did that crash knock some confidence into you?" She smiled, almost happy.

"Not the crash, the fall." I brushed my hand against hers.

She grabbed my fingers, locking them together. "Whatever did it, I like it." She kissed me softly.

Our lips parted after the most magical moment I had ever experienced.

Before I could speak, she kissed me again, harder and longer. Blood rushed throughout my aching limbs. "Now get to work," she said, smiling as our eyes met.

I wanted to kiss again, but I also wanted to hurry up so we could get out of the room. There were too many alions stalking the halls to stay put for very long. I began pressing random buttons and tuned the orange knob.

Static blasted from a speaker in the console.

Penelope twisted all the knobs within range, and after several failed tries, found the volume. "I can barely hear as it is right now," she said, rubbing her ears.

I kept turning the knob until a voice came on. It was a person's voice. "I can't understand it."

"It's Portuguese, I think," she said. "Keep tuning it."

I turned the knob a little bit more, then a little bit more, slowly twisting it until finally a woman speaking English came over the broadcast.

A microphone-looking device jetted out of the console, and I quickly grabbed it, holding down the yellow button on it. "Can anyone hear me?" I released the button. Nothing. "This is Darrel Reid, can anyone hear me?"

"I read you loud and clear, Darrel Reid. This is Private Albores of the U.S. 56th Infantry Division. Please describe your location and situation."

"What should I say?" I asked Penelope.

"What do you mean? Tell her we're on a ship!"

"In outer space?"

"Yes in outer space!"

I clicked the button. "Private Albores, I, along with Penelope Whitestone, are onboard an alion vessel in outer space above North America. We are in extreme danger." I released the button.

"Say over," she yelled at me.

"Over," I added quickly.

"And don't call them alions, she won't know what you're talking about."

"Repeat your transmission, Darrel. I couldn't understand your message. And you don't have to say over, that's what the beep indicates."

I repeated what I had said, using alien instead of alion.

"We have a team heading out the gates as we speak. They have a plan to fly classified spaceships to try to power up the Planetary Defense Network, so we can destroy all extraterrestrial threats. I will relay your transmission to them. They'll be your best bet at a rescue."

I looked at Penelope, wide-eyed. "Did you hear that," I said, excited beyond control. "Rescue. RESCUE!"

"Rescue!" she repeated the glorious word.

I gripped the microphone and clicked the button. "Thank you! Thank you, Private Albores. I have a transmitter that I think will help you find us. Do you know how to calibrate locator beacons?"

"Describe the locator to me, and we'll see what we can do."

"It's alien technology, but I'll describe it as best I can." Penelope handed me the silver device. I began to detail the locator, and she walked me through programming the beacon to send a certain frequency they could pick up.

"We have your signal."

I jumped in the air, then kissed Penelope, completely ecstatic. "Great! We'll try to find a safe place to hide while we wait."

Static overtook the transmission for the first time since beginning the conversation. "Repeat transmission. You cut out—what?" The voice filled with alarm. Gunfire boomed in the background. Then the channel went dead.

"You think they were under attack?" I asked.

"Sure sounds like it," she said. "They have our signal, we should get back to the duct."

I nodded. "That's certain." A spark of light caught my attention to my left. The wall, covered in individual displays—the very picture of a security room from any casino heist film—came to life, streaming video footage as if monitoring the ship. The screens shifted coverage.

Penelope pointed to a screen showing the duct system and a dead alion. "That's where we were." She saw another place where we had left a sign of our escape, then another and another. "They've been watching us this whole time."

I tapped the screen with our pods on view. "If they know where we are, why have they let us roam the ship?"

"They hunted us on the ground, on our own territory . . . maybe they wanted to see how we would react in their domain. You know, testing us . . ."

"You think we've been set up from the beginning?" I asked, disconcerted.

"How else can you explain our survival? You don't think they have sensors that can pick us up? I mean it makes sense, doesn't it?"

"Maybe they never developed the technology." I regretted saying that; it was too unlikely . . . and the more I thought about, the more it made sense, with the alion's delay when holding Penelope captive. They wanted to see what I could and would do to rescue her. A shudder stopped the mental images. I didn't want to think about being a lab rat.

"Doubtful," she scoffed.

I ignored her scathing tone. Scanning the screens, I saw another familiar room, the concealed camera rotated until the back of Penelope's head came into the scene. A furry body stood a few meters behind it. "But that would mean—" I started.

Both of us had been too distracted to notice the silent footfalls of the alion creeping up behind us.

Reacting, Penelope shouldered the bazooka and launched a stasis-orb. The alion froze. "Run!" she commanded.

We bolted out the room and down a long hall. An alion blocked our path in the next hall we entered. Sprinting up behind us, a company of alions readied bazookas.

I fired the alion gun, both barrels spinning, ejecting black globe after black globe. Blood splattered the walls all around.

Penelope shot more stasis-orbs until a mechanized noise signaled that it was empty. She cursed and threw it at the company of alions. A stasis-orb suspended the bazooka in the air, just short of smashing an alion's skull.

Several more stasis-orbs flew our way. Before I could say a word, I was trapped again, trapped in a frozen world of blue. The lightning struck my body. My pain peaked, to the point that I thought I would pass out.

But instead, I watched as the alions strode over to me; one tapped its bazooka and the field disappeared.

Another alion ran up and stuck a needle in my elbow.

I screamed as my surroundings descended into a warm darkness that no light could penetrate.

10
Off the Ground
Maggy

Maggy! Maggy!"

Tortilla's voice belled in my ears. I couldn't distinguish the words, I just recognized the voice . . . that comforting voice. I opened my eyes, and there he was, stooping over me.

"Tortilla?" I rasped. My sore voice ached, and my throat was so dry that every syllable took great effort to get out. "Tortilla?"

"I'm here, Maggy. I'm here." He grasped my hand, gently squeezing my fingers. "Do you need water?"

I heard gunfire next. The repetition of burst rounds rent the air. The roars of alions rushed by my ears as dread attacked my stomach. "What's happening?"

"We're under attack," Tortilla replied. "Do you need some water?" he repeated.

"I need a gun," I answered.

"The third jeep is still running," another voice yelled. "We need to get to it if we want to get the hell out of here."

"I think she's hurt, Burnhammer," Tortilla shouted back.

"Can you carry her?" Burnhammer's voice registered in my head.

"I think so," Tortilla replied. "I'll have to."

I noticed Burnhammer's back, then her face as she glanced down at me. She returned her attention to something in the distance. The sound of her assault rifle rattled my eardrums.

Tortilla wrapped an arm under my knees and one around my back, lifting me with a grunt. He smiled. "Does this hurt?"

"No," I whispered.

Blackness swooped in again.

The thunder of machine guns broke my sleep.

"On your nine! Nine! Nine!" someone screamed. "To your six!"

A stone in the road sent a jolt of pain down my back. The uneven terrain rocked the jeep side to side. I could feel every little bump. I tried to sit up.

Tortilla put a hand to my chest to restrain me. "Rest now. There's nothing you can do for us. Let the soldiers handle it."

Each word became clearer as I listened. I opened my mouth to talk, but nothing coherent came out, just a gasp for air.

A bump sent Tortilla into the ceiling of the back of the jeep and his glasses fell off. He cursed, but then smiled at me, feigning cheeriness. He retrieved his crooked spectacles. "We're gonna get there, don't you worry."

Screams from the soldiers continued to burst forth uninhibited: they used every swear word in the book, and they never stopped.

"These jeeps were made for rides like this." Burnhammer's voice rang loud and clear. "And we'll take down every SOB out there, you have my word on that."

I shifted my head to the right and found Burnhammer firing out an open side window. She was yelling as loud as the rest of her comrades. With deft fingers, she endlessly fed her assault rifle clip after clip.

I smiled up at Tortilla. "How does it look out there?" I asked hoarsely.

Tortilla glanced out the tinted window. "Like a world of fire . . . with monsters jumping out of the flames. It's not a world like it used to be." He put a water bottle to my lips and poured relief down my throat.

"Or maybe it's the same," I said, with a slightly smoother voice. "It's not like we never napalmed forests before."

"I guess that's certain." He leaned down to my ear. "I love you." He wore a face full of uncertainty, not about his love for me, but about our future together.

I squeezed his hand. "I love you, too." But when I closed my eyes, I could feel sleep taking hold again.

When I woke up next, we were driving on a smooth, paved road. I looked up. Tortilla was gazing out the window with a look of reflection in his eyes. "What ya thinking about?" I asked him.

He smiled down at me. "I was thinking about how we met."

"In sixth grade?"

"Yeah," he replied. "How shy we both were."

"You're still shy," I said.

"At least I can get words out around you now." He grinned as he touched my hand. "Took a while, but I got there."

I laughed. "A while . . . it took years."

"Well, I've always heard that the tortoise wins the race." He stroked my fingers with his thumb. "I think it's true this time. If we became friends earlier, and started dating in junior high or something, who knows, we probably would have broken up a month later and never talked again."

I had thought about that a dozen times the last few days and fell upon the same conclusion.

"I guess I was meant to accidentally trip and grab your boob," he said.

"And I guess I was meant to throw my applesauce in your face."

We both laughed hard, remembering the incident that assured my relentless silence towards him for the next couple of years.

"We're on highway 2 now," he informed me. "They haven't attacked us in a half hour or so, we lost them before we came to the blacktop."

Burnhammer glanced down at me. "We should be there in under an hour."

I nodded at her as I slowly sat up with the help of Tortilla. Every muscle felt stiff, especially my mid-back and neck. When the jeep came to a roadblock of dead cars, the driver simply went off road, hurtling around the obstacle. I stared at the passing trees. A brilliant blue sky hung above the sea of green. The day was warm and pleasant. The air from the open windows allowed for deep, peaceful breaths.

"How did we get out of the jeep? How did we survive?"

"Not all of us did . . ." Burnhammer said, pain thick in her voice. "The helmets probably lessened most of the impact that would have crushed our skulls in, and when we flipped, I had caught myself, ready to recover. I pulled you two from the wreckage, along with Private Paola." She pointed to the unconscious woman lying in the seat in front of us. "No one from the first jeep made it. Lieutenant Laffrado . . . Sergeant Goldward . . . even the two scientists. Most from our jeep didn't make it, including Sergeant Loritz. Eleven in total fell. There are only ten of us left, twelve with you two. Hopefully that's enough to do what we need to do." She rotated her tense jaw from side to side and it cracked with the most gruesome sound imaginable.

I hung my head. "I'm sorry about your comrades."

"Don't worry, I plan on avenging their deaths," she said. "We'll show these alion bastards what we're made of soon enough."

A HOOAH echoed in the jeep.

Every time the soldiers said the battle cry made me feel like yelling my own cry, but I didn't think they would appreciate it since I wasn't really one of them.

The hour went by, and Paola had woken halfway through, complaining of severe aches in her back. We eventually pulled off the highway, taking a left on to Foothill Boulevard, then another left at Oak Grove Drive. We drove past several signs with JPL in bold red font. There were too many buildings, and none of us had a clue where such a classified project would be located, though my guess had been near a runway. A few of the soldiers agreed, including Sergeant Henderson, who had taken over command of the platoon, or more precisely, incorporated the three soldiers from 1st squad into the 3rd squad.

The only problem, the directory we found pointed out five runways. "This one looks like it's the largest, sir," Burnhammer said. She directed a finger to the fourth one on the map.

Henderson examined the map with a critical eye. "I would have to agree with you there," she said. From a large pocket, she pulled out a PocketPad, powered by the sun, and jotted down the directions to the runway.

Her assistant, Sergeant Geisler, was behind the wheel, awaiting our return. We all climbed back into the jeep. "Find where we're going?" he asked.

"Think so. Take the next right," she told him.

The maze of roads led us to a long black tarmac at the base of a giant hill. Geisler busted through a chain-link gate, heading for a massive hangar far in the distance. The tarmac was flat and without a bump to be found. It didn't even feel like a regular road at all, but something special, something probably made specifically for what we were searching to find.

Geisler stopped at a normal-sized door in the hangar. Soldiers, including a grumbling Paola, took position all around the vehicle, securing the immediate ground, then the perimeter.

Henderson led Tortilla and I, along with a couple of soldiers, into the locked hangar. The sergeant made easy work of the door with the same automatic shotgun Burnhammer had given Tortilla before we left on our suicide mission.

Henderson kicked the door; it swung wide.

My heart sank in disappointment. There was nothing within the hangar but an empty slab of gray concrete.

"Dammit," Burnhammer cursed.

"Sweep the interior," Henderson ordered.

The soldiers fanned out in pairs. Tortilla and I stayed close to Burnhammer. She had given me another of the same machine gun. I held it up, ready to fire. Tortilla also held one, but his was across his chest as we sped along the bare walls.

I glanced at the door as a soldier ran in to the hangar and whispered in Henderson's ear. When we returned to her, all the soldiers reported the same: there was nothing in the building; it had all probably been taken or destroyed somehow.

"Well, we may not have wasted all of our time," Henderson said. "Fox says she found what looks to be a door built into the hill. It could be a bunker. We'll take a look and find out." At that, she raced out the door, following Corporal Fox.

Fox led the way to a small camouflage door built into the hillside, almost mistakable for rock, except for the large rust spots that gave away the door when standing close enough to it. "I couldn't get it open, sir. I thought your shotgun might help."

"With these door-blastin' rounds, I'd be surprised if it held." She waved us back a step. The door handle busted in with one try. The door hid a narrow, unlit passageway, descending every couple of steps with a short flight of stairs.

The soldiers switched on the headlamps built into their helmets. I couldn't find my switch until Burnhammer pointed to my left temple. I nodded a thank you to her.

Without Henderson commanding it, the Stalkers went silent. Tortilla and I breathed noisily. He didn't say anything though, and neither did I, but I wanted to hold his hand for comfort. The space didn't allow for that. I didn't think Henderson would approve either.

The passage wound back and forth, steadily descending the entire way. At last, our luck turned for the better. We entered an enormous room that still had auxiliary lights. Strips of little lights lined the floor and the ceiling.

Everyone gasped when we saw what hid inside. I was completely shocked.

Row upon row of sleek white fighter planes lay before us. The triangular shape of the planes resembled that of stealth fighters, only much smaller in its build. USAF SQ-1 Whitedragon was etched into the right side of the planes, barely visible.

"There must be a hundred of these," Geisler commented.

"At least," Fox agreed.

"There's a console over there." Henderson pointed to the left. Upon closer inspection, there were a couple consoles, and four large flat screens built into the wall.

Geisler located the button that supposedly turned on the power. "It's dead." He broke open a panel under one of the consoles and started working on fixing the power. A moment later, he pressed the button again; this time lights turned on all over.

The room was much bigger than I had thought. Three larger planes, also resembling stealth fighters, sat at the far end. They looked as if they could be manned, and that renewed my hope that we really could rescue Jelly and Penelope.

Computers booted up as displays came to life. A few soldiers began to type away.

"Sergeant, there is a list of the planes," Geisler said, waving his commander over. "Only they're not just aircrafts, they're spacecrafts. These are the unmanned fighters . . . there are so many."

"Does it give an inventory?" Henderson asked.

"Yes, sir. There are 221 SQ-1s. It also lists three SF-1s."

"Those must be the big boys in the back." She glanced back at the spaceships with desire in her eyes. "Are they manned fighters?"

"Looks that way, sir," Geisler answered. "I think the SQ-1s are controlled from these four consoles alone."

"Four consoles for over 200 ships," she said, stunned. "Can you operate them?"

"I think so," he replied. "The system looks like it was designed so grade-schoolers could do the job."

"My kind of engineering. Nice and simple," she said, grinning. "But how the hell do we get them out of here? We must be 30 meters under the surface."

"Oh, right," Geisler said. After a second of typing, he pressed a combination of buttons on the console.

The ground started to shake. Then suddenly, the entire floor was ascending to the surface, and as we climbed, the concrete ceiling parted from its center.

"Is that the ceiling of the hangar?" Tortilla asked, surprised.

"I think so," Burnhammer responded.

When the floor ceased moving, we were even with the ground, exactly where we had started at in the hangar. The exit to the jeep was now right behind us.

"That's some crazy shit," Henderson said. She wasted no time. "Guylas, Paola, and Corporal Mu, you'll stay behind with Geisler and fly these babies. We'll take one of the manned ships and attempt to succeed at this ludicrous mission of ours."

A wave of, "Yes, sir," filled the room.

Before anyone took a step, a panicky voice came over the radio clipped at Henderson's waist. She snatched it up, raising it to her ear.

"Lieutenant Laffrado, please come in," the voice said.

"This is Sergeant Henderson, who am I talking to?"

"This is Private Albores at Mount Baldy. I'm looking for Lieutenant Laffrado; I have an urgent message for him."

"Lieutenant Laffrado was killed in an ambush soon after we left the compound. I have taken over his command. What is the message?"

"No one told me about the ambush. I'm sorry, Sergeant Henderson. We had an attack of our own, but we wiped out what they threw at us. Can you confirm your identification code?"

Enraged, she waved the radio in the air. "Goddammit, what do you need my code for?"

After a short silence the private said, "It's procedure when a command is exchanged. Please, sir, your code."

She sighed. "Hotel, India, November, Delta, Uniform."

"Confirmed, Sergeant Henderson. I'm being told you've been field promoted to lieutenant. Sorry it's not under better circumstances . . ."

"Me too, private. What's the message?"

"Message reads: two civilians trapped on the spaceship above North America. They are awake and have a locator beacon tuned so that we can find them. They are looking forward to seeing some friendly, non-furry faces."

"Two civvies onboard a spaceship . . ." Henderson said to us.

"Did they give their names?" I asked, hope growing in my heart.

"Did the civvies give their names, private?"

"They did, sir. Darrel Reid and Penelope Whitestone."

"Tho—those are our friends!" I screamed with joy. "We have to rescue them, we have to." I turned to Tortilla and hugged him.

He squeezed me hard. "I knew it . . . I knew they were alive!"

The Stalkers stared at us, speechless.

Henderson frowned. "I'm sorry, Maggy, but we have a mission to fulfill. We don't have the time, resources, or the intel to pull off a rescue mission."

I was taken aback by her words. "But they're our friends . . ."

"Sir, what would you like me to relay to them?" Albores asked.

Henderson held down the button, about to give her decline, when Burnhammer stepped forward.

"Sir, I believe I can do it."

Henderson eyed the corporal. "Alone? Are you melted?"

"No, sir. Not alone . . . with these two." Burnhammer pointed at Tortilla and I. "There are three of the big ships, we can take one of those. If they have a locator beacon, it might be as easy as pick n' go."

"It might be as hard as a thousand automated weapons blowing you to smithereens."

"I would like to take the chance, sir."

Henderson weighed the options in silence. Her face scrunched as she decided upon what course to take. "Do me a favor?"

"What's that, sir?" Burnhammer asked.

"Do some damage while you're at it."

"I will try, sir. Thank you."

A smile lit up my face. Tortilla showed all his white teeth.

"Private Albores, tell the civvies a team will be by to extract them shortly. Send me the locator frequency."

"Done, sir. So you found the ships?"

"A whole company's worth. But first, private, explain to me what happened at the compound. You said you were attacked."

"Yes, sir. We were. Heavily. They broke through the wall and made it into the first level, one even made it here, into the communications room, but don't worry, we got 'em all. No civvies in the lower levels were touched."

"Sounds like quite a battle. I'm glad to hear operations are still running. Inform General Kramer that we have found 221 drone space fighters and three manned ships. Wish us luck; we're going to need it. Over and out."

"I will have the message relayed, sir. Good luck. Over and out."

Henderson replaced the radio and drew her PocketPad from a pouch. "Sending you the frequency," she told Burnhammer. "All right, so that leaves Rivera, Fox, Lakes, and Tasper with me. Hopefully the controls of the ships were designed for grade-schoolers too."

Geisler winked at his commander. "With some luck, sir. You'll need these." He handed Burnhammer and Henderson each a keycard he had found. "Radio me when you're in the cockpit."

The eight of us left the four soldiers sitting at the consoles, as Geisler instructed his comrades what to do.

When we were close enough, I could make out the etchings on the manned ships: USAF SF-1 Spacefalcon. The white bird looked eager to see some action.

Burnhammer lowered a ramp at the rear of the ship by sliding the keycard through a scanner. She waved for us to find a seat. The six-seater cockpit was arranged with two seats to the right, two at the front, and two to the left. After inspecting the rest of the ship, she took a seat at the helm. I sat to the right of Burnhammer. Tortilla sat in the closest chair at my back on the right.

All of the buttons had labels, detailing what to do, and in what order to do it. "This looks easy enough," Burnhammer uttered.

"What's the plan?" I asked her.

"We'll hang back with the squad for a bit, as they head for the International Space Station, then we'll break off. There's a spacesuit, some cutting tools, and a sealing tube in the back, so I think the best plan would be to land on the alion ship and cut a hole big enough for a person, then connect the sealing tube from our ship to the alion's ship."

I stared at her, amazed. "How do you know how to use the sealing tube; I've never even heard of a sealing tube."

"I don't really. I watched a documentary about them: space operations use them to save crews with damaged suits." She flipped a line of switches and the engines powered up. Before I could reply, she grabbed her radio. "Geisler, I've got the bird roaring, how about some sunlight?"

The massive door behind us started to withdraw to the ceiling. Without warning, all 221 of the unmanned space fighters turned on in unison, generating a boom that thundered in the hangar.

I gazed out at all the white fighters, disbelieving my eyes.

"Cool," Tortilla said.

"Way cool," I agreed. I turned back to Burnhammer. "We've never been in space; don't you have to be trained to use the suits?"

She nodded. "You also have to be trained to fly one of these, but all of those people have been taken. We'll just have to wing it." She winked at me. "You two ready?"

I nodded hesitantly.

"I've always wanted to go into space," Tortilla said, smiling. "I can't believe we're going into space . . ."

"Burnhammer, we're all ready," Henderson said over the radio. "How's your team?"

"Good to go, sir," Burnhammer replied. "Ready to find their friends."

"I hope that you do. Good luck." Henderson's ship rolled forward into the sunlight. We followed, giving the planes some distance.

"What do you think these things run on?" I threw out the question.

"I have no idea," she responded. "But my guess is something new and experimental."

"Hopefully not too experimental," Tortilla said nervously.

We watched as Henderson's plane started driving down the runway, picking up speed at an unimaginable rate. Within moments, the ship was racing to break the atmosphere.

Burnhammer glanced over at us. "Here we go."

"Engage," Tortilla said. He burst out in laughter.

A laugh was pushing its way up when Burnhammer punched it. The ship sped away and my gut sank in, roiling. The next thing I knew, I was staring at the sky and swirling white clouds, flying straight up.

Then a barrier of color folded over the nose of the ship. Red dominated my vision. Then the hard vacuum of outer space engulfed my eyes, black speckled with dots of white. Dozens of satellites flew by us, circling the planet.

Burnhammer pressed a button labeled Gravity Stabilization.

My butt instantly sank into my chair while my arms and legs dropped like bricks. "Genius."

She tittered. "I guess it beats floating around all day."

"We're in space . . . we're actually in space," Tortilla said, astonished. "I think we're the first teenagers in space."

"What about Jelly and Penelope?" I asked.

"They don't count," he replied. "They were abducted. We came into space in a man-made craft by our own free will."

"Then we're the first teenagers in space . . ." I gazed out the front window. "It's even more incredible than I imagined it to be."

"You two are pretty fascinated with space," Burnhammer observed.

"Aren't you? You said you watched documentaries," I said.

"I like to see technology, but I never wanted to go into space—"

"The mother ship," I gasped. I pointed to the right where the alion spaceship orbited, red against the blackness. "It's the biggest machine I've ever seen." It was similar to the smaller ones hovering above the cities, but redder and instilling more trepidation.

"It's the scariest machine I've ever seen," Tortilla stated.

"Just imagine how many alions are waiting for us," Burnhammer said, as if trying to frighten us in a joking manner.

On a display hanging between Burnhammer and I, a hundred triangles appeared behind us. "Can you turn the ship around?" I asked.

Burnhammer rotated the controls and we spun around, finding an array of white ships tailing in formation. It was a remarkable sight.

"How are the birds doing?" Geisler asked over the radio.

"They look beautiful," Burnhammer said. "I just hope they're enough."

As if in response to her statement, an alarm drew our attention to the display. Dozens of unidentified objects were approaching fast. She spun the ship so that we faced the alion mother ship. From it, fighters launched from two hangars, zooming our way.

"We have company," Henderson announced over the radio. "Geisler, engage the drones."

"Yes, sir." The drones burst ahead. The Whitedragons shot hoards of missiles. The alion fighters launched the yellow balls of death. Ships exploded in huge clouds of fire that evaporated an instant later; shrapnel was ejected from the detonations, cutting into the frames of nearby ships. The drones performed with precision, dodging attacks and returning fire, pursuing alion fighters in tight well-formed packs.

"We have to help them make it to the ISS," Burnhammer yelled. "Find the weapon systems."

Frantically, I searched the console, but there was nothing. "Anything?" I glimpsed at Tortilla.

"No, nothing over here," he replied. He jumped to the other console. "This says laser over here."

I dashed to the seat beside him. "Laser," I exclaimed. I scrutinized the labels on the console. There were missile and laser controls, along with machine gun cannons.

"So you have the laser and I have the machine guns . . . wanna switch?" I asked him, but I already knew his answer.

"Switch a laser for a machine gun?"

"Just thought I'd ask, you know, to make sure." I smiled.

He laughed as he gripped the controls, examining the screen in front of him.

The screen before me presented ten alion crafts near us. I grasped the wheel that controlled the turret. The bullets shot out in a flash of light. I only managed to damage two of the targets, the rest raced after Henderson's ship.

Two more disappeared off the display, signaling that their ship was in the fight. "We're nearing the station," Burnhammer informed us. "There are still six ships tailing them."

"On it," Tortilla shouted. I watched as he pressed a button that targeted a ship with a laser, then he fired a beam of light where the other laser directed it. The ship vanished from the display. "Got one," he announced.

"Still five more," Burnhammer said.

I found the button that switched the machine gun display to missile controls. I let five fly.

Burnhammer cheered at the explosions. "Took them all down."

"Burnhammer, we are set to dock with the station. Cover our asses," Henderson requested.

"Yes, sir." Burnhammer circled the great silver station, maneuvering between two more fighters.

I switched back to the machine gun, blasting round after round. I caught the wing of one, and it collided into the second, blowing them both to bits.

Tortilla fired the laser again, targeting the rear of a fighter, and the crimson gas that jetted out behind it; it exploded into fragments.

Burnhammer dipped the craft, and I briefly lost focus, as my eyes drifted from the screen. Once my eyes adjusted, I found a new target, destroying the fighter by clipping its fuel source. Our ship dipped again, then twirled, dodging a yellow ball that combusted on a drone.

"Our ship is secured to the station," Henderson informed us. "Go get those civvies. The drones will get our backs."

"Copy that," Burnhammer replied. "On route to the mother ship."

We flew through a melee of fighters; it was a field of short explosions, as dangerous dogfights blasted each other out of existence.

"We have four on our tail," Burnhammer yelled back to us.

I licked my lips and pulled down the machine gun trigger. "Got one."

"Got another," Tortilla called out.

Then suddenly we flipped over. I about threw up, but it stopped halfway up my throat, rushing back down, burning as it descended.

"Sorry. Not familiar with the controls," Burnhammer said. "It's easier than I thought it would be but still difficult. I'll get the hang of it though, don't worry." She dodged another attack. Her reflexes were impressive to say the least, if only my stomach could keep up.

I fired two missiles to finish the chasing fighters.

Eventually we left behind the fray. No more fighters hunted after us. I was glad for that, but I didn't drop my guard, eyeing the screen as it continuously updated.

"Look at that," Burnhammer gasped.

My gaze was drawn for a moment. A colossal hole, only now visible, stretched across the far side of the mother ship. Blue lights sparked all around the damage. We flew close enough to see alions in suits performing repairs on the devastated section. "What do you think caused it?"

"Hard to say," Burnhammer said. "Maybe a missile attack. Whatever it was did some serious havoc."

"This could be good for us," I said, assessing the situation. "One thing we never thought about was if they have proximity or anticollision alarms."

"And you're just thinking of this now?" Tortilla said.

"*None* of us thought of it." I gave him a nasty look. "Anyway, let me finish. Maybe since they're doing repairs, maybe those systems are down, taken out by whatever caused the hole."

"We're about to find out." Burnhammer found a flat surface large enough to land on, and she touched down the Spacefalcon as gently as she could, but it still jolted my body. "Sorry about that."

"No problem," I told her. "We're still alive, and the ship is running, so I'd say you did a hell of a job piloting." I unbuckled the seatbelt that strapped over my shoulders, chest, and waist, hopping out of the comfortable chair. "It does feel good not to be moving so fast." I smiled at her. "I thought you would wait for me to finish telling you my reasoning."

"Whether their systems are down or not, this is our mission, to risk our lives to save your friends. Was there another option?"

"No," I replied. "No, I guess not. Let's just hope they're not right there waiting for us."

She grabbed my shoulder and squeezed. "That's all we can do."

Tortilla stood and wobbled a couple of steps. "Whoa. That's weird."

"That's certain," I agreed. "Messes with your system."

Burnhammer rushed to the aft compartment. We followed behind. "I'll need some help putting on the suit, and it might take some time, but don't worry, I don't think I'll need any help out there."

I nodded as she started to garb herself in the spacesuit.

Tortilla counted the minutes going by, arriving at thirteen when the suit was finally all put together, hopefully the correct way. "All right, head back to the cockpit, I'll communicate with you with the ship's radio."

"Okay. You sure you can do this by yourself?"

"Not entirely, but I think it's for the best," she said. "I'll see you in a bit."

"Good luck," Tortilla said.

I echoed his words.

She nodded. "Thanks." She waited to make sure our door was sealed before she opened the hatch in the middle of the compartment. We watched, as she held on tight to a bar while the room depressurized. A mechanized ladder lowered a meter from the hatch. She waved to us before she disappeared into space.

"Come on, let's get back to the controls," I said. I ran off and Tortilla trailed behind. I grabbed a headset to communicate to the spacesuit. "Burnhammer, this is Maggy, can you hear me?"

"A little too loud," Burnhammer said.

"What?"

"You're a little too loud in my ear, take it down a notch," she replied.

"Sorry. How is outer space?" I asked, excited to hear a personal account.

"It's a bit spooky," she replied. "I can say I'm not a fan. But everything is moving along. I'm almost done cutting the hole."

"Well try not to worry us too long," I said. I fidgeted, twirling my thumbs around each other. She gave no reply. I got up and paced back and forth. The space was cramped, and I could only take a couple of steps from one side to the other. "You think she's all right?" I asked Tortilla.

"I'm sure she's fine," he responded calmly. "She's secured to the ship; she's not going anywhere."

"Fine? Don't you know how dangerous space is? A little tiny pebble could kill her, and it wouldn't even have to be going that fast. And the explosions . . . those particles could pierce a hole in her oxygen, or cut her tether . . ."

I could tell he could see the anxiety festering in my mind. "There's nothing we can do for her. Just relax."

I hated when people told me to relax; it never helped. In fact, it had the opposite effect it was supposed to have on me, tensing my muscles even more. "I don't like this small space. I didn't mind the Apocalypse Room because I couldn't see, but this . . . we're in space!"

He sprung from his chair and wrapped his arms around me. He must have held me for fifteen minutes, or close to it, and when I realized how long it had been, I heard the hatch door close. I sprinted to the aft compartment. The door to it was still shut, but I could see through the window.

Burnhammer stood in the far right corner, putting away the gear, dismantling the suit with several CLANGS, which I had thought was the hatch. She noticed me and waved me in.

I hit a button and the door unlocked. "Did you do it?" I asked.

She pointed to the open hatch door. "We're connected and pressurized. It's a go."

"You're amazing," Tortilla said, inspecting the tubing that joined our ship with the alion's. "It didn't even take you long, less than an hour."

I walked over and began helping her remove the suit. "Pretty impressive, I agree. Especially since you've had no training. Your nerves must be made of neo-plastic."

"Thanks." She slid out of the magnetic boots. "But everything had directions on how to handle and set up the equipment. It really wasn't much . . . I need to rest before we board those bastards though."

"Sure. Can I see the signal?" I asked.

She withdrew the PocketPad from a pouch and offered it to me.

I accepted it with greedy fingers. "Thanks." I zoomed in on the signal emitted from Jelly's locator beacon. It was close but farther than I had hoped. I showed Tortilla.

"Well I'm ready to kill every last one," he said with ire in his tone.

Burnhammer got up after a half hour or so. "Gather your weapons, we're goin' in."

"If only I still had my axe," I said, saddened by the thought. "But I guess a submachine gun will do." I grinned at Tortilla.

"You mean two submachine guns." He nodded at the second one I held in my left. He raised both of his KRISS VP55s to his narrow shoulders.

"Well I heard two is better than one when killing alions," I said, laughing. "If the futuristic Gimli were with us, I bet he'd say: 'Let's hunt some alion!' don't you think?"

He laughed as he checked his pockets for spare ammo. "That's certain."

"You two ready?" Burnhammer asked.

We nodded.

"Stay behind me unless I say otherwise. Clear?"

"Clear," we said simultaneously.

"Then let's hunt some alion!" she shouted in an animated voice. Assault rifle in hand, she ran off to the hatch, then down the ladder, falling three meters or so through the tubing.

Tortilla and I stopped at the hatch, staring down at the drop. The ladder didn't extend nearly far enough, which meant chance stepped in the rest of the way. "I'll go first," I told him. I climbed down until I was hanging from the last bar, nervous about the descent. "All right, here I come." I released my fingers in a flash of boldness. Burnhammer tried to catch me, but I dragged her down to the floor. When I glanced up at Tortilla, he was smiling.

"Fun?" he asked.

"You'll find out," I said. "Hurry up." I clambered to my feet, using a wall to steady my shaking body.

He dropped like a boulder, despite his feathery weight. Burnhammer and I both had our hands out ready to catch him, but we still managed to fall to the floor. We all jumped to our feet.

"Rough," he spoke in a hushed voice.

I nodded at him, then turned my attention to Burnhammer, who scouted out the next room.

She returned. "It's just an empty hall like this one. I guess you were right about the detectors being down, unless they're waiting in ambush somewhere else." She paused, her head bent down and her ears cocked up, listening. "Come on," she grunted a moment later.

We were at her heels through the next four corridors, until we came to a long, long hall with sleek black capsules. I gasped when I saw what lay trapped inside: humans; they were men, women, and children of all ages. Placid eyes stared at us through transparent white doors. No plea for release fought its way out, as if content.

I put my hand to the capsule. The eyes did not follow. "So this is what they do with us," I said, shocked and horrified. "Should we try to free them?"

"Of course we should," Tortilla shouted. "We can't let them stay here . . . not like this."

"Look, there's a console." Burnhammer pointed to a station with buttons that were lit up. She pressed a couple, but nothing happened, then she hit them all, earning the same results.

"We'll just have to break them open," I said.

Burnhammer nodded and struck the nearest capsule with the butt of her rifle. The white material was thick and strong, and it did not break with the impact. She smashed it repeatedly. It began to look like a cracking eggshell, until at last, the material gave, and a blue fog rushed out, dissipating soon after. She began using her gloved hands to clear the jagged pieces, creating a hole large enough for the man within to climb out.

An alarm rang out: RAWRK . . . RAWRK . . . RAWRK.

The man's body started to violently convulse. Burnhammer grabbed him and pulled, but he was stuck inside, secured by some unknown means. It was a painful sight, watching his body contort within the cell. Then he lay motionless. She checked his pulse. "He's dead."

I gasped. "We killed him."

"He was dead already," Tortilla said. "Trapped in there, waiting for the alions to consume him . . . he was dead already."

"We should move. This area will probably be crawling with alions soon," Burnhammer predicted. She headed down the corridor, turning left at the end through an open door.

We rushed right behind. "Won't we get lost?" I yelled.

"The PocketPad is mapping out where we go, so we should be able to find our way back." She shifted down another corridor filled with capsules. When we entered the next hallway, a group of alions stood at a console, touching a display with their humanlike hands. Burnhammer unstrapped a grenade at her hip and tossed it in the middle of the room, spinning on her heels. "Back, back, back!"

Smoke filled the room behind us as we hurried into another corridor. Burnhammer followed the signal on the PocketPad, pressing buttons on its touch screen. "We're getting close, should be just a few more rooms away," she apprised us.

The alarm faded into nothing.

In the next corridor, two alions guarded a door, their guns raised. In a panic, I pulled the triggers of my guns. The bullets punctured the alions' furry chests. The door was locked, so we backtracked until we found an open route, circumventing the barred door.

We met opposition in every room after that, bullets whizzing in the confined space. Their black bullets bounced off the Dragon Scale armor.

I dodged a blue orb, as Tortilla aimed a stream of well-aimed shots at the threat. The alion flew back from the force. It slammed into a wall, collapsing to the grating under our feet. "Thanks for the save." I kissed his cheek, a quick peck like a viper strike. That's all I had time to do.

An alion burst through a door, wildly shooting.

Burnhammer took care of the alion with one bullet to its head. She had switched over to the smaller assault rifle with the folding stock. It proved effective in the tight quarters, especially when she needed to whip around and fire in the opposite direction. Her skills in combat comforted my trembling nerves.

We stopped before a locked door. She stretched her hand holding the PocketPad so that we could see. "The signal is coming from inside this room, I'm sure of it."

"How are we going to get in?" I asked. I slid my fingers across the door, feeling its smooth texture. "Can we shoot the door open like Henderson did."

"No, that was a special round, designed for human doors with human locks," she responded. She studied the door. "These doors are all reinforced and slide into a gap between rooms; they're not the same at all."

"So we can't open it?" Tortilla asked, his hopes audibly sinking.

"I didn't say that." She unlatched a square container from her jacket. Opening the box, a light brown block waited to fulfill its purpose. "A more powerful version of C4."

"What if it kills them?"

"It shouldn't, but it's our only way in, unless you have a key."

I hung my head.

"They would rather die in a rescue attempt than be eaten by these beasts," Tortilla said. "Do it."

Burnhammer attached the explosive to the top and bottom of the door. "Get back." She ran to the end of the corridor. Once we had found cover, she blew it. The detonation filled the room with wisps of smoke. We ran up to view the damage. The door was blown off, fallen less than a meter away in the other room. She rushed through the gap, rifle primed.

I followed with Tortilla behind me.

Four alions crouched underneath large blue slabs of shiny metal. Reacting, we all fired our weapons, releasing a wave of death.

I gasped, pointing.

"Darrel." Tortilla rushed to one of the slabs where Jelly lay, still, as if sleeping. "Bromigo, wake up."

I hurried to Jelly's other side and shook his shoulder. "Wake up."

"He must be sedated," Burnhammer said, drawing a pen-shaped object from a pouch. "This will wake him." She gripped his arm and stuck the needle end into his elbow. A brief pressurized sound filled my ears.

Jelly shot straight up, screaming. He was loosing curse after curse. His eyes didn't seem to notice us, as he blankly stared ahead.

"Jelly, it's all right. Calm down," I said. "We're here to rescue you."

He began wheezing, which quickly transformed into a harsh cough. He whipped his head in my direction and fell back, as if utterly shocked to see me. "I'm dead!" he shouted. "I'm dead, I'm dead, I'm dead!"

"No, bromigo." Tortilla grabbed Jelly's hand. "You're not dead. Snap out of it."

Jelly squinted at us, skeptical of our presence. He calmed his breathing, focusing hard on a routine. "The alarm," he said suddenly. He scanned the room this way and that. Most of the electronics were dead.

"The explosion must have fried some of the systems," Burnhammer observed. "But it's still unwise to stay here for much longer."

Jelly glanced at all of us. "You're really here to save us."

"Yeah," I spoke softly. "We're really here to save you. Now get your butt in gear."

He slid from the slab. "Penelope!" he squeaked as he ran to another slab.

Penelope lay unconscious on the blue metal, her chest rising and falling peacefully. A shoe was off her foot, and her skin was marked with black lines running from between her toes to her ankle.

"What were they doing to you in here?" Tortilla asked.

"Experimenting, torturing . . . at least that's what they did to others," Jelly explained. "I think they were going to cut open her foot to map out the structure of it. They did that to another woman . . . but," he stammered. "But it was her brain . . ."

"Do you have another one of those pens?" I asked Burnhammer, but she was already snagging it from her pouch.

She injected the substance into Penelope's elbow, and instantly her eyes popped open.

Jelly stood over her, gently stroking her arm. "Hey . . . it's okay. We're finally getting the hell off this ship." He smiled at her.

Her breaths were relaxed and regular "Darrel?" she said, as if her mind was catching up to her senses. She glanced around. "Maggy? Félix? How?"

"They found us . . ." He turned to me. "How did you find us?"

"Your signal," I replied.

"Signal? The locator beacon . . ." He reached into a pocket and pulled it out. "They didn't take it; they must have missed it when they took everything else." He replaced it in his pocket and turned his attention back to Penelope. "We're going home."

She smiled. "Or die trying," she rasped.

"Or die trying," he echoed.

Burnhammer handed her a canteen of water.

Penelope drank a few sips and gave it back. "Thanks."

"Ready to move?" Burnhammer asked.

All of us nodded.

Burnhammer dispensed her handguns to Jelly and Penelope. "The route back is going to be rough since we made such a ruckus to get here. We came across a lot of locked doors, so we only have one path—"

"We could use a key," Jelly blurted.

"A key?" I asked.

"The things around the alions' necks, those are keys," he stated. He walked over to an alion carcass and snatched a green disk hanging around its neck. "These disks open the doors."

"Well that might make it a little easier," Burnhammer said. "But don't count on it."

"I'm sorry, who are you?" Penelope asked, staring at Burnhammer.

"Corporal Burnhammer of the 56th Infantry Division, United States Army." She smiled. "The woman who's going to rescue your scrawny ass."

Penelope smiled back at her. "And I'm glad for it."

"Good, now let's get a move on." PocketPad in hand, she navigated the maze of corridors. Three rooms away, Jelly opened a locked door, only to find a group of alions, but our firepower made quick work of the surprised beasts.

That occurrence happened four more times, but every time we killed the unsuspecting alions before they could sound any alarm.

A few times the alions rushed us from behind, scouting. One of the alions wore a funny helmet, which Penelope seized, fitting it on her head.

"Oh, by the way, they can make themselves invisible," she said in a nonchalant tone. "But I think they also have a way of detecting invisible objects with these nifty helmets. I just have to figure out how to use them." She pressed a button. "There are several different types of vision. Even a heat sen—" She screamed before she could finish her sentence, firing an entire clip into the air behind us.

"Was it an alion?" Jelly asked, picking up two alion guns. He handed one to Penelope.

"Two," she replied. She returned the empty handgun to Burnhammer. "How close are we to the ship?"

"The hallway should only be two or three rooms away," Burnhammer said, regarding the PocketPad screen.

Inhaling a deep breath, we continued on, sprinting the rest of the way.

We huddled under the hole in the ceiling. "How are we going to get back up?" I asked.

"I wish you would have asked that before we left the ship," Tortilla spat.

"It's okay," Burnhammer assured us. Using the PocketPad, she sent a signal to the ship, and out of a compartment below the hatch ejected a tether used for the spacesuits. The tether fell down the sealing tube, hitting the grating of the alion ship. "Climb," she ordered.

We didn't hesitate. Penelope ascended first, then Jelly, and next went Tortilla. Burnhammer eyed me, and I knew not to argue, so I climbed up the tether as fast as I could. Burnhammer threw a grenade to each end of the corridor, then began scrambling up until she was aboard the ship.

I closed the hatch.

When we sat down in the cockpit, the radio started spitting out words muffled by static.

Burnhammer clutched the radio. "Repeat transmission. I say again, please repeat transmission."

The static disappeared for a second and I recognized Geisler's voice. I listened carefully as the static dropped in and out. "They—all—dead—sur—attack—they're all dead!"

11
Alions, Offline
Darrel

Who is dead? Geisler, what are you talking about?" Burnhammer
spoke into the radio.

I sat in a chair to the right of the front chairs. Penelope
had plunked down next to me. Everyone in the room listened with
attentive ears.

"Henderson, Fox–vera, Lakes, Tasper, they're all dead." The soldier Burnhammer called Geisler was cutting out less frequently now.
"You have to turn on the Planetary Defense Network . . ."

Burnhammer flopped back in her chair. "They're all dead . . ." she
said quietly, directed at no one in particular. She looked over at Maggy.
"What do ya say, are you up for it?" She glanced around at all of us.

"Hell yes we are," Maggy spoke up.

"Wait, what are we up for?" Penelope asked.

Maggy explained the plan, how they had intended to destroy all the
alion vessels by powering up the inoperative PDN, and also how the
alions were permitted to abduct a percentage of humans before they
went and took almost everyone. The brief story made my stomach
queasy.

Eventually Penelope and I agreed to the mission. We didn't really
have a choice, though.

"Geisler, inform command at Mount Baldy that we'll finish the
job," Burnhammer told the soldier on the other side of the radio.
"Geisler, there is something you should know . . . there are hundreds

of people trapped on the ship in some sort of suspended animation, we can't just kill them . . ."

I wanted to correct her and tell her that there were probably millions aboard the ship, but I kept my mouth shut instead.

"Can you rescue them?" Geisler asked.

"We tried, but we couldn't figure out how. Maybe if we could get some help, someone who knows electronics and mechanics better."

"This is our only chance, you have to power up the PDN. Do I have to order you to do it?"

"No, sir. We'll be back to celebrate before you can say hold on to your panties. Over and out." Burnhammer replaced the radio on the console. Geisler gave no reply, or if he did, the radio was turned down enough so that I couldn't hear it.

"So we're going to leave those people there to die?" Penelope asked.

"We would have to know how to work the alion systems," Maggy said. "Otherwise the people die if we try to release them any other way. Trust me, we tried; it was terrible."

"Which brings us to the question: how did you escape the capsules?" Félix asked.

"Uhrm. The capsules, you mean the pods?" I asked.

"Sure, whatever, the pods. How did you get out of them? Or were you never in them?"

"Oh, we were in them all right," I told him. "But there was a *malfunction*"—I air quoted—"with Penelope's pod, and she escaped, killed an alion, then by some great luck, released me. We think they were testing us, letting Penelope loose on purpose, to see what she would do, like an experiment. But we don't really know."

Burnhammer disengaged from the alion mother ship, zooming through space. It was unbelievable, the stars, the orbiting satellites, the dead Solar Stations, the mother ship, everything within view astounded me.

Luckily no alion space fighters hunted us, as there had been an epic space battle earlier, one Félix described with fondness and enthusiasm, telling us how he had operated the ship's laser system.

I supplied them with the story of how we escaped, living in the duct systems, finding the alion technology, the flight deck, killing the alion admiral, the freezer, the wall of security footage that displayed our every move, squeezing in every agonizing detail that I could remember. Penelope helped out when I misremembered something, but kept quiet for the most part, growing more irritated the more times Maggy called me Jelly. Her jaw was clenched, and I could see how much she disliked the nickname.

"We're nearing the ISS," Burnhammer apprised us of our closing proximity. "There are still drones circling the station, and I don't see any alion ships docked, so the alions that killed the rest of the platoon must have already been on there. Hopefully that's a good thing for us."

"A good thing?" Maggy questioned. She prepared her gear. She wore a full-length suit of body armor, which she related as Dragon Scale, a bullet-stopping suit of magic.

"If they were already there, then maybe that means only a few are monitoring the station," Burnhammer said. "Posted there to make sure a group like us doesn't come along with a bright idea like ours. They probably never actually thought we'd be coming since they took away almost everything we had to fight them with."

"They're probably cloaked," Penelope chimed in.

"Makes sense," Burnhammer replied. "It would explain how such a well-trained team was taken down without a large number of alions on board. Unless of course I'm wrong and a whole company of the beasts await our arrival."

"And if there is a whole company of alions, what do we do then?" Félix raised the question.

"We'll give 'em everything we've got," Burnhammer answered.

"Or die trying," Penelope said, as if a motto.

"That's certain," I said. "Does anyone know what to do once we land?"

Burnhammer slowed the ship, pulling up alongside the giant station. She approached a landing platform that resembled a helicopter pad. "Someone is supposed to guide us through the process. Geisler will patch us through to somebody with some expertise, or at least a manual."

"All right, I guess that's something," I replied.

The ship felt like it was barely moving when she touched down. Automatic clamps locked us in place. "Geisler, this is Burnhammer, we've docked on the ISS."

"Glad to hear it. I'm ready to patch you through to command. Communications say they have a small team working through the manuals, and one person who has actually been aboard the ISS. So this is good luck from the rest of the Stalkers, we hope to see you soon. HOOAH."

"HOOAH," Burnhammer shouted into the radio.

"Corporal Burnhammer, this is command at Mount Baldy, please respond," a familiar female voice said over the radio.

I turned to Penelope. "I recognize that voice."

She scrunched her brow. "How?"

"I'm not sure," I replied.

"This is Burnhammer. Who am I talking to?"

"Private Albores. I had the pleasure of talking to your platoon leader, Henderson. Are you ready for docking instructions?"

"I am, Albores. Proceed."

"I guess normally someone inside the station would engage the docking tunnel, so you'll have to board the ISS and do it manually. There will be a button on the inside of the docking portal. You can use your PocketPad to send a code to open the doors. Transmitting code now . . ."

"Oh great, another trip outside. Just what I wanted to do."

" . . . Life support and artificial gravity are still online, along with secondary lights and some other minor systems."

"All right, thanks, private. I'll radio you when we're secured. Over and out."

"Over and out."

"I can do it," Maggy shouted with excitement. She sprung from her chair. "Let me do it."

"Sorry, Maggy, but I can't let you," Burnhammer said. "Now help me put on the suit." Heading towards the aft compartment, we watched Burnhammer gear up in the spacesuit. We had to wait behind a door in another compartment as she disappeared out the hatch.

"I could have done it," Maggy muttered.

"We all know that," Félix said. "But it's her charge to protect us, so let her do her job."

Maggy eyed him disapprovingly.

"So tell me what happened after we were taken?" I asked. Maggy had already related that Penelope's sisters were safe at some secret military base, but she hadn't mention Jacob at all. "How is Jacob?"

The two began to tear up at Jacob's name. "He uh . . . he didn't make it," Félix said with a lump in his throat. "He died in Portland."

I cleared my throat. "Died . . . how?" I sat down, waiting for an answer.

"He had gotten pretty sick, and he was exhausted, which slowed him down," Maggy said. "He was put in, well it's hard to describe, but

it was like a big blue cloud—"

"Yeah, we know those," I interrupted.

"Okay, well, after they trapped him . . . yeah." She sniffled. "I . . . I watched it happen. I thought he was right behind me, but when I turned . . . he was so far back. I should have kept a closer eye on him."

Félix grabbed her and put her head to his shoulder.

I reflected on my friendship with Jacob. I hadn't known him all too well, but still, his death pained me a great deal.

I jerked as the ship moved.

"I think something hit us," Penelope said. She ran to the window between compartments, searching the aft for Burnhammer. "She's not back."

My memories of Jacob were put to the back of my mind as I looked through the window. "Uhrm. How long should we wait?"

"No more than an hour," Maggy said. "There's another suit." She pointed to the white spacesuit hanging in a cubby. "I'll go investigating by then."

"You won't have to," Penelope said. "There she is now."

I glanced through the window and saw Burnhammer stepping out of the hatch. She gave us the thumbs up.

Maggy tapped a button that pressurized the room. Opening the door a moment later, we scooted inside, peering down the hatch. A long pipe had extended up to connect the ISS to the ship.

I stared down at a walkway into the ISS, something I had never thought I would do. The ladder spaced the entire distance, so we didn't have to worry about a tether, which I had trouble climbing up from the alion mother ship. I was certainly grateful for the sturdy bars.

Once we helped Burnhammer remove the spacesuit, she walked up to Penelope. "Do you mind if I wear your helmet. I'm trained and I should be the one to go first."

Penelope nodded, stripping off the helmet and handing it over to the soldier.

"Don't worry, we'll get all the furry bastards," Burnhammer declared. "I promise." She stared at Maggy for a moment. "Since I'll be busy watching our front, you'll have to navigate us." Unclipping her radio, she handed it to Maggy, along with her PocketPad. "Can you handle it?"

"Yes, sir," Maggy quickly replied.

"Ready?" Burnhammer glanced around at us.

I nodded, raising my alion gun. Everyone else signaled that they

were prepared as well.

With the go-ahead, Burnhammer descended the ladder. Her feet planted on the ISS and she scanned the area. Looking up, she yelled, "Clear."

Eventually we all found our way down, huddling together in the confined space, elbows bumping occasionally. The stale air was tainted with rot, but holding the guns, there was nothing any of us could do about the horrible reek.

Burnhammer crept forward down the narrow corridor. "Radio command and ask for instructions."

Maggy nodded. "Private Albores, this is Maggy Li, one of the civilians with Corporal Burnhammer. She is preoccupied leading us and requests that you communicate instructions to me."

"Copy that, Ms. Li. Are you secured to the ISS?"

"We are secured and have boarded. Now we need to know where to go."

"I'm being told you need to take the first left, following a skinny red pipe, taking the next right. You'll come to a door."

The radio was loud enough that we all could hear, and Burnhammer began tiptoeing down the corridor, turning left, then right.

We stopped at a door with foreign words displayed across a high-tech screen.

"Language set to English," Burnhammer said. Instantly the words translated into English, reading: Welcome. Laboratory 1 ahead.

"Albores, we're at the door. It says Laboratory 1 ahead."

"All right, I'm transmitting the code to open it."

The PocketPad lit up, flashing: Download Complete. I lined up the device with the scanner next to the door and transmitted the code. The door slid open. A room filled with dead consoles greeted us. "Okay, where to now?"

"Go through the laboratory, continuing straight for the next three doors, I'll give you the codes for each."

We continued on. With every advancing step, my nerves grew more frightened, and my entire body tensed. I could feel knots of dread building up in my shoulders. I scanned behind me every other second, sweating.

The third door was marked: Control Room. Maggy lifted the PocketPad to the scanner and the door slid up, just like all the rest, but the room on the other side was larger and much darker than the previous ones. A fetid odor accompanied the black; the smell was so bad my

stomach threatened to climb up my throat.

I spooked myself gazing into the shadows of the room. My throat closed. I tried to relax, breathing slowly.

Penelope wandered into the darkness. "The smell gets worse over here," she said. A heartbeat later, the sound of bones snapping echoed in the compartment. "It's a human!" She sprinted back into the light of the walkway that connected the rooms.

"In military gear?" Burnhammer asked.

Penelope nodded, bending over and resting her hands on her knees, ready to puke.

"I wonder where the rest are—" Burnhammer started.

"Did you hear that?" Félix shrieked.

"Yes," I replied. "I think it came from over there." I pointed to my left, behind several consoles engulfed in darkness.

Burnhammer shifted in the direction of the consoles. "Down," she yelled.

I ducked.

Using a small assault rifle, she fired one bullet. One bullet was all it took. "Target eliminated." She crept forward towards a furry body and kicked. "Yeah, it's dead." Earlier, she had advised not to shoot unless we had a clear shot, since a bullet could damage vital equipment, or possibly even pierce through the hull, venting our oxygen and exposing us to the deadly vacuum that surrounded the station.

Burnhammer inspected the room, while Maggy asked for further instructions.

"Okay, here you'll need to power up the solar panels," Albores said. "Go to the console labeled 4."

We fanned out in search of the console.

"Here," Penelope shouted. She stood to the right of the door, next to a lifeless control panel. On a shelf beside the panel, a vibrant-colored display propped against the wall, resembling a tablet computer except inexplicably more sophisticated. Images rapidly flashed on its screen. "Those are pictures of humans."

"They're studying us," Burnhammer speculated.

"Looks like it," Maggy supported the notion.

Penelope gasped. "That's probably why they didn't destroy the ISS. They're researching us using the world archives, the one place where information from across the globe is continuously backed up."

"But why study us?" I asked. "They took what they wanted."

"To better learn how to hunt us down in their training," Burn-

hammer guessed. "But who knows? We don't, and we sure as hell don't have time to find out. Get on that radio."

Maggy nodded. "Found it," she informed Albores.

"Good. Under the console there is a group of wires," he explained. He detailed what to do, and Maggy followed his directions, as we stood guard.

After several failed attempts to power up the station, she finally got it right. A moment of excitement washed over all of us, especially Maggy. The lights flickered on. Consoles lit up with colorful buttons. Machines started beeping and thrumming with life. I hadn't even noticed how silent the halls of the ISS had been until irritating noises attacked my ears from all directions.

The ISS demanded an experienced crew to silence the equipment. Sadly, it wasn't us, and the sounds drowned out our communications. Until one by one, most of the noises quit, falling into a standby status.

By the time the racket from the machinery died down, another note took its place, one that rattled my chest. I had heard the sound all too often.

A roar resonated through the halls.

My heart shifted into overdrive.

"Which way are they coming from?" Félix asked.

"Cover both entrances," Burnhammer ordered.

"Maggy, are you there?" Albores's voice came over the radio.

"Hold on!" Maggy replied. She lifted her gun and aimed at the door we had entered from, the same one I pointed my weapon at.

Burnhammer altered between doors, glancing back and forth, checking to make sure nothing invisible snuck up on us.

Suddenly a giant mass filled the hallway in front of me. "This door!" I screamed. I fired the alion gun, spitting black rounds at the beasts.

"This door!" Félix shouted, shooting at the opposite door.

As soon as the skirmish had started, it had ended, with two dead alions by each door. The canisters of my alion gun still spun around, my fingers clenching down the triggers, but they fired nothing.

"It's okay, Jelly." Maggy patted my shoulder. "They're dead, bromigo."

I gaped at the alions. "Right," I said, releasing the triggers.

Penelope bent down and tossed me a new alion gun to replace the empty one I held.

"Thanks," I told her, shooting her a smile.

She grabbed my hand and squeezed. "We're gonna get through this."

"Get Albores on the radio!" Burnhammer commanded.

Maggy knelt, resting her gun on the floor and snatching up the radio. "Albores, come in. We need to know what to do now."

"From the control room, take the next two rights. That should be the Planetary Defense room."

"You heard the woman, move!" Burnhammer yelled.

Two rights later we entered a skinnier room filled with consoles. Buttons blinked all around. It didn't look like anything special, but apparently most of the world's defense network was run from these few essential consoles.

"Here," Maggy said. "Now what?"

"Hold on," Albores replied. After a long pause, she came back on the radio. "Go to a console labeled 2."

"Found it," Maggy informed her.

"There should be a green—"

Albores's words were lost in a powerful roar that quaked the room. Terror ran throughout my body. Again there were two doors to defend.

"Maggy, keep going," Burnhammer ordered. "Darrel and Penelope, watch that door." She pointed behind us. "Félix get that door. I'll make sure nothing invisible gets the upper hand."

I positioned myself off to the side of the door, so that the alions would have to turn before they attacked, instead of head-on, where I had mistakenly placed myself the previous time.

Penelope knelt on the opposite side of me, alion gun targeted in the middle of the entrance for prime destruction.

Insanity struck a second later. Roars threatened my grip on the weapon, as the awkward hold loosened in sweat, my nerves shaking nearly out of control. I held down the triggers. Blood splashed my eye.

Alion claws reached out for my face, lashing and swiping in fury. The beasts were just too quick. The second one that entered slapped the gun from my clutch, sending it to the wall. I dove to the side.

Penelope launched a stream at the alion's back.

I rolled over before the alion crashed on top of me. Its body fell, smashing into a console.

"Help! Help!" I heard Félix cry out. Then I heard a soaring scream.

I spotted my gun and rushed to pick it up. Gun in hand, I shifted back to the door, blasting teeth out of a furry head.

"I got it! I got it!" Maggy's voice rang in my ears. "What next?"

A gut-wrenching roar deadened any reply from Albores. I clenched the trigger until nothing fired. "Out of bullets," I yelped. I could see the instruments that would carry out my death sentence: five scything claws so long and sharp they put my mom's cutlery to shame. The paw darted for my chest, aimed at my wildly pumping heart, less than a meter away. A strong arm controlled it, corded muscles flexing, throwing enough force my way to knock me back ten meters.

I couldn't breathe.

Suddenly blood showered me once more. Before I could close my eyes, I saw the paw explode, as several bullets tore it to pieces. A bullet penetrated the alion's head, and its body wrenched to the side before its bulk collided into me.

Penelope stared at me. The cylinders of her gun rotating endlessly but ejecting nothing.

I heard Maggy yelling, "Online! The network is online!"

The deafening noises of the alions ceased. No more advanced, and I hoped it was because they were all dead.

We all turned to Maggy. "It's done?" Burnhammer asked, covered in blood.

"Albores said ground control will take over," Maggy reported. "They have control of the system now."

"We can go home?" Penelope asked.

"Maggy, help Félix." Burnhammer pointed to Félix, who was lying on the floor with a gash down his shin, bleeding. "Let's get the hell out of here."

Maggy eyed Félix with horror. "Are you okay? I didn't know . . . I should have . . ."

"You did what needed to be done," Félix responded, coughing.

Maggy took off her vest and ripped her sleeve from the shirt she wore. She wrapped Félix's leg. Helping him to his feet, she carried most of his weight.

He screamed in agony when they took a step.

I rushed over to his other side, positioning my body so that he didn't put pressure on his leg at all. "You're gonna be all right, dude."

He nodded at me, blood smeared across his face.

Burnhammer grabbed the PocketPad off the floor and handed it to Penelope. "Get us back."

Penelope nodded. She navigated the route back to the docking pad.

A skinny tunnel never looked appealing to me, but all I wanted to

do was climb through this one. I saw safety on the other side. I ascended the ladder faster than I had ever moved in my life.

With everyone aboard, I closed the hatch, and Burnhammer was running for the flight deck. Quickly, Penelope and I tailed her.

A scream echoed throughout the ship as an invisible claw sliced at Burnhammer's elbow. With her short assault rifle, she shot the air, until a body bumped me, sending me to the ground.

I groaned under the weight.

Burnhammer howled, blood pouring out her severed limb.

Penelope glanced between us and decided to help me first. She took up Burnhammer's fallen helmet and found the alion corpse that was crushing me. She kicked the body off me as I pushed.

Freed, I turned to Burnhammer, who had blacked out. Her detached forearm and hand rested nearby. "We have to stop the bleeding," I yelled.

"There are rags in the same cubby as the spacesuit," Penelope said, running off. She returned, jumping down to her knees and blocking the bleeding stump.

I squeezed around the end, attempting to stop the outpour, but it was little use. Blood soaked through all the rags. "What do we do?" I asked.

Maggy entered the cockpit. Her eyes grew at the messy scene. "What the hell—"

"An alion hid up here, invisible," Penelope replied. "We have to get her to a hospital . . . to the facility you came from." She directed her speech at Maggy.

"To Mount Baldy?" Maggy shook her head. "I have no idea where it is."

"Well someone has to fly us there," she replied. "Darrel, you could do it while I keep the pressure around her wound."

I stared at her. "Maggy would—"

"Maggy has to take care of Félix. You have to fly us there. Use the radio to ask for coordinates to the base. Hurry!"

I leapt up. "Okay." The controls on the console confused me at first, until I read the labels on each button. A couple detached the ship from the ISS and we floated away. I was searching for the engine start up when I noticed movement out the window. Satellites around earth started to reposition themselves towards the mother ship.

Nothing visible shot out of the satellites, but a second later, sections of the mother ship exploded. Fires blew out into space, lasting a

mere second before evaporating. Missiles launched from other satellites, zipping through the black, detonating upon impact. Giant chunks of the ship broke off. More missiles rocketed towards the disconnected pieces.

It was the best firework show that anyone could ever watch.

Penelope and Maggy were observing the phenomenal event, mouths parted.

"Infrared lasers," Maggy gasped, gazing at the aimed satellites. "Undetectable to our eyes."

Suddenly the realization of all the deaths taking place struck me. "All those people," I whispered.

"There was nothing we could do . . ." Penelope reassured me. With the daze fading, she returned her attention to Burnhammer. "Get us out of here, Darrel."

"Yeah, all right. I'll try to." I located the correct button and the engines fired up. The controls were surprisingly easy, designed similar to a computer game.

"I'll be with Tortilla," Maggy said.

Focused on the controls, I barely heard what she had said. I flew over the satellites aimed at the mother ship and the invisible lasers destroying it. Turning towards the Earth, hundreds of black clouds came into view across North and South America.

A smile broke on my face.

We were blasting the beasts across the entire world. Unprepared, their ships felt the full force of our weaponry, most of which I had never known existed, but I was glad it did.

I grabbed the radio, trying to remember the woman's name before I asked for help. It popped into my head a moment later. "Albores, come in . . . Albores, please come in."

"This is Albores, who am I talking to?"

"This is Darrel Reid from the ship. Burnhammer is out of commission, and she desperately needs medical attention. I'm flying the ship right now, how do I get to your base?"

"Copy that, Darrel. Hold on a second," Albores said. "I'm transmitting our coordinates to your PocketPad. You'll have to transfer them to the ship's navigation system."

"Okay, thanks." I turned to Penelope behind me. "Where is the PocketPad?"

"I had it here somewhere," she replied. Still clutching Burnhammer's stumpy elbow, she searched her pockets. She found it on the

ground a short distance away, blood pooling around its casing. "Hope it still works." She tossed it.

I caught the slippery device, wiping it on my shirt, then began trying to send the coordinates to the computer. A window kept popping up on the ship's display in front of me, requiring a code to transfer the data. I hadn't a clue what it was.

I had to put the transfer on hold as the ship started to enter the atmosphere. The blinding light made it difficult to make out anything on the screen.

When the intensity dwindled, I glimpsed a yellow ball fly right past the right wing. Several more zoomed past. "We're under attack!"

"Fire back," Penelope yelled.

"I don't know how!"

"Maggy! Maggy!" Penelope cried out.

Maggy rushed into the room. "What is it?"

"We're under attack," I panted. "Do you know how to use the weapon systems?"

"Yeah, hold on." She plunked herself down in a chair behind me and buckled up.

I rolled the ship. My stomach hated that. A ball nearly hit the left wing. I started to curse as my panic peaked. I dipped the ship this way and that, suddenly changing directions, barrel rolling and diving.

I looked back. Penelope had Burnhammer pinned down as she held on to a bar. I'm sure Penelope's stomach despised me as much as mine did.

"Missiles away!" Maggy called out.

"There's another," I informed her.

"We're out of missiles." She began cursing but didn't stop working at the terminal before her.

"What do we do?"

Her fingers were speeding as rapidly as the ship was bolting through the air. "There's a machinegun and a laser. Don't worry. I'll get it."

The next thing I knew, debris was hurtling past the ship, wreckage colliding with the tail. The minimal damage did not slow our blazing-fast pace.

"Can you transfer the coordinates to the navigation?" I asked Maggy.

Unbuckling, she sprung from her chair and set about the transfer. "Done," she said a blink later.

A dot appeared on the navigation screen. Circles expanded from the dot like ripples in a pond.

"I have to get back to Tortilla." She patted my back and dashed away.

I followed the navigation arrow. I pulled back on the yoke and leveled out: the attitude indicator showed the wings even across a blue-sky horizon. The crust of the Earth lay a hundred meters down. Smoke clouds blackened the real horizon. We were closing fast upon the coordinates. Hills began to populate the terrain underneath the ship. The hills soon grew into mountains, spots of white snow upon black rock and dark evergreens. The dot pointed me to a valley below the snow-line.

"Albores, I'm approaching the base. Where do I land?"

A long pause ate away at my nerves, worried that no response would come. I radioed again.

"This is Albores, Darrel. There is a landing strip below the base. Some of the tarmac has been demolished, but there should still be enough for you to land safely. I cannot give you the coordinates; you'll just have to keep an eye out for it. It's not far."

That wasn't music to my ears. "I don't know how to land a spaceship!" I shouted. "Can't it be done by an autopilot system?"

"Negative. I'll try to find a pilot to talk you through it, but it's chaotic down here, so I can't promise I'll find one. Just circle the base until I get back to you. Over and out."

I didn't bother with a reply.

Satellite towers of the base appeared soon after Albores parted. The complex itself was harder to find, hidden well within the tall needled-trees. Hangars, as well as a long, thick wall gave away the base's location. I flew south down the mountain, hunting for the airstrip.

I circled the area over and over without a sign of the runway. The trees concealed it too well for my exhausted eyes. I desired sleep more than food or water, or anything else that I could think of, except for maybe one last kiss from Penelope.

I decided to try my luck at a lower altitude, though I was shaking as it was, and I didn't want to accidentally dive and hit a tree. I glided along the treetops, and at last, a strip of black materialized out of nowhere. Climbing a little to get a better view, I could see the yellow lines that divided the tarmac evenly.

Then the waiting began. I passed over the airstrip a couple more times before Albores came over the radio.

"Darrel, you there?"

"I'm here! I'm here!" I screamed into the radio. "I can see the runway. What do I do now?"

"I found a crop pilot who says he knows everything there is to know about landing a plane, big or small. I'm going to pass you over to Lenny Gortel. Here he is."

A harsh smoker's voice took over Albores's soft, musical one. "You there, kid?"

I had never agreed with the term kid, not since I was ten. "You the crop duster?"

"Sure am, kid. I hear ya need some advice about how to land a plane."

"Not a plane, a spacecraft."

"Does it have wheels?" he asked.

"Yeah," I replied. "It has wheels."

"Then it's the same damn thing," he said curtly. "All ya need to do is listen and not jerk the controls. Don't jerk the damn controls. Ya hearin' me, kid?"

I didn't want to answer him; his tone irritated me. "I hear you, crop duster." I could hear my voice faltering over the words. Even though I couldn't see him, he made me nervous. I tried to emphasize *crop duster* the way he was calling me *kid*, but I didn't think it was working.

"All right, good. This is probably goin' to be a rough landin', but you'll survive. Line up with the tarmac."

"I did but the wings keep dipping," I reported.

"Bring her around and hold her steady."

I looked back at Penelope.

"Just land it, Darrel!" Penelope shouted. "She's going to die!"

I circled again. I swallowed hard at her tone, aligning the ship with the tarmac. "Aligned," I told the crop duster.

"Now pull back on the throttle," he said. "Ya may have to push the yoke to dive. Keep the airspeed within the green arc."

I pulled the throttle and dipped the nose of the ship, pushing on the yoke. I held my breath.

"Breathe," Penelope encouraged.

I exhaled until my lungs were empty. "Done."

"Good. Now to slow the plane without losin' lift, you'll have to use the slats and flaps next to the throttle. Almost there, just hang on, kid." He guided me well enough and the plane slowed. "Just before ya touch

down, ya have to flare the nose, or raise it, pullin' back on the yoke. Not too much now."

The ship must have been centimeters from the ground, though it was hard to tell. I breathed out again as the back tires touched down. The front tires seemed to take forever to connect, but eventually they tapped the ground, bouncing up, then touching down for good. "Down," I yelled into the radio.

"Activate reverse thrusters!"

I did as told. Rapidly decelerating, the ship rocked from side to side as I held the yoke as straight I could, and every second I hoped that the plane wouldn't fall apart or hit a lethal object to pop a tire. My nerves calmed when the wheels came to a stop. I saw the sign labeled idle and pulled the throttle all the way back. "We've stopped and the engines are idling."

"Well hey, ya sound like ya got it under control there, kid."

"Thanks. Thanks for everything, crop duster. Could you put Albores back on?"

"Sure thing, kid. And you're welcome. Glad ya made it all right."

"Darrel, this is Albores. A team is waiting for you at the end of the runway."

"Got it," I said crisply, though it was not my intent.

"Help me carry her," Penelope said, almost as if an order.

Without another word to Albores, I darted to Burnhammer's side. I groaned from the effort necessary to lift the soldier. The ramp at the tail was already down when we lugged her back there. A group of soldiers rushed up and grabbed Burnhammer with ease, running her down to a stretcher on wheels. She was loaded into a van that drove away before I could barely glimpse it.

Félix was moaning, drenched in sweat. "What about me? They forgot me."

A soldier walked up the ramp. "Maggy Li?" he said, eyeing Maggy. The man was a tower.

"Yes?" she answered.

He stuck out a strong hand. "I'm Major Henry Higgans. I cannot tell you the debt this country . . . this world owes you. Without the Planetary Defense Network, we would be sitting ducks, with a snowball's chance in hell in defeating the enemy. You saved us, Maggy Li."

Maggy accepted his massive hand and gripped.

"And that goes for each of you up there—"

"My leg," Félix interrupted the major. "My leg, my leg, my leg!"

The major swiveled around. "Privates, get this man to the base ASAP!"

Two soldiers bolted up the ramp and hauled Félix away to a nearby jeep. The entire way he complained about the gash in his leg.

"Let's get you three some food and water, and anything else you need."

"A shower would be nice," Penelope said. "And a comb."

The major nodded, pointing the way down the ramp. He followed behind us, jumping into the front of the jeep once we were all loaded and secured.

I fell asleep on the ride to the complex.

Night passed and a new morning arrived. I met Maggy, Penelope, and her sisters in a cafeteria several floors below the ground. The complex amazed me. If the elevators were to be believed, then it spanned near 75 levels. It was monstrous.

"You ready to go visit Tortilla?" Maggy asked, finishing a plate of spaghetti.

The cooks had made us special meals that morning, anything we desired. Penelope had ordered a bison steak and a plate of vegetables. The twins had ordered a stack of giant pancakes. I had ordered my favorite cereal: a bowl of sugarcoated wheat flakes.

"Yeah, I am," I said. I pushed aside the empty bowl. "You?" I turned to Penelope.

"Yeah, hold on. Two more bites." She stuffed a huge chunk of bison meat into her mouth.

We headed down to a lower level, to an infirmary where they were keeping Félix and Corporal Burnhammer. We met Burnhammer first, who was in an isolated recovery ward. At her elbow, only a stump was left, but the arm had been saved. I had feared they would have to amputate the entire limb.

She greeted us with a warm smile. "I may have lost part of my arm, but we saved the world," Burnhammer spoke softly.

"Not completely," Maggy said. "Even with the ships destroyed, there are still alions on the ground that need to be dealt with. I've signed up to make sure we get them all."

"Good for you . . . I'll probably join you if you save some for me." Burnhammer winked at Maggy.

"I'll try," she responded.

We left Burnhammer to check on how Félix fared. He had a slight

fever, but the attending doctor assured us that it was normal and would decline within the day.

"How's the food down here?" I asked him.

"Had vegetables and bread this morning." He grinned. "But I enjoyed them."

"Have you heard about the new colony starting up in Santa Barbara?" Maggy asked.

"Yeah, I did, where survivors are going to rebuild. I'm not sure why they aren't going to hunt down the remaining alions." He adjusted a new pair of black spectacles. "That's what we're doing, right?"

"That's right," Maggy answered. "Soon as your leg starts to mend."

"Actually . . ." I started, taking a breath. Penelope seized my hand. "Uhrm. Actually, Penelope and I are going to help out in Santa Barbara."

"What?" Maggy spat. "You never said anything before."

"I didn't think you would like the idea . . . but it's safer for the twins . . . It's where we need to be."

"You need to be with us, Jelly," Maggy said.

Penelope squeezed my hand. "Uhrm. Maggy, you have to stop calling me that. It was . . ." I paused. "It was cute at first, but it's not anymore. If you want to call me a nickname, think of a new one, or just call me Darrel."

She gaped at me. "You don't like the name?"

"I never really have, I just . . . I just couldn't gather up the courage to tell you."

Her eyes saddened. "When are you leaving?"

I cleared my throat. "A caravan is leaving in an hour or so, we're going with them," I told her.

"I can't believe you're leaving, bromigo," Félix said, completely shocked. "When will we see you again?"

"Probably when you finish off all the alions, I'd imagine," I said. I gripped his arm and embraced him. "But who knows, man, maybe sooner."

I hugged Maggy.

"I'm going to miss you, bromigo," she said with a snuffle.

"It's not goodbye forever, just for a while. We'll see each other soon enough, you'll see."

"It's just weird to think of you going away," she said, grinning. "Especially since we just got you back."

I patted her shoulder. "We'll grow old as neighbors . . . I'll save you

two a plot of land." I smiled as we parted.

"I'll hold you to that." Her grin expanded, enveloping her face from ear to ear.

After the long goodbyes, Penelope and I packed up some fresh clothes and headed for a jeep preparing to depart for Santa Barbara. The twins settled, with their bags stuffed full with new clothes, and a few other things they couldn't leave behind.

Shafts of light penetrated the dark clouds. The sky was mostly black and smoky. I searched the horizon to the west. "Do you think . . . do you think people fifty years from now will be playing video games about the invasion like WWII games at the turn of the century?"

"You can count on it," Penelope said, gazing out into the hills. "You can count on it."

A large black bird flew through a sunbeam, lit up like some magical creature, then it disappeared a second later, lost in the shadow that haunted L.A. I smiled, hopeful for the days when sunshine prevailed, and I could lie outside like a lizard and bathe in the peaceful warmth with Penelope by my side.

End of Book One of The Road to Extinction Trilogy

Acknowledgements

I would like to thank:

My parents for their continuing support.

My friends and family, who have always been there for me and endured my prolix talks detailing the world of The Cry of Havoc.

The fans that have enjoyed my work, especially to those who took the time to review Life Descending.

My bromigo Eric Schlect, who read Life Descending faster than the speed of light.

My bromigo Brett Carlson, whose remarkable talents as a graphic designer shine with At the End's cover art and design.

A special thanks goes out to Dennis Hoff, who showed me the path of self-publishing, and without whom my stories might still be collecting dust on my hard drive.

And finally, my loving fiancée Katherine, who told me that the story was worth pursuing.

About the Author

Born in 1988, John Hennessy became entranced by the world of fantasy and sci-fi at a young age, playing video games and reading books for many long nights/early mornings. He recently graduated from Western Washington University, and now lives in the Rose Lands of Portland, OR, at work finishing The Road to Extinction Trilogy. Visit his website at: http://www.johnhennessy.net